初級
挑戰單字 1500

千盼萬盼,常春藤全民英檢系列叢書終於出版了!

事實上,從數年前政府實施全民英檢第一天起,常春藤便密切注意後續的發展,並全心研究各項試題的內容及形態,裨使系列叢書的品質永保領先地位。

我們的系列叢書分初級(國中學生程度)、中級(高中學生程度)、中高級(大學學生程度)三級,每一級的系列叢書包含:

單　　字:附例句、衍生字、反義字及重要字詞片語用法。	
片　　語:附例句、及其他相關片語。	
閱讀測驗:附譯文、字詞用法、難句解析。	
段落填空:附譯文、選項精解、百分之百鎖定考題趨勢。	
文　　法:掌握所有出題重點,採條例式解說,清晰易懂。	
聽　　力:由常春藤資深外籍編輯編纂,完全仿真,並附 CD 提供無限次的練習機會。	
模擬試題:精撰仿真模擬試題,裨使讀者充分了解全民英檢試題的全貌,培養臨場作答的經驗。	

我們相信,讀者在打開本系列叢書的第一頁起,便會感覺常春藤所出的書就是跟其他出版社出的書不一樣,因為我們相信我們付出的心力比別人多出甚多。嚴謹的寫作態度一向是常春藤的寫照,也因為我們的這種態度,行政院特委託常春藤負責行政院各部會科長以上各級長官的英語培訓。這項殊榮不啻是對常春藤的一項肯定,也更鞭策常春藤要更加努力,出版更多好書。

全民學英語,大家一起來!

于台北常春藤

錄

如何使用本書

1. 本書每個單字之後均附音標，按此音標及音節唸出正確的發音，重複唸五次。換言之，憑聲音記單字，而不要按字母記單字。

    茲以 beautiful 為例：

    不要按字母記此字： b-e-a-u-t-i-f-u-l（×）

    而要按音標及音節記此字：

    beau‐ti‐ful

    [bju] [tə] [fḷ]

2. 細讀單字的中文解釋及相關字詞、片語的用法。

3. 熟唸例句五遍，唸完一遍，思考整句中文的意思。

4. 按自己的英文程度自設進度。例如，每天要求自己記六頁單字。

5. 每晚就寢前，複習一天所記的單字。方法如下：

    a. 將英文例句用筆或便條紙遮住，留出中文的譯文。

    b. 將中文譯文反譯成英文，並核對例句的原文。可重複這個過程，直到無誤為止。（雄哥當年就是利用此法記單字，不知不覺中大大提升中翻英及英翻中的能力。）

6. 隨時攜帶本書，隨時複習。

1. **abroad** [ə'brɔd] adv. 在國外

study abroad　　留學

travel abroad　　出國旅行

例: I plan to study abroad next year.

（我計劃明年出國深造。）

2. **absent** ['æbsənt] a. 缺席的

be absent from...　　未出席……

反義字: present ['prɛznt] a. 出席的

例: Mary is absent from class because she has a cold.

（瑪麗沒來上課，因為她感冒了。）

3. **accept** [ək'sɛpt] vt. 接受

accept one's gift　　接受某人的禮物

例: I cannot accept your gift for nothing.

（我不能無緣無故接受你的禮物。）

4. **accident** ['æksədənt] n. 意外; 意外事件 (多指車禍)

by accident　　意外地

a car accident　　車禍

例: I didn't do it on purpose. It was an accident.

（我不是故意的。那是個意外。）

5. **account** [ə'kaʊnt] n. 帳戶

bank account　　銀行帳戶

open (up) an account　　開戶頭

例: I will open up an account at the bank across the street.

（我要在對面的銀行開立一個帳戶。）

6. **ache** [ek] n. & vi. 疼痛

a headache　　頭痛

a stomachache　　胃痛

例: My heart aches whenever I see those poor children on TV.
(每當我看到電視上那些可憐的兒童時，就覺得心痛。)

7. **active** [ˈæktɪv] a. 活躍的　

例: The little girl is very active and often gets into a lot of trouble.
(這小女孩很活潑，常惹不少麻煩。)

8. **activity** [ˌækˈtɪvətɪ] n. 活動

例: There are many activities to take part in after school.
(放學後有很多活動可參與。)

9. **action** [ˈækʃən] n. 動作; 行動

take action　　採取行動

例: Let's take action before it is too late.
(咱們採取行動以免太遲。)

10. **across** [əˈkrɑs] prep. 越過

across from...　　在……對面

例: Mary lives across from me.
(瑪麗住在我對面。)

11. **address** [əˈdrɛs] n. 地址; 演講

make an address to...　　對……演講

例: What is your address?
(你住在哪裏？)

12. **adjust** [əˈdʒʌst] vt. & vi. (使) 適應

adjust (oneself) to...　　(使自己) 適應……; 習慣於……
= get used to

例: He has adjusted to the weather in Taipei.
(他已經適應了台北的天氣。)

13. adopt [ə'dɑpt] vt. 領養; 採取 (意見, 方案)   a

例: Mr. & Mrs. Peterson have adopted five children in all.
(彼得遜夫婦共領養了五個孩子。)

14. advertisement [ˌædvɚ'taɪzmənt] n. 廣告 (常縮寫成 ad [æd])   a

classified ad   分類廣告
put/place an advertisement   登廣告
例: I put an advertisement in the paper for a roommate.
(我在報上刊登廣告徵求室友。)

15. adventure [əd'vɛntʃɚ] n. 冒險   a

例: Life is full of adventures.
(人生充滿了冒險。)

16. advice [əd'vaɪs] n. 勸告, 建議 (不可數)   a

an advice (✗)
a piece of advice   一項勸告 (○)
例: She gave me a piece of advice on how to study English.
(有關如何學英文方面, 她給了我一項建議。)

17. afford [ə'fɔrd] vt. 有足夠的 (錢、時間)去買/做……   a

(一定與 can 或 cannot 並用)
can/cannot afford + 名詞/to V   有能力/無能力負擔/從事……
例: I can't afford such an expensive car.
(這樣貴的車我買不起。)

18. afraid [ə'fred] a. 害怕的   a

be afraid of...   害怕……
例: I am no longer afraid of the dark.
(我不再怕黑了。)

19. afterwards [ˈæftɚwɚdz] adv. 之後 (= then)

例: We went out for dinner. Afterwards, we went to the movies.
（我們外出吃晚飯。之後便看電影去了。）

20. again [əˈgɛn] adv. 再一次

again and again　　一再地

例: I phoned you again and again, but there was no answer.
（我一再打電話給你，可是都沒人接。）

21. against [əˈgɛnst] prep. 反對, 違抗

例: It is against the law to steal.
（偷竊是違法的。）

22. age [edʒ] n. 年齡

be + 年 + of age　　……若干歲
= be + 年 + old

例: My daughter is two years of age.
（我女兒兩歲了。）

23. agree [əˈgri] vi. 同意

agree with sb　　同意某人

例: I don't agree with you on this matter.
（有關這件事，我不同意你的看法。）

24. ahead [əˈhɛd] adv. 在前面

go ahead　　向前走; 請便

例: "Can I use your car?"
　　"Go ahead."
（『我可以使用你的車嗎？』）
（『請便。』）

25. air-conditioned [ˈɛrkənˌdɪʃənd] a. 有空調的 ⓐ

air-conditioner [ˈɛrkənˌdɪʃənɚ] n. 冷氣機

例: This room isn't air-conditioned. I'm so hot.
(這房間沒冷氣。我好熱喲。)

26. airport [ˈɛrˌpɔrt] n. 機場 ⓐ

例: He went to the airport to see his friend off.
(他到機場為朋友送行。)

27. album [ˈælbəm] n. 相簿; (唱片的) 專輯 ⓐ

例: Father gave me a photo album for my birthday.
(爸爸給我一本相簿當做我的生日禮物。)

28. alarm [əˈlɑrm] n. 警鈴 ⓐ

alarm clock 鬧鐘
fire alarm 火警警鈴

例: Please set the alarm clock for eight.
(請把鬧鐘設在八點。)
The fire alarm went off.
(防火警鈴響了。)

29. alive [əˈlaɪv] a. 活著的 ⓐ

本字通常置於 be 動詞之後, 但亦可修飾名詞, 不過要放在該名詞後, 而
不可置於該名詞之前。

例: The plant is still alive even though I forgot to water it for two
weeks.
(即使我有兩個星期忘了澆水, 這植物仍活得好好的。)
The police found two alive people in the traffic accident. (✗)
→ The police found two people alive in the traffic accident. (○)
(警方發現車禍中有兩名生還者。)

30. allow [əˈlaʊ]vt. 允許

allow sb to V　　允許某人從事……

例: Will you allow me to go with you?
(你會讓我跟我去嗎？)

31. almost [ˈɔlmost] adv. 幾乎, 差不多

例: It's almost time to leave.
(差不多是動身的時候了。)

32. alone [əˈlon] a. 單獨的

例: Leave me alone. (= Mind your own business.)
(別管我。／管自己的事就好了。)

33. along [əˈlɔŋ] prep. 沿著

get along　　過日子

例: He walked along the street and turned left at the first intersection.
(他沿街而行，在第一個十字路口左轉。)
　　How are you getting along?
(你近來如何？)

34. already [ɔlˈrɛdɪ] adv. 已經

例: I am already finished with my work.
(我工作已做完了。)

35. although [ɔlˈðo] conj. 雖然

= though [ðo]

中文常用『雖然……但是……』，唯在英文中『雖然』(although/though) 是連接詞，『但是』(but) 亦是連接詞。由於兩個子句只可使用一個連接詞，因此，寫英文句子時, 使用 although/though, 就不可同時使用 but, 反之亦然。

例: Although he is nice, but I don't like him. (✗)
→ Although he is nice, I don't like him. (○)
= He is nice, but I don't like him.
(雖然他人不錯，可是我並不喜歡他。)

36. **always** [ˋɔlwez] adv. 始終, 一直

= at all times
例: Todd is always busy with his work.
(陶德一直忙著他的工作。)

37. **a.m./am** [͵e ˋɛm] n. 上午 (是拉丁字 ante meridiem 的縮寫)

p.m./pm [͵pi ˋɛm] 下午 (是拉丁字 post meridiem 的縮寫)
例: We set out at 10 a.m. and arrived in Tainan at 2 p.m.
(我們上午十點出發，下午兩點抵達台南。)

38. **amazed** [əˋmezd] a. 感到驚訝的

be amazed at...　　對……感到驚訝
= be surprised at...
例: We were amazed at how well the girl sang.
(這女孩子歌唱得很好，令我們驚訝。)

39. **ambulance** [ˋæmbjələns] n. 救護車

fire truck [ˋfaɪr ͵trʌk] n. 消防車
例: Call an ambulance. Somebody's hurt.
(叫救護車來。有人受傷了。)

40. **American** [əˋmɛrɪkən] n. 美國人 & a. 美國人/籍的

Chinese 一字亦採相同用法。
例: She's an American (n.), but she lives in France.
= She's American (a.), but she lives in France.
(她是美國人，不過都住在法國。)

41. among [əˈmʌŋ] prep. 在……之中 (三個以上)

between [brˈtwin] prep. 在……之中 (兩個)

例: Among the three girls, she is the most beautiful.
(她是三個女孩中最美的一個。)

There is no trust between the two students.
(這兩個學生彼此之間不能互信。)

42. angry [ˈæŋgrɪ] a. 生氣的

be angry with sb　　生某人的氣
be angry at sth　　對某事不悅

例: Don't worry. I'm not angry with you.
(別擔心。我沒生你的氣。)

43. animal [ˈænəmḷ] n. 動物

例: Animals are not allowed in this restaurant.
(本餐廳不准帶寵物進來。)

44. another [əˈnʌðɚ] a. & pron. 另一個, 再一個

例: May I have another hamburger, please?
(麻煩您再給我一份漢堡,好嗎?)

45. answer [ˈænsɚ] vt. 回答 & n. 答案 (與 to 並用)

answer the phone　　接電話
answer the door　　應門

例: If you know the answer to the question, raise your hand.
(你若知道這個問題的答案,請舉手。)

46. ant [ænt] n. 螞蟻

例: There were hundreds of ants in the sugar jar.
(糖罐裏有好幾百隻螞蟻。)

47. apartment [ə'pɑrtmənt] n. 公寓

例: The apartment is for rent.
(本公寓出租。)

48. appear [ə'pɪr] vi. 出現

= show up

例: He didn't appear until five minutes ago.
(他直到五分鐘前才出現。)

49. apple ['æpḷ] n. 蘋果

apple 亦可喻『最受喜愛的人』，只用於下列片語中：
be the apple of one's eye (此處 eye 用單數)

例: Mary is the apple of her father's eye.
(瑪麗是她爸爸的掌上明珠。)

50. appliance [ə'plaɪəns] n. 家電用品

例: We went to the appliance store to buy a new rice cooker.
(我們到電器行去買一只新電鍋。)

51. apply [ə'plaɪ] vi. 申請 (與介詞 for 並用)

apply for a job　　應徵工作

例: I'd like to apply for a job. Do you have any openings here?
(我想求職。您這裡有空缺嗎？)

52. appreciate [ə'priʃɪˌet] vt. 感激; 欣賞

例: I really appreciate your help
(我真的很感激你的幫助。)

53. appropriate [ə'propriɪt] a. 適當的

例: The dress is not appropriate for work.
(這件洋裝不適合上班穿。)

The dress is not appropirate for work.

 讀者有信心 **9**

54. April [ˈeprəl] n. 四月

下列是各月份的英文說法:

January [ˈdʒænjʊɛrɪ] n. 一月

February [ˈfɛbrʊɛrɪ] n. 二月

March [mɑrtʃ] n. 三月

May [me] n. 五月

June [dʒun] n. 六月

July [dʒuˈlaɪ] n. 七月

August [ˈɔgəst] n. 八月

September [sɛpˈtɛmbə] n. 九月

October [akˈtobə] n. 十月

November [noˈvɛmbə] n. 十一月

December [dɪˈsɛmbə] n. 十二月

例: Nina is getting married in April.

（妮娜將在四月份結婚。）

55. aquarium [əˈkwɛrɪəm] n. 水族館 (箱)

例: The aquarium is full of fish.

（水族箱裏都是魚。）

The aquarium is full of fish.

56. argue [ˈɑrgju] vi. 爭論

argue with... 與……爭論

例: You should never argue with your family members.

（你絕不應與家人起爭執。）

57. around [əˈraʊnd] adv. 四周; 大約 (之後加數字)

fool around 游手好閒

around ten dollars 大約十元

= about ten dollars

例: Don't fool around. Get down to work.

（別鬼混。好好工作。）

58. arrange [əˈrendʒ] vt. 安排

arrangement [əˈrendʒmənt] n. 安排

make an arrangement 做安排

例: I will arrange the party for the class.

（我要為全班籌辦一個派對。）

59. **arrive** [əˈraɪv] vi. 到達   a

arrival [əˈraɪvl] n. 到達
arrive at + 建築物 (如飯店, 車站)   到達……
arrive in + 城市   到達……
例: I arrived at the station at ten, but the train had already left.
（我十點到達車站，但火車已開了。）

60. **article** [ˈɑrtɪkl] n. 文章   a

an article on...   有關……的文章
= an article about...
例: Did you read the article on pop music?
（你看過那篇有關流行樂的文章了嗎？）

61. **arrow** [ˈæro] n. 箭   a

shoot an arrow at...   用箭射……
例: He shot an arrow at the deer.
（他用箭射那隻鹿。）

62. **asleep** [əˈslip] a. 睡著的   a

fall asleep   入睡
比較: sleepy [ˈslipɪ] a. 想睡的
feel sleepy   想睡覺
例: When did you fall asleep last night?
（你昨晚什麼時候睡著的？）

63. **assistant** [əˈsɪstənt] n. 助手   a

be an assistant to sb   是某人的助手
teaching assistant   助教
例: She is an assistant to our teacher.
（她是我們老師的助手。）

64. **attack** [ə'tæk] vt. & n. 攻擊

attack sb　攻擊某人

= make an attack on sb

例: A stray dog attacked a little boy yesterday.
　　(昨天有隻流浪狗攻擊小男孩。)

65. **attend** [ə'tɛnd] vt. 參加

attend school　　上學

= go to school

例: Where do you attend school?
　　(你在哪兒唸書?)

66. **attention** [ə'tɛnʃən] n. 注意

pay attention to...　　注意……

例: You should pay attention to every word I say.
　　(我所說的每個字你都應注意。)

67. **aunt** [ænt] n. 姑姑; 阿姨; 嬸嬸

uncle ['ʌŋkl] n. 舅舅; 叔叔; 伯父

例: Gina's aunt is coming for a visit soon.
　　(吉娜的阿姨很快就要來訪。)

68. **autumn** ['ɔtəm] n. 秋天

= fall [fɔl]

例: In autumn leaves start to fall.
　　(秋天樹葉開始掉落。)

69. **available** [ə'veləbl] a. 有空的; 可用的; 可買得到的

be available　　有空

= be free

= have time off

例: I will be available this afternoon.
（我今天下午有空。）

　Is that new book available here?
（那本新書你這兒有賣嗎？）

70. **avoid** [əˋvɔɪd] vt. 避免

avoid + N/Ving　　避免……

例: You should avoid to eat too much fat. (✗)

→ You should avoid eating too much fat. (◯)
（你應避免攝取過多的脂肪。）

71. **awake** [əˋwek] a. 醒著的 & vt. 叫醒 & vi. 醒來 (= wake up)

awake 作動詞時三態為: awake、awoke、awoken。

例: I was awake all night long.
（我整晚未眠。）

I │woke up│ at ten this morning.
　│awoke　│
（我今天早上十點醒來。）

72. **babysit** [ˈbebɪsɪt] vi. & vt. 看護嬰兒　　**b**

babysitter [ˈbebɪˌsɪtɚ] n. 保姆

例: Can you babysit my daughter tonight?

(妳今晚可以照顧我女兒嗎？)

73. **bacon** [ˈbekən] n. 培根　　**b**

例: I had a bacon sandwich for breakfast this morning.

(今天早上我吃了一個培根三明治當早餐。)

＊此處 for 表『當做』之意。

74. **bag** [bæg] n. 袋子　　**b**

＊魔術師變魔術時,先展示一只空袋子,然後叫助手偷偷將一隻貓放在袋子裏,在適當時間再把貓從袋子裏變出來。在處理的過程中,魔術師會叮嚀助手: "Don't let the cat out of the bag." (可別讓貓從袋子裏跑出來,以免穿幫。) 現在英美人士就用這句話比喻『千萬不要洩密』之意。

＊老張,小賴的爸爸是個人妖。但可千萬不要告訴別人喲！

"Don't let the cat out of the bag."

例: I left my book bag on the bus this morning.

(今天早上我把書包遺留在公車上了。)

75. **baggage** [ˈbæɡɪdʒ] n. 行李 (不可數)　　**b**

= luggage [ˈlʌɡɪdʒ]

a baggage (✗)

→ a piece of baggage 　一件行李 (○)

例: Don't leave all your baggage at the front desk.

(不要把你所有的行李放在櫃檯處。)

76. **bake** [bek] vt. 烘培　　**b**

bakery [ˈbekərɪ] n. 麵包店

例: My mother baked a cake for my birthday.

(我媽媽為我的生日烤了一個蛋糕。)

77. balloon [bə'lun] n. 氣球

例: The little boy had a red balloon in his hand.
(小男孩手中抓了一個紅色的氣球。)

78. banana [bə'nænə] n. 香蕉

a bunch of bananas　一串香蕉

例: He bought a bunch of bananas.
(他買了一串香蕉。)

＊複數的 bananas 亦可作形容詞, 等於 crazy ['krezɪ] (瘋狂的)。

go bananas　瘋了

= go crazy

例: He went bananas when Mary left him.
(瑪麗離開他時,他便瘋了。)

79. bandage ['bændɪdʒ] n. 繃帶

例: He has a bandage on his left arm.
(他左手臂貼了一塊繃帶。)

80. bank [bæŋk] n. 銀行

例: I went to the bank to open an account.
(我到銀行開戶頭。)

81. barbecue ['bɑrbɪˌkju] vt. 烤肉

例: Gary barbecued hamburgers and hotdogs for dinner.
(蓋瑞烤漢堡及熱狗當晚餐吃。)

82. barber ['bɑrbɚ] n. 理髮師

a barbershop　(男) 理髮店
a beauty parlor　(女) 美容院

例: I asked the barber to cut my hair.
(我要理髮師替我理髮。)

83. bark [bɑrk] vi. 吠

bark at... 對……吠叫

例: Barking dogs never bite.
(會叫的狗不咬人。——諺語)

84. baseball [ˈbesbɔl] n. 棒球

例: Matt will go to a baseball game on Sunday.
(星期天馬特會去看棒球賽。)

85. bat [bæt] n. 蝙蝠; 球棒

例: We saw a bat fly through the air.
(我們看到一隻蝙蝠飛過天空。)

86. bathroom [ˈbæθrum] n. 浴室, 廁所

例: He's in the bathroom taking a bath.
(他在浴室洗澡。)

87. battle [ˈbætl] n. 戰役

war 指全面的『戰爭』; battle 指在戰爭中一場一場的『戰役』。

例: The battle took the lives of two hundred people.
(這場戰役奪走了兩百條人命。)

88. beach [bitʃ] n. 海灘

comb the beach 在海邊撿貝殼

comb [kom] 原為名詞, 表『梳子』, 作動詞時則表『用梳子梳』, 如:
"comb your hair"』(梳頭髮)。我們到海邊常會用手或樹枝挖洞找貝殼,
這個動作在英語中就說"comb the beach"。

例: I like to go swimming at the beach.
(我喜歡到海邊游泳。)

89. beak [bik] n. 鳥的嘴, 喙

　哺乳類動物的嘴則用"mouth"表示。

　例: The bird hit the ground with its beak.
　（這隻鳥用嘴啄地。）

90. bean [bin] n. 豆子

　例: Tom ate beans and rice for dinner.
　（湯姆晚餐吃豆子及米飯。）

91. bear [bɛr] vt. 忍受 & n. 熊

　＊bear 作動詞時, 三態為: bear、bore、borne。

　例: I can't bear his bad temper anymore.
　= I can't put up with his bad temper anymore.
　（我再也受不了他的壞脾氣了。）

92. beat [bit] vt. 打 & n. 節拍

　beat 作動詞時, 三態為: beat、beat、beaten。

　例: We danced to the beat of the music.
　（我們隨著音樂的節拍起舞。）

　Father beat me up for lying.
　（我因為說謊被爸爸揍了。）

93. beautiful [ˈbjutəfəl] a. 美麗的

　例: That dress looks beautiful on you.
　= You look beautiful in that dress.
　（那件洋裝穿在妳身上很好看。）

94. because [bɪˈkɔz] conj. 因為

　中文常說『因為……所以……』, 但在英文中不可說"Because...so...",
　因為在英句中, 只可使用一個連接詞, 故使用 Becuase 時, 就不可以
　使用 so; 若使用 so, 就不可以再使用 Because。

例: Because he is polite, so I like him. (✗)
→ Because he is polite, I like him. (○)
= He is polite, so I like him.
(因為他很有禮貌，所以我很喜歡他。)

95. **become** [bɪˋkʌm] vi. 變成

例: After a few months, we became good friends.
(幾個月後，我們就成了好友。)

96. **bedroom** [ˋbɛdrum] n. 臥房

例: My bedroom is next to my sister's.
(我的臥房就在我妹妹的隔壁。)

97. **bee** [bi] n. 蜜蜂

be (as) busy as a bee　　忙得要命

例: I just got stung by a bee.
(我剛才被蜜蜂螫到了。)

＊ stung [stʌŋ] 是 sting 的過去式及過去分詞。
sting [stɪŋ] vt. 叮，螫

98. **beef** [bif] n. 牛肉

例: My favorite food is beef noodle soup.
(我最愛吃的食物就是牛肉湯麵。)

99. **begin** [bɪˋgɪn] vi. & vt. 開始 (= start)

三態為: begin、began、begun。

例: The movie began an hour ago.
(電影一個小時前開演。)

100. **behind** [bɪˋhaɪnd] adv. 落後 prep. 在……之後

fall behind　　落後了

例: Mary is falling behind in her schoolwork.

(瑪麗的功課落後了。)

Do not speak ill of others behind their backs.

(不要在別人背後說壞話。)

---

101. **believe** [bɪˈliv] vt. & vi. 相信

belief [bɪˈlif] n. 信仰

believe in...　　相信……的存在; 信奉 (宗教)

例: Mary doesn't believe in Santa Claus.

(瑪麗不相信有聖誕老公公。)

＊ believe 亦可用於下列片語中:

make believe that...　　假裝……

例: He made believe that he was rich.

= He pretended that he was rich.

(他假裝很有錢。)

---

102. **bell** [bɛl] n. 鈴; 鐘

ring a bell　　聽起來很熟

例: When the bell rang, students rushed out of the classroom.

(鐘聲響起，學生全都衝出教室。)

The name rings a bell.

(這個名字聽起來很熟。)

---

103. **belong** [bɪˈlɔŋ] vi. 屬於

belong to sb　　屬於某人

例: All the things you see here belong to me.

(你在這兒所看到的東西都屬於我的。)

---

104. **below** [bəˈlo] prep. 在……之下

例: When the temperature is below zero, water becomes ice.

(溫度降至零下時，水就結冰。)

105. **belt** [bɛlt] n. 腰帶, 皮帶

例: These pants are too big. I need to wear a belt.
(這條褲子太大了。我需要繫皮帶。)

106. **bench** [bɛntʃ] n. (公園內的) 長板凳, 長椅

例: I saw a couple sitting on a bench kissing.
(我看到一對情侶坐在長椅上接吻。)

107. **bicycle** [ˈbaɪsɪkl] n. 腳踏車 (= bike [baɪk])

例: Every morning, I ride my bicycle to school.
(我每天早上騎單車上學。)

108. **bill** [bɪl] n. 帳單

pay the bill   付帳
= foot the bill
例: Don't worry. I'll take care of the dinner bill.
(別擔心。晚餐的帳單我來付。)

109. **billboard** [ˈbɪlˌbɔrd] n. 廣告牌

例: The billboard is a large sign for Coca-Cola.
(這塊廣告牌是可口可樂的大型看板。)

110. **birthday** [ˈbɝθˌde] n. 生日

give sb sth for his/her birthday   給某人某物當生日禮物
= give sb sth as his/her birthday present
例: Father gave me a watch for my birthday.
(爸爸送我一只錶做為我的生日禮物。)

111. **bit** [bɪt] n. 少量

a bit of...   一點點的……
例: Can I get a bit of help with my homework?
(可否請你幫我一點小忙教我做功課?)

112. **bite** [baɪt] vt. 咬 & n. 一口咬下的食量 **b**

grab a bite to eat　　匆匆吃點東西

例: Don't bite off more than you can chew.

(量力而為。——諺語)

I grabbed a bite to eat before going to school.

(我匆匆吃點東西便上學去了。)

113. **bitter** [ˈbɪtɚ] a. 苦的 **b**

例: The juice tastes bitter.

(這果汁嚐起來有苦味。)

114. **blackboard** [ˈblæk͵bɔrd] n. 黑板 **b**

例: The teacher wrote the answer on the blackboard.

(老師把答案寫在黑板上。)

115. **blank** [blæŋk] n. 空格 **b**

例: Fill in all the blanks on the test paper.

(把考卷上的空格填妥。)

116. **blanket** [ˈblæŋkɪt] n. 毛毯 **b**

例: The baby was wrapped in a warm blanket.

(小寶寶被包裹在溫暖的毛毯裏。)

117. **blind** [blaɪnd] a. 瞎的 **b**

turn a blind eye to...　　對……視若無睹

= be blind to...

例: My old aunt is going blind.

(我年邁的阿姨就要眼盲了。)

The boy turned a blind eye to all of his girlfriend's mistakes.

(男孩對他女友所有的錯誤視若無睹。)

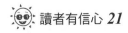

118. **block** [blɑk] n. 街區

例: Go straight two blocks and turn right.
(直走過兩個街區再右轉。)

119. **blood** [blʌd] n. 血

bleed [blid] vi. 流血 (三態為: bleed、bled、bled)
blood type　　血型
例: There's blood on the floor. What happened?
(地板上有血跡。怎麼回事？)
His wound is bleeding.
(他的傷口在流血。)

120. **blouse** [blaʊz] n. (女用) 圓領襯衫

shirt [ʃɝt] n. (男用) 襯衫
例: It's OK for a girl to wear a blouse or shirt, but it's strange for
a boy to wear a blouse.
(女孩子穿什麼襯衫都可以，但男孩子若穿女生的襯衫那就怪了。)

121. **blow** [blo] vt. 吹

三態為: blow、blew [blu]、blown [blon]。
blow out...　　將……吹熄
blow up...　　將……炸掉
例: The girl blew out the candles on the cake.
(女孩把蛋糕上的蠟燭吹熄了。)
The soldiers blew up the bridge.
(士兵們把橋炸了。)

122. **blue** [blu] n. 藍色 & a. 藍色的; 憂鬱的

例: I saw birds flying in the blue sky.
(我看到碧藍的天空中有鳥兒在飛翔。)
Why are you feeling so blue?
(你為什麼如此憂鬱？)

123. **board** [bɔrd] vt. 登上 (火車、船、飛機等大型交通工具)   b

　例: We boarded the train (that was) bound for Taichung.
　　(我們登上開往台中的火車。)
　　＊be bound for＋地方　　開往某地

124. **boat** [bot] n. 船   b

　例: The boat turned over and sank.
　　(船翻了之後接著便沈入水中。)

125. **body** [ˈbɑdɪ] n. 身體; 屍體   b

　in body and mind　　身心方面
　例: Traveling is good for you in both body and mind.
　　(旅遊對你身心有益。)

126. **boil** [bɔɪl] vt. 煮沸 & vi. 沸騰   b

　例: Please boil the water before you make tea.
　　(請把水煮開再泡茶。)
　　＊make tea/coffee　　泡茶/咖啡
　　= fix tea/coffee

127. **bone** [bon] n. 骨頭; 魚刺   b

　bony [ˈbonɪ] a. (魚) 多刺的
　例: I broke the bone in my left leg when I jumped down.
　　(我跳下來時,把左腿的骨頭折斷了。)
　　Be careful when eating the fish. It's bony.
　　(吃這魚的時候要小心。它刺很多。)

128. **book** [bʊk] n. 書 & vt. 預訂   b

　hit the books　　K 書
　例: I have to hit the books tonight, so I can't go out with you.
　　(我今晚必須 K 書,因此無法跟你外出。)
　　I'd like to book a room for three nights, please.

(我想訂房住三個晚上。)

129. **boot** [but] n. 靴子

例: Gene has on a pair of black boots.
(阿金穿了一雙黑馬靴。)
　＊have on...　　穿著……
　　＝ wear...

130. **bored** [bɔrd] a. 感到乏味的

be bored with...　　對……感到厭倦
＝ be tired of...
　例: I was bored with the same work every day.
　(每天做同樣的事令我煩死了。)

131. **boring** [ˈbɔrɪŋ] a. 令人乏味的

例: My math teacher is very boring.
(我的數學老師很無趣。)
＊ bored 及 boring 均源自動詞 bore。
　bore [bɔr] vt. 使……厭倦
　例: His speech bored me to death.
　(他的演講乏味得要命。)

132. **born** [bɔrn] a. 出生的

be born into ＋ 家庭　　出生在……的家庭
be born of ＋ 夫妻　　由某對夫妻所生
　例: He was born into a poor family.
　(他出生寒門。)
　　He was born of a poor couple.
　　(他是一對貧窮的夫妻所生的。)
＊ born 與 borne 均源自動詞 bear (三態為: bear、bore、borne), 但用法不同。born 是形容詞, borne 則是過去分詞, 僅用於兩種情況:
　a. have borne ＋ 受詞

例: She has born five children in all. (✗)

→　She has borne five children in all. (○)

（她共生了五個小孩。）

b. be borne by...　　被……所生

例: She was born by Mary. (✗)

→ She was borne by Mary. (○)

（她是瑪麗所生的。）

133. borrow [ˈbɑro] vt. 借入　　b

lend [lɛnd] vt. 借給 (三態為: lend、lent、lent)

borrow sth from sb　　向某人借東西

lend sth to sb　　借東西給某人

= lend sb sth

例: Can I borrow some money from you?

（我可以向你借錢嗎？）

He lent $500 to me.

= He lent me $500.

（他借給我五百元。）

134. both [boθ] pron. 兩者　　b

例: Both of my sisters are very tall.

（我兩個姊姊個子都很高。）

135. bottle [bɑtḷ] n. 瓶子　　b

a bottle of...　　一瓶……

例: There is a bottle of juice on the table.

（桌上有一瓶果汁。）

136. bottom [ˈbɑtəm] n. 底部　　b

from the bottom of one's heart　　打自內心

例: I respect him from the bottom of my heart.

（我打自內心尊敬他。）

137. **bowl** [bol] n. 碗; 保齡球

　　a bowl of rice/noodles　　一碗飯/麵

　　例: How much does a bowl of beef noodles cost?
　　（一碗牛肉麵多少錢？）

138. **box** [bɑks] n. 盒子

　　a box of...　　一盒……

　　例: My older sister bought me a box of chocolate for my birthday.
　　（我姐姐買了一盒巧克力給我慶生。）

139. **boxing** [ˈbɑksɪŋ] n. 拳擊

　　boxer [ˈbɑksɚ] n. 拳擊手

　　例: I'm not interested in boxing at all.
　　（我對拳擊一點興趣都沒有。）

140. **boy** [bɔɪ] n. 男孩; int. 哇 (之後多採倒裝句)

　　例: Boy, is she beautiful!
　　（哇塞，她真有夠美！）

141. **branch** [bræntʃ] n. 樹枝

　　例: I heard a bird chirping on the tree branch.
　　（我聽到樹枝上有鳥叫聲。）

142. **brand** [brænd] n. 品牌

　　brand-new [ˌbrændˈnju] a. 全新的

　　brand-name [ˈbrændˌnem] a. 名牌的

　　例: John's brand-new car was stolen two days after he bought it.
　　（約翰的新車買了兩天後就被偷了。）

　　　 Mary only buys brand-name products.
　　（瑪麗只買名牌貨。）

143. **bread** [brɛd] n. 麵包 (不可數)　　b

a piece of bread　　一塊麵包

例: Carrie baked some bread for her children.

(凱莉烤了些麵包給孩子吃。)

144. **break** [brek] n. 休息 & vt. 打破　　b

三態為: break、broke、broken。

take a break　　休息一下

a tea/coffee break　　喝茶/咖啡/休息時間

例: Tell me who broke the vase.

(告訴我是誰把花瓶打破了。)

Let's take a break.

(咱們休息一下吧。)

145. **breakfast** [ˈbrɛkfəst] n. 早餐　　b

lunch [lʌntʃ] n. 中餐

supper [ˈsʌpɚ] n. (家中) 晚餐

dinner [ˈdɪnɚ] n. (正式或在餐廳的) 晚餐

例: I'd like a cup of coffee and two boiled eggs for breakfast, please.

(早餐給我來杯咖啡及兩顆水煮蛋。)

146. **bridge** [brɪdʒ] n. 橋　　b

例: We walked over the bridge.

(我們步行過橋。)

147. **bright** [braɪt] a. 明亮的; 聰明的　　b

例: The moon was very bright last night.

(昨晚的月亮真明亮。)

Thank you for such a bright idea.

(謝謝你給我這麼一個好點子。)

148. bring [brɪŋ] vt. 帶來

三態為: bring、brought [brɔt]、brought。

例: What brings you here?

(什麼風把你吹來的?)

149. broadcast ['brɔdˌkæst] n. & vt. 廣播 (三態同形)

例: I listen to the news broadcast every morning.

(我每天早上收聽新聞廣播。)

The show was broadcast live [laɪv].

(這個節目現場播出。)

150. broken ['brokən] a. 已破的; 已壞的

例: The broken TV needs to be fixed.

(這架壞電視機需要修理了。)

151. broom [brum] n. 掃帚

例: I swept the floor with a broom.

(我用掃帚掃地板。)

152. brown [braʊn] a. 棕色的

例: The rug is brown and white.

(地毯的顏色棕白相間。)

153. brush [brʌʃ] n. 刷子 & vt. 刷

brush one's teeth　刷牙

例: I forgot to brush my teeth last night.

(我昨晚忘了刷牙。)

＊ brush 亦可作不及物動詞, 有下列重要用法:

brush up on...　複習……

例: You should brush up on what I have taught you.

(你應該複習我教過你的東西。)

154. build [bɪld] vt. 建造 (三態為: build、built、built) **b**

例: We built a new park in memory of the hero.
(我們建立一座公園以紀念這位英雄。)

155. building [ˈbɪldɪŋ] n. 建築物, 大樓 **b**

例: That building is on fire.
(那座大樓起火了。)

156. bump [bʌmp] vi. 碰撞 **b**

bump into...　　碰到……; 與……不期而遇
例: Pat bumped into the table.
(派特撞到桌子。)

I | bumped into | Peter on my way home.
  | ran into |

(我回家途中與彼得不期而遇。)

157. bun [bʌn] n. 圓麵包 (可數) **b**

bread [brɛd] n. 麵包 (集合名詞)
a bun　　一個麵包
a piece of bread　　一塊麵包
例: The warm buns were delicious.
(這些熱騰騰的麵包好好吃喲。)

158. bunch [bʌntʃ] n. 束 **b**

a bunch of...　　一束; 一群; 一串
a bunch of bananas　　一串香蕉
a bunch of people　　一小群人
a bunch of flowers　　一束花
例: He gave her a bunch of flowers on her birthday.
(她生日那天, 他送了一束花給她。)

159. **burn** [bɜn] vt. 燙傷; 燃燒

(三態為: burn、burned/burnt、burned/burnt)

burn up...　　燒掉 (紙張, 文件等)

burn down...　　燒毀 (建築物)

例: Be careful not to burn your hands.

(小心別燙到手。)

She burnt up all the letters he had sent her.

(她把他寄給她的所有信都燒掉了。)

The fire burnt down the house, killing all the people in it.

(大火燒毀房子，裏面的人全都喪命。)

160. **bus** [bʌs] n. 巴士

get on the bus　　上公車

get off the bus　　下公車

catch the bus　　趕搭公車

例: I have to catch the bus in ten minutes.

(十分鐘後我得趕搭公車。)

161. **bush** [buʃ] n. 樹叢

beat around the bush　　繞著樹叢兜圈子, 喻『講話兜圈子』

例: There is a small bush in front of my house.

(我家前面有片小樹叢。)

Don't beat around the bush. Get to the point.

(別拐彎抹角。直接講重點。)

162. **business** [ˈbɪznɪs] n. 生意; 事務

mean business　　當一回事

be on business　　出差

例: I'm not joking. I mean business.

(我可不是開玩笑。我是當真的。)

He is on business in Japan.

(他正在日本出差。)

163. **busy** [ˈbɪzɪ] a. 忙碌的

be busy with + 名詞　　忙於……

be busy + Ving　　忙著從事……

例: We were busy with our homework last night.

（我們昨晚忙著做功課。）

I'm busy to do the work, so I can't answer the phone now. (✗)

→ I'm busy doing the work, so I can't answer the phone now. (○)

（我忙著做事，因此現在不能接電話。）

164. **but** [bʌt] conj. 但是

例: I want to go, but I can't.

（我想去，但卻無法成行。）

165. **butter** [ˈbʌtɚ] n. 奶油

例: We are out of butter and milk.

（我們的奶油跟牛奶用完了。）

166. **butterfly** [ˈbʌtɚˌflaɪ] n. 蝴蝶

例: A butterfly flew by my window.

（一隻蝴蝶飛過我窗邊。）

167. **button** [ˈbʌtn̩] n. 鈕扣; 按鈕

push the button　　按按鈕

例: Help me undo the buttons.

（幫我把鈕扣解開。）

168. **buy** [baɪ] vt. 買 (三態為: buy、bought、bought)

例: I need to buy some food.

（我需要買些食物。）

169. cab [kæb] n. 計程車 (= taxi)

cabbie [ˈkæbɪ] n. 計程車司機 (= taxi driver)

例: Tim took a cab to work this morning.

(提姆今晨搭計程車上班。)

170. cabbage [ˈkæbɪdʒ] n. 包心菜

例: The fried cabbage tasted very good.

(這道炒包心菜味道不錯。)

171. cabin [ˈkæbɪn] n. 小木屋

例: There is a cabin by the river.

(河邊有一座小木屋。)

172. cabinet [ˈkæbənɪt] n. 櫥櫃

例: I put my dishes away in the cabinet.

(我把盤子收到櫥櫃內。)

＊put away... 　將……放好/歸位

173. cage [kedʒ] n. 籠子

例: The bird in the cage is a parrot.

(籠中的鳥是隻鸚鵡。)

174. cake [kek] n. 蛋糕

a cake 　一整個蛋糕

a piece of cake 　一塊蛋糕

例: May I have a piece of your cake?

(我可以吃一塊你的蛋糕嗎?)

＊be a piece of cake 　是很簡單的事

= be quite easy

例: To me, singing is a piece of cake.

(對我而言,唱歌是很簡單的事。)

175. calendar [ˈkæləndɚ] n. 日曆　　　C

   the solar calendar　　陽曆

   the lunar calendar　　陰曆

例: I looked at the calendar to find out what day it was.

（我看日曆以了解那天是星期幾。）

176. calf [kæf] n. 小牛 (複數為 calves)　　　C

   cow [kaʊ] n. 母牛

   bull [bʊl] n. 公牛

例: The little calf stood next to its large mother.

（小牛站在體型碩大的母牛身旁。）

177. call [kɔl] n. 電話 & vt. 叫喊; 打電話給 (某人)　　　C

   give sb a call　　打電話給某人

= give sb a ring

例: There is a call for you on the other phone.

（另外一支電話有人找你。）

   Give me a call when you have time.

= Call me (up) when you have time.

（有空打電話給我。）

   ＊call on...　　拜訪⋯⋯

   = visit...

例: I'll call on him tomorrow.

（我明天會去看他。）

178. camera [ˈkæmərə] n. 照相機　　　C

例: The camera is used to take pictures.

（照相機是拍照用的。）

179. camp [kæmp] n. & vi. 露營　　　C

   go camping　　去露營

例: We went camping in the mountains last week.
(上星期我們到山中露營。)

180. **cancel** [ˈkænsḷ] vt. 取消　　C

= call off...

例: We cancelled our trip to Japan.
(我們取消了日本之行。)

181. **candle** [ˈkændḷ] n. 蠟燭　　C

例: I made a wish and then blew out the candles on the birthday cake.
(我許了願，然後把生日蛋糕上的蠟燭吹熄。)

＊blow out...　　將……吹熄

182. **cap** [kæp] n. 帽子; 瓶蓋　　C

例: How much does that baseball cap cost?
(那頂棒球帽多少錢？)

183. **captain** [ˈkæptn̩] n. 隊長; (飛機) 機長　　C

例: My older brother is the captain of the soccer team.
(我哥哥是足球隊隊長。)

184. **capital** [ˈkæpətḷ] n. 首都　　C

例: The capital of the U.S. is Washington, D.C.
(美國首都是華盛頓。)

185. **car** [kɑr] n. 汽車　　C

例: I'm tired. It's your turn to drive the car.
(我累了。輪到你開車了。)

186. **card** [kɑrd] n. 卡片; 撲克牌　　　　　**c**

play cards　　　玩紙牌

例: We killed time by playing cards.
（我們藉玩牌消磨時間。）

187. **care** [kɛr] n. 小心 & vi. 關心; 喜歡 (使用於下列片語中)　**c**

take care of...　　照顧……
care about...　　關心……
care for...　　喜歡……

例: Would you take care of my baby while I'm away?
（我不在的時候，可否請你照顧我的小寶寶？）

I really care about you.
（我真的關心你。）

Would you care for some wine?
= Would you like some wine?
（要不要喝點酒呀？）

188. **careful** [ˈkɛrfəl] a. 小心的　　　　　**c**

be careful with + 東西　　小心處理某物
be careful about + 言行　　謹言慎行

例: Be careful with that vase. It may break.
（小心處理那花瓶。它容易破。）

Be careful about what you say and do.
（說話行事要謹慎。）

189. **careless** [ˈkɛrlɪs] a. 粗心的　　　　　**c**

例: The careless man caused the car accident.
（那名粗心的男子造成這起車禍。）

190. **carpenter** [ˈkɑrpəntɚ] n. 木匠　　　　**C**

例: The carpenter is good at making bookshelves.
（這個木匠擅長製作書架。）

191. **carpet** [ˈkɑrpɪt] n. (鋪滿整個地板的) 地毯　　**C**

rug [rʌg] n. 方型地毯; (一小塊的) 地毯

例: The small girl spilled juice on the carpet.
（小女孩把果汁濺到地毯上了。）

192. **carriage** [ˈkærɪdʒ] n. 馬車　　　　**C**

例: People used to travel by carriage.
（以前大家都是乘馬車旅行。）

193. **carrot** [ˈkærət] n. 胡蘿蔔　　　　**C**

例: Carrots are rich in vitamin A.
（胡蘿蔔含有豐富的維他命 A。）
＊be rich in...　　含有豐富的……

194. **carry** [ˈkærɪ] vt. 攜帶　　　　**C**

例: Will you help me carry my bag?
（請你幫我提我的袋子好嗎？）

195. **cart** [kɑrt] n. 手推車　　　　**C**

例: The cart was full of vegetables and fruit.
（手推車上滿是蔬果。）
＊be full of...　　充滿著……
= be filled with...

196. **carton** [ˈkɑrtn̩] n. 紙盒　　　　**C**

a carton of...　　一盒……

例: I need to buy a carton of milk and some eggs.
(我需要買一盒牛奶和幾顆雞蛋。)

197. **cartoon** [kɑr'tun] n. 卡通　　　　C

例: I enjoy watching cartoons.
(我喜歡看卡通片。)

198. **case** [kes] n. 情況; 刑案　　　　C

in case of...　　萬一有……

例: Keep a fire extinguisher at hand in case of an emergency.
(準備一支滅火器放在附近，以便緊急狀況使用。)

The police are still looking into the case.
(警方仍在調查該案。)

＊look into...　　調查……

199. **catch** [kætʃ] vt. 捉; 感染 & vi. 趕上　　　C

三態為: catch、caught、caught。

catch a cold　　感冒

catch up with...　　趕上……

例: I caught a cold last week.
(我上星期感冒了。)

You're walking too fast; I can't catch up with you.
(你走得太快，我趕不上你。)

200. **cattle** ['kætl̩] n. 牛群 (複數名詞)　　　　C

cattle 一字如同 people (當『人』解釋時) 一樣, 只可用 two 以上的數詞修飾。

one/a cattle (✗)

one/a cow/bull (○)　　一頭母牛/公牛

two cattle (○)　　兩頭牛

five cattle (○)　　五頭牛

many cattle (○)　　許多牛

one/a people (✗)
one/a person (○)　一個人
two people (○)　兩個人
five people (○)　五個人
many people (○)　許多人
例: The farmer raises many cattle.
(這個農夫養了許多牛。)

201. **cause** [kɔz] vt. 引起 & n. 原因　　C

cause sb to V　促使某人……
例: His carelessness caused the accident.
(他的粗心造成了這起意外。)
The sad story caused me to cry.
(這悲傷的故事使我哭了。)
What was the cause of that car accident?
(那起車禍的原因是什麼？)

202. **cave** [kev] n. 洞　　C

例: The cave was dark and scary.
(這個洞既黑且嚇人。)

203. **ceiling** [ˈsilɪŋ] n. 天花板　　C

hit the ceiling　大發雷霆
例: The ceiling was painted white.
(天花板被粉刷成白色。)

204. **celebrate** [ˈsɛləˌbret] vt. 慶祝　　C

celebration [ˌsɛləˈbreʃən] n. 慶祝
in celebration of...　慶祝……
例: How will you celebrate your birthday?
(你的生日將怎麼慶祝？)

We threw a party in celebration of his birthday.
(我們舉行派對以慶祝他的生日。)

205. **cellular phone** [ˌsɛljələˈfon] n. 行動電話   c
= cell phone [ˈsɛl ˌfon]
= mobile phone [ˌmobḷ ˈfon]
> 例: My cellular phone doesn't work. Can I use yours?
> (我的大哥大壞了，可以用你的嗎？)

206. **cent** [sɛnt] n. 一分 (美金)   c
> 例: One hundred cents equal one US dollar.
> (一百分等於美金一元。)

207. **centimeter** [ˈsɛntəˌmitə] n. 公分   c
> 例: That bug is two centimeters long.
> (那隻蟲長兩公分。)

208. **center** [ˈsɛntə] n. 中心   c
> 例: This city is the center of business.
> (本市是商業中心。)

209. **century** [ˈsɛntʃərɪ] n. 世紀   c
> 例: A century is a hundred years long.
> (一世紀有一百年之久。)

210. **cereal** [ˈsɪrɪəl] n. 麥片   c
> 例: My favorite breakfast is cereal and milk.
> (我最喜愛的早餐是麥片加牛奶。)

211. **certain** [ˈsɜtṇ] a. 某些 (= some); 確定的   c
certain + 複數名詞   某些……

a certain + 單數名詞　　某個……

例: Certain answers are not correct.
(若干答案有誤。)

I'm certain that he is right.
= I'm sure that he is right.
(我確信他是對的。)

212. **certainly** [ˈsɝtn̩lɪ] adv. 當然地

= surely [ˈʃʊrlɪ] adv.

例: I will certainly call you if I need any help.
(我若需要幫助,一定會打電話給你。)

213. **chair** [tʃɛr] n. 椅子

例: She sat down in the chair by the window.
(她在靠窗的椅子上坐了下來。)

214. **chalk** [tʃɔk] n. 粉筆 (不可數); 石膏粉 (不可數)

a piece of chalk　　一根粉筆

例: The teacher wrote on the blackboard with a piece of white chalk.
(老師用一根白粉筆在黑板上寫字。)

215. **chance** [tʃæns] n. 機會

by chance　　偶然間 (= by accident)
take chances　　冒險

例: You have a good chance of winning the contest.
(你贏得比賽的勝算很大。)

Do not take chances while driving.
(開車時不要冒險。)

I found the secret by chance.
(我無意間發現這個秘密。)

216. change [tʃendʒ] vt. & vi. 改變 & n. 改變; 零錢 (不可數)　　Ⓒ

　　keep the change　　零錢免找
　　change A into B　　將 A 變成 B
　= turn A into B
　　例: The mother changed her baby's diaper.
　　　(這位媽媽替小寶寶換尿片。)
　　　　The magician changed the mouse into a bird.
　　　(魔術師把老鼠變成一隻鳥。)
　　　　How much change do you have?
　　　(你有多少零錢?)

217. character [ˈkærəktɚ] n. 角色; 人物　　Ⓒ

　　the main character　　主角
　　例: The main character in the book is a boy named Charlie.
　　　(書中的主角是個名叫查理的小孩。)

218. charge [tʃɑrdʒ] vt. & n. 記賬; 充電; 收費　　Ⓒ

　　例: Will that be cash or charge?
　　　(您付現還是刷卡?)
　　　　They charged me $10 for the service.
　　　(他們向我收十元的服務費。)

219. chase [tʃes] vt. 追趕; 追求 (女孩子)　　Ⓒ

　　例: The cat chased the mouse around the room.
　　　(貓把老鼠追得滿屋跑。)
　　　　John wasted a lot of time chasing girls.
　　　(約翰浪費很多時間追女孩子。)

220. chat [tʃæt] n. & vi. 聊天　　Ⓒ

　　have a chat with...　　與……聊天
　= chat with...

例: I had a pleasant chat with my father yesterday.
（我昨天跟我爸爸聊天聊得很愉快。）

221. **cheap** [tʃip] a. 便宜的; 小氣的 (= stingy [ˈstɪndʒɪ])

expensive [ɪkˈspɛnsɪv] a. 昂貴的

例: Matt is very cheap. He doesn't like spending money.
（馬特很小氣。他不喜歡花錢。）

I bought the shirt because it was very cheap.
（襯衫很便宜，所以我就買下來了。）

222. **cheat** [tʃit] vt. 欺騙 & vi. 作弊

cheat sb　　欺騙某人

cheat on sb　　對某人感情不忠

例: Tom cheated on the examination.
（湯姆考試作弊。）

Mary left Peter when she found he had cheated on her.
（瑪麗發現彼得對她感情不忠時，便離他而去。）

223. **check** [tʃɛk] vt. & vi. 檢查; 登記

check out　　退房

check in　　住房

例: You need to check in at the hotel first.
（你得先在飯店辦理住房手續。）

When will you check out of the hotel?
（你何時退房？）

224. **cheek** [tʃik] n. 面頰 (因有左右兩邊, 故常用複數)

例: The girl's cheeks turned red when the boy touched her hand.
（那男孩觸碰女孩子手時，她面頰紅了起來。）

225. cheerful ['tʃɪrfəl] a. 高興的　　**C**

= happy

例: Mary became cheerful at the sight of her boyfriend.

(瑪麗一看到男友，便高興起來。)

226. cheese [tʃiz] n. 乳酪, 起司　　**C**

例: Do you want cheese on your hamburger?

(你的漢堡要不要加起司？)

227. cherry ['tʃɛrɪ] n. 櫻桃　　**C**

例: My mother made a cherry pie for dessert.

(我媽媽做了一個櫻桃派當甜點。)

　　＊dessert [dɪ'zɝt] n. 甜點

228. chest [tʃɛst] n. 胸腔　　**C**

例: The ball hit him in the chest.

(那個球打到他的胸部。)

　　＊hit sb on the + 硬的部位

　　hit sb in the + 軟的部位

例: He hit me on the back.

(他打我的背。)

　　He hit me in the nose/stomach.

(他打我的鼻子/肚子。)

229. chicken ['tʃɪkən] n. 雞 (可數); 雞肉 (不可數)　　**C**

例: That restaurant is known for its fried chicken.

(那家餐廳以炸雞出名。)

230. child ['tʃaɪld] n. 小孩 (單數)　　**C**

children ['tʃɪldrən] n. 小孩 (複數)

例: Mr. and Mrs. Smith will take their children to the zoo tomorrow.
(史密斯夫婦明天會帶孩子到動物園去。)

231. chimney [ˈtʃɪmnɪ] n. 煙囪　C

例: Smoke was coming out of the chimney.
(煙囪正在冒煙。)

232. Chinese [ˌtʃaɪˈniz] n. 中國人; 中文 & a. 中國 (籍)的; 中文的　C

例: He is a Chinese. (Chinese 是名詞)
= He is Chinese. (Chinese 是形容詞)
(他是中國人。)

233. chocolate [ˈtʃɑkəlɪt] n. 巧克力　C

例: The chocolate candy melted in the sun.
(巧克力在陽光下融化了。)

234. choir [ˈkwaɪr] n. (教堂或學校的人聲) 合唱團　C

band [bænd] n. (熱門音樂) 合唱團
orchestra [ˈɔrkɪstrə] n. 管絃樂團

例: I want to join my school's choir next year.
(我明年要加入學校的合唱團。)

235. choose [tʃuz] vt. 選擇　C

choice [tʃɔɪs] n. 選擇
make a choice　做選擇
have no choice but to V　除了……別無選擇

例: There are not many things for me to choose from.
(我可以選擇的東西並不多。)
I have no choice but to leave you, honey.
(親愛的,我除了離開你外別無選擇。)

236. chop [tʃɑp] vt. 切, 砍

例: The chef chopped the carrots into small pieces.
(廚師將胡蘿蔔切成小塊。)

237. chopstick ['tʃɑpˌstɪk] n. 筷子

a pair of chopsticks　　一雙筷子

例: Chopsticks are hard for many foreigners to use.
(對許多外國人來說，使用筷子很困難。)

238. Christmas ['krɪsməs] n. 聖誕節

例: Santa Claus comes on Christmas Eve.
(聖誕老人在聖誕夜降臨。)

239. church [tʃɝtʃ] n. 教堂

go to church　　做禮拜

例: Every Sunday we go to church.
(每個星期天，我們去做禮拜。)

240. cigarette [ˌsɪgə'rɛt] n. 香煙

a cigarette butt　　煙屁股

例: Phil is trying to stop smoking cigarettes.
(菲爾正設法戒煙。)

241. cicada [sɪ'kɑdə] n. 蟬

例: With the coming of spring, we can hear cicadas singing everywhere.
(隨著春天的到來，我們可以聽到蟬到處鳴唱。)

242. circle ['sɝkl̩] n. 圓圈

例: The students formed a circle and started to dance.
(學生圍成圓圈開始跳舞。)

243. circus ['sɝkəs] n. 馬戲團

例: At the circus we saw clowns and animals like tigers and lions.
(馬戲團裏，我們看到小丑和老虎、獅子等動物。)

244. clap [klæp] vt. 拍 (手)

clap one's hands　　拍手

例: Everyone clapped their hands when the singer finished singing.
(歌手唱完歌時，大家都拍手。)

245. class [klæs] n. 班級; 課程

cut class　　蹺課
attend class　　上課
= go to class

例: A good student never cuts class.
(好學生從不蹺課。)

246. classmate ['klæsmet] n. 同班同學

schoolmate ['skulmet] n. 同校同學

例: My classmates and I went on a trip to Hualien last week.
(我同班同學和我上星期到花蓮玩了一趟。)

247. classroom ['klæsrum] n. 教室

例: The teacher was angry because the classroom was a mess.
(老師很生氣，因為教室內一團亂。)

248. claw [klɔ] n. 爪子 & vi. 抓

claw at...　　猛抓……

例: The cat keeps clawing at the ground.
(這隻貓猛在地上抓。)

The bird held a leaf in its claw.
(這隻鳥的爪上抓住一片葉子。)

249. clean [klin] vt. 清潔 & a. 清潔的 **C**

clean up... 將……清理乾淨
keep...clean 把……保持乾淨
例: Clean up the table after dinner.
(餐後把桌子清乾淨。)

250. clear [klɪr] a. 透明的; 晴朗的 & vi. (天空) 放晴 (與 up 並用) **C**

clear up (天空) 放晴
例: The water is so clear that I can see fish swimming around.
(水好清,我可以看到魚兒游來游去。)
The rain has stopped and the sky is clearing up.
(雨停了,而天空也漸漸放晴了。)

251. clever ['klɛvɚ] a. 聰明的 **C**

例: Frank is very clever. In fact, he is the smartest boy in our class.
(法蘭克很聰明。事實上,他是我們班上最聰明的孩子。)

252. climb [klaɪm] vt. & vi. 爬 **C**

例: The monkey climbed the tree looking for bananas.
(猴子爬樹找香蕉吃。)

253. clinic ['klɪnɪk] n. 診所 **C**

dental clinic [ˌdɛntl̩ 'klɪnɪk] n. 牙醫診所
例: The mother took the baby to the clinic to see the doctor.
(媽媽帶小寶寶到診所看醫生。)

254. **clock** [klɑk] n. 鐘

around the clock　一天二十四小時

例: The clock says it is 6:25.

(鐘顯示現在時間是六點二十五分。)

The soldiers are on guard around the clock.

(軍人全天候保持警戒。)

255. **close** [kloz] vt. 關閉, 結束 & [klos] a. 靠近的 & adv. 靠近

come close to + Ving　差一點……

例: The bookstore is now closed. It will be open tomorrow.

(書店現在打烊了。明天會營業。)

We came close to winning the contest.

= We almost won the game.

(我們差一點贏了這場比賽。)

256. **closet** [ˈklɑzɪt] n. 壁櫥 (靠牆連壁的衣櫥)

例: My coat is in the closet.

(我的外套在衣櫥裏。)

257. **cloth** [klɔθ] n. 布料 (不可數)

a piece of cloth　一塊布

唯 cloth 表『桌布』或『抹布』時, 則可數:

a tablecloth　一張桌布

a cloth　一張抹布

例: I like cloth that feels smooth.

(我喜歡觸感平滑的布料。)

258. **clothes** [kloz] n. 衣服 (恆為複數, 不可數)

例: Those clothes are dirty. Take them off and wash them.

(那些衣服很髒。把它們脫下來洗一洗。)

259. clothing ['kloðɪŋ] n. 衣服 (= clothes, 亦不可數)　　Ⓒ

例: All of the clothing in this department store is on sale.
= All of the clothes in this department store are on sale.
(百貨公司所有的衣服都在打折。)

260. cloud [klaʊd] n. 雲　　Ⓒ

cloudy [klaʊdɪ] a. 多雲的, 陰天的

例: The clouds are gray and it looks like it will rain.
(雲灰灰的，看起來要下雨的樣子。)
You should carry an umbrella. It's really cloudy outside.
(你應帶把傘，外頭天色好陰喲。)

261. clown [klaʊn] n. 小丑　　Ⓒ

例: The funny clown made all of the children happy.
(滑稽的小丑讓所有的孩子很開心。)

262. club [klʌb] n. 俱樂部; 社團　　Ⓒ

例: There are many clubs to join at my school.
(我學校有好多社團可以參加。)

263. coach [kotʃ] n. 教練　　Ⓒ

例: The basketball coach yelled at his players.
(籃球教練大罵他的球員。)
＊yell at...　對……吼罵

264. coal [kol] n. 煤　　Ⓒ

例: Some people still use coal to heat their homes.
(有些人仍使用煤炭提供房間的暖氣。)
heat [hit] vt. 加熱

265. coast [kost] n. 海岸

on the coast 　在海岸邊

例: The east coast of Taiwan is full of beautiful views.
(台灣東海岸盡是些美景。)

C

266. coat [kot] n. 外套

例: Hang up your coat after you take it off.
(脫下外套後把它掛好。)

C

267. coffee [ˈkɔfɪ] n. 咖啡

例: I'm really tired. I need a cup of coffee.
(我好累,需要一杯咖啡。)

C

268. coin [kɔɪn] n. 硬幣

例: I need some coins to make a phone call.
(我需要一些硬幣打電話。)

C

269. cold [kold] a. 寒冷的 & n. 傷風感冒

catch/have a cold 　感冒

例: It's so cold outside. You'll have to wear heavy clothes when
you go out.
(外頭真冷。你外出時要穿厚衣服。)

＊ heavy clothes [ˌhɛvɪ ˈcloz] n. 厚衣服 (非 thick clothes)
light clothes [ˌlaɪt ˈcloz] n. 薄衣服 (非 thin clothes)

C

270. collar [ˈkɑləˌ] n. 衣領

例: The collar of this shirt is too small. I can't breathe.
(這件襯衫的領子太小了。我不能呼吸。)

C

271. collect [kəˈlɛkt] vt. 收集

collection [kəˈlɛkʃən] n. 蒐藏

C

a large collection of...　　有大量的……蒐藏

例: The teacher asked me to collect everyone's homework.
（老師要我收大家的作業。）

John has a large collection of stamps.
（約翰蒐集很多郵票。）

272. college ['kɑlɪdʒ] n. 學院, 大學 (= university [ˌjunə'vɝsətɪ])　C

go to college/university　　唸大學

例: John went to college with my brother.
（約翰和我哥哥唸同一所大學。）

273. collide [kə'laɪd] vi. (車輛) 撞擊　C

collide with...　　與……相撞

例: The car collided with the truck; fortunately, no one was hurt.
（小車與卡車相撞；所幸無人受傷。）

274. color ['kʌlɚ] n. 顏色; 色彩　C

例: Brown is my favorite color.
（棕色是我的最愛。）

275. comb [kom] n. 梳子 & vt. 梳 (頭)　C

comb the beach　　在海邊撿貝殼 (用樹枝如梳子般在海邊刮來刮去
找貝殼)

例: Comb your hair after you brush your teeth.
（刷完牙之後要梳頭。）

We had a good time combing the beach last weekend.
（上個週末我們在海邊撿貝殼。）

276. comfort ['kʌmfɚt] vt. 安慰 & n. 舒適 (不可數)　C

comforts ['kʌmfɚts] n. 舒適的設備

例: The mother comforted her child after he fell off his bike.
(孩子從腳踏車上摔下來之後，媽媽便安慰他。)

The hotel has all the comforts of home.
(這家飯店擁有家中一切的舒適設備。)

277. **comfortable** [ˈkʌmfɚˌtəbḷ] a. 舒適的; 自在的　　C

例: I feel comfortable when you're around.
(你在場的時候，我感到很自在。)

278. **comic** [ˈkɑmɪk] n. 漫畫　　C

例: I enjoy reading comics in my free time.
(我休閒時喜歡看漫畫。)

279. **common** [ˈkɑmən] a. 共同的; 普通的　　C

common sense　　常識
have something in common with sb　　與某人有某種共同點

例: This flower is very common in our country.
(這種花在我國很普遍。)

Even though we are twins, we have nothing in common (with each other).
(即使我們是雙胞胎，我們卻沒有共同點。)

280. **company** [ˈkʌmpənɪ] n. 同伴 (集合名詞, 不可數); 公司 (可數)　　C

例: Don't keep bad company.
(不要結交壞朋友。)

The company is going out of business soon.
(這家公司就要倒閉了。)

＊表『同伴』時, company 為不可數名詞, 但 companion
[kəmˈpænɪən] 則可數。

He had many companions with him on the trip.
(他有許多同伴隨行旅遊。)

281. compare [kəm'pɛr] vi. 比較

compare A with B   比較 A 與 B

例: Don't compare me with my sister. We're very different.
(別把我與我老姐作比較。我和她大不相同。)

282. complain [kəm'plen] vi. 抱怨

complaint [kəm'plent] n. 抱怨

complain of/about...   抱怨……

例: There is nothing to complain about.
(沒啥好抱怨的。)
    Stop making complaints about life.
(別再抱怨人生了。)

283. computer [ˌkəm'pjutɚ] n. 電腦

例: We use computers to send emails to our friends.
(我們使用電腦向朋友傳送電子郵件。)

284. communicate [kə'mjunəˌket] vi. 溝通; 通訊

communicate with...   與……溝通

例: I communicate with Mark by telephone.
(我藉電話與馬克通訊。)

285. concentrate ['kɑnsənˌtret] vt. & vi. 專心

concentrate on...   專注於……

例: Turn off the TV! I can't concentrate on my work.
(把電視關掉！我無法專心工作。)

286. condition [kən'dɪʃən] n. 狀況; 條件

be in good condition   狀況良好
= be in good shape

例: The car, though old, is still in good condition.
（這輛車雖然老舊，車況仍不錯。）

287. consider [kən'sɪdə] vt. 考慮

consider + Ving　考慮……

例: I'm considering taking a trip to Japan.
（我正考慮到日本走一趟。）

288. consideration [kən,sɪdə'reʃən] n. 考慮

take...into consideration　考慮……
= consider...

例: You should take his ability into consideration before asking
him to do it.
（你要他做這事之前應先考慮他的能力。）

289. continue [kən'tɪnju] vt. 繼續

continue Ving　繼續……
= continue to V
= go on Ving

例: They continued talking after the meal.
（用餐後他們繼續談。）

290. control [kən'trol] vt. & n. 控制

be under control　掌控中
be out of control　失控

例: Don't worry. Everything is well under control.
（別擔心。一切都在掌控中。）

291. container [kən'tenə] n. 容器

例: Put the extra food in a container. Don't throw it away.
（把多餘的食物放在容器裏。不要丟棄。）

292. **convenient** [kən'vɪnɪənt] a. 便利的　　C

It is convenient for sb to V　　某人從事……很方便

例: Will it be convenient for you to take me home?

(你載我回家方便嗎?)

293. **conversation** [ˌkɑnvɚ'seʃən] n. 會話　　C

have a conversation with...　　與……談話

例: I just had a great conversation with my younger sister.

(我剛才與我妹妹談得很愉快。)

294. **cook** [kʊk] n. 廚子, 會做菜的人 & vt. 烹調　　C

chef [ʃɛf] n. (餐廳) 大廚師

例: My dad is a really good cook. He is a chef in a famous hotel.

(我爸爸很會做菜。他是某知名飯店的大廚師。)

295. **cookie** ['kʊkɪ] n. 餅乾　　C

例: Chocolate cookies are my favorite.

(巧克力餅乾是我的最愛。)

296. **cool** [kul] a. 涼的; 正點的 (= great)　　C

例: Wow! That shirt is really cool. Where did you get it?

(哇塞!那件襯衫真棒。你在哪兒買的?)

297. **copy** ['kɑpɪ] vt. & vi. 抄寫; 複製 & n. 副本　　C

copy down...　　抄下……

make a copy of...　　影印一份……

例: Copy down everything I say.

(抄下我說的每句話。)

Please make five copies of this paper.

(這份文件請替我影印五份。)

298.　corn [kɔrn] n. 玉米　　C

例: The farmer grows corn, wheat, and soybeans.
（這個農夫種植玉米、小麥及黃豆。）

299.　corner [ˈkɔrnɚ] n. 角落　　C

on the corner 　　（戶外）轉角處
in the corner 　　（室內）角落裏
be around the corner 　　快要到了
= be coming soon
例: There is a post office on the corner.
（轉角處有一家郵局。）
　　Christmas is around the corner.
（聖誕節就快到了。）

300.　correct [kəˈrɛkt] a. 正確的 & vt. 糾正　　C

例: The teacher will correct our homework.
（老師會批改我們的作業。）

301.　cost [kɔst] vt. 花費 (三態均為 cost) & n. 成本　　C

at the cost of... 　　以……的代價
例: How much does that book cost?
（那本書花多少錢買的？）
　　He bought that book at the cost of $100.
（他花一百元買了那本書。）

302.　cotton [ˈkɑtn̩] n. 棉花　　C

例: We put cotton in our ears because the noise was too loud.
（噪音太大，我們便把棉花塞在耳朵裏。）

303. cough [kɔf] vi. & n. 咳嗽

例: I couldn't stop coughing when I had a cold.
(我感冒時一直咳嗽。)

304. count [kaʊnt] vt. 計算 & vi. 重要

例: Count the money for me.
(替我算錢。)
　　What he says counts.
=　What he says is important.
(他的話算數/很重要。)

305. counter [ˈkaʊntɚ] n. 櫃台

例: Check out at the counter.
(在櫃台處辦理退房。)

306. country [ˈkʌntrɪ] n. 國家 (可數); 鄉村 (不可數)

例: I love visiting the country on weekends.
(週末時我喜歡到鄉下走走。)

307. course [kɔrs] n. 課程; 路徑

of course　　當然

例: Next month I'm taking a writing course.
(下個月我要修寫作課。)
　A: Can I use your car?
　B: Of course./Certainly.
(甲：我可以用你的車嗎？)
(乙：當然可以。)

308. cousin [ˈkʌzn] n. 堂/表兄、弟、姊、妹

例: Karen is my cousin, who is fond of singing.
(凱倫是我表妹，她很喜歡唱歌。)

＊fond [fɑnd] a. 喜歡的
　be fond of...　　喜歡……
＝ enjoy

309. **cover** [ˈkʌvɚ] vt. 覆蓋 Ⓒ

be covered with...　　被……所覆蓋
例: In winter, the mountain is covered with snow.
（冬天時，整座山被白雪覆蓋。）

310. **cow** [kau] n. 乳牛 Ⓒ

例: We saw over a dozen cows in the field.
（我們看到田野裏有十幾隻乳牛。）

311. **crab** [kræb] n. 螃蟹 Ⓒ

例: A crab has two large claws.
（螃蟹有兩個巨螯。）
　＊claw [klɔ] n. 螯; 爪子

312. **cram** [kræm] vi. & n. 填鴨, 死背 Ⓒ

a cram school　　補習班
cram for a test　　為考試臨時抱佛腳
例: Tonight I have to cram for a test.
（今晚我得為考試臨時抱佛腳。）

313. **crash** [kræʃ] vi. & n. 撞擊 Ⓒ

an air crash　　空難
例: The car crashed into a tree.
（車子撞到樹。）

314. **crawl** [krɔl] vi. 爬行　**C**

例: You have to crawl before you can walk.
(你得先爬才會走。)

315. **crayon** [ˈkreən] n. 蠟筆 (可數)　**C**

例: I bought a pack of crayons for my child.
(我買了一盒蠟筆給孩子。)

316. **crazy** [ˈkrezɪ] a. 發瘋的 (= mad); 熱愛的　**C**

be crazy about...　　熱愛……
= be mad about...

例: That man is out of his mind. I think he's crazy.
(這男子腦筋不正常。我想他瘋了。)

John is crazy about the girl he met two days ago.
(約翰很迷戀他兩天前認識的那個女孩。)

317. **cream** [krim] n. 奶精; 奶油　**C**

ice cream　　冰淇淋

例: I'd like my coffee with cream and sugar.
(我的咖啡要加奶精和糖。)

比較: I'd like my coffee black.
(我的咖啡什麼都不加。)

318. **create** [krɪˈet] vt. 創造; 造成　**C**

例: His bad behavior created a lot of trouble.
(他的惡行造成很多麻煩。)

319. **credit** [ˈkrɛdɪt] n. 信用　**C**

a credit card　　信用卡

例: Sorry, we don't accept credit cards here.
(抱歉，我們這裏不收信用卡。)

320. crop [krɑp] n. 農作物　　　C

例: Rice is the main crop grown in Asia.
(米是亞洲栽種的主要農作物。)

321. crowded [ˈkraʊdɪd] a. 擁擠的　　　C

be crowded with...　　擠滿了……
= be packed with...
例: The meeting room is crowded with reporters.
(會議室擠滿了記者。)

322. cry [kraɪ] vi. & n. 哭　　　C

burst out crying　　突然放聲大哭
= burst into tears
例: I couldn't help but cry after I heard the bad news.
(我聽到壞消息之後忍不住哭出來。)

323. culture [ˈkʌltʃɚ] n. 文化　　　C

例: This city is full of culture and exciting things to see.
(本市含有豐富的文化及刺激的事物可看。)

324. cup [kʌp] n. 杯　　　C

glass [glæs] n. 玻璃杯
a cup of coffee/tea　　一杯咖啡/茶
a glass of milk/water　　一杯牛奶/水
be not one's cup of tea　　非某人中意的東西 (用於否定句中)
例: Music is not my cup of tea. I like dancing instead.
(音樂不是我的所愛。我反而喜歡跳舞。)

325. cure [kjʊr] n. & vt. 治療　　　C

cure sb of a disease　　治療某人的疾病

例: Prevention is better than cure.
(預防勝於治療。)
The doctor cured him of asthma.
(醫生醫好了他的氣喘。)
＊asthma ['æzmə] n. 氣喘

326. **curtain** ['kɝtn̩] n. 窗帘　　C

例: Open the curtains. It's too dark in here.
(打開窗帘，這裏面太暗了。)

327. **custom** ['kʌstəm] n. 風俗, 習慣　　C

例: During Chinese New Year, it is a custom to give out red
envelopes to children.
(農曆新年中，發壓歲錢給孩子是個習俗。)

328. **customer** ['kʌstəmɚ] n. 顧客　　C

例: "Will you help that customer over there?" asked the manager.
(經理問道:『你可不可以幫那邊的那位顧客一下?』)

329. **cute** [kjut] a. 可愛的　　C

例: That puppy is so cute. I wish I could take him home.
(那隻小狗狗好可愛，我真希望能帶牠回家。)

330. **cyber** ['saɪbɚ] a. 與網路有關的　　C

cyber café [ˌsaɪbɚ kæ'fe] n. 網路咖啡店
例: There are many cyber cafes in my neighborhood.
(我家附近有很多網咖。)

331. **daily** [ˈdelɪ] a. 每日的 & adv. 每日 (= every day)

例: I always make a daily list of things to do.
(我總是將每日要做的事列成一張表。)
＊make a list of...　將……列表

332. **damage** [ˈdæmɪdʒ] vt. 損害 & n. 損害 (不可數)

do/cause damage to...　損害……
例: The storm did a lot of damage to the city.
(暴風雨對城市造成很大的損害。)

333. **damp** [dæmp] a. 濕的

例: I used a damp cloth to clean off the table.
(我用濕抹布把桌子清乾淨。)

334. **dance** [dæns] vi. 跳舞 & n. 跳舞; 舞會

dance to the music/beat　隨著音樂/節拍起舞
dance with sb　與某人共舞
例: Would you like to dance with me?
(跟我跳舞好嗎?)
We danced to the music.
(我們隨著音樂起舞。)

335. **danger** [ˈdendʒɚ] n. 危險

be in danger　處於危險中
例: That old man is in danger of being hit by a car.
(那名老人有被車子撞的危險。)

336. **dangerous** [ˈdendʒərəs] a. 危險的

例: Drinking and driving is very dangerous.
(酒後駕車很危險。)

337. **dark** [dɑrk] a. 黑暗的

例: It's dark in here and we should turn on the light.
(這裡頭很暗，我們應該把燈打開。)

338. **date** [det] n. & vt. 約會

go on a date with sb　　與某人約會

date sb　　約某人

例: I went out on a date with Mary last night.
(我昨晚與瑪麗約會。)

339. **daughter** [ˈdɔtɚ] n. 女兒

son [sʌn] n. 兒子

daughter-in-law　　媳婦

son-in-law　　女婿

例: The woman has three daughters and one son.
(這名婦女有三個女兒、一個兒子。)

340. **deaf** [dɛf] a. 聾的

turn a deaf ear to...　　對……充耳不聞

turn a blind eye to...　　對……視若無睹

= be blind to...

例: He turned a deaf ear to what I said.
(他對我的話充耳不聞。)

Ian is deaf and he can't speak.
(伊恩既聾且啞。)

341. **deal** [dil] vi. 對付, 處理 & n. 划算的東西

deal with...　　處理……

deal in...　　從事……的買賣 (= buy and sell...)

例: This week, I have a lot of work to deal with.
(這個星期我有很多工作要處理。)

His father deals in used cars.
(他的父親從事中古車買賣。)

The car you've bought is a good deal.
(你買的車很划算。)

342. **dear** [dɪr] a. 親愛的

例: You are a dear friend of mine.
(你是我的摯友。)

343. **debate** [dɪˈbet] vt. & n. 辯論

例: I'm on the debate team at my school.
(我是學校辯論隊的一員。)

We debated whether we should do the work or not.
(我們辯論是否要做這工作。)

344. **decide** [dɪˈsaɪd] vt. 決定

decision [dɪˈsɪʒən] n. 決定

decide to V　　　決定要……

= make a decision to V

例: I've decided to study abroad.
(我決定要出國深造。)

345. **decorate** [ˈdɛkəret] vt. 裝飾

be decorated with...　　　被裝飾著……

例: The whole room was decorated with roses.
(整個房間都以玫瑰裝飾著。)

346. **deep** [dip] a. 深的

例: The swimming pool is 25 meters long and 4 meters deep.
(游泳池長廿五公尺,深四公尺。)

347. delicious [dɪˋlɪʃəs] a. 美味的, 好吃的

= tasty [ˋtestɪ]

例: This food is delicious. Can I have another helping?
（這道菜真好吃。我可以再來一份嗎？）

348. deliver [dɪˋlɪvɚ] vt. 運送; 發表 (演講)

deliver/make a speech to...　　對……演講

例: Postmen do not deliver mail on Sundays.
（星期天郵差不送信。）

I feel honored to deliver a speech to you.
（我很榮幸能對諸位演講。）

349. dentist [ˋdɛntɪst] n. 牙醫師

dental [ˋdɛntḷ] a. 牙科的
a dental clinic　　牙科診所

例: I need to go to the dentist for my toothache.
（我牙痛，必須去看牙醫。）

350. department store [dɪˋpɑrtmənt ˏstɔr] n. 百貨公司

例: Do you know where the department store is located?
（你知道這家百貨公司位於何處嗎？）

351. depend [dɪˋpɛnd] vi. 依靠

depend on...　　依靠……

= rely on...

例: You can depend on him for help.
（你可以指望他幫忙。）

352. desert [ˋdɛzɚt] n. 沙漠

例: The desert is hot, dry and covered in sand.
（沙漠又熱又乾燥，全被沙覆蓋。）

353. describe [dɪˈskraɪb] vt. 描述　　**d**

description [dɪˈskrɪpʃən] n. 描述

beyond description　　難以形容

例: The woman described the thief to the police.
(這名婦女向警方描述小偷的模樣。)

She is beautiful beyond description.
(她美得難以形容。)

354. dessert [dɪˈzɝt] n. 甜點 (不可數)　　**d**

eat/have sth for dessert　　吃某物當甜點

例: We ate ice cream for dessert last night.
(昨晚我們吃冰淇淋當甜點。)

355. develop [dɪˈvɛləp] vt. 發展　　**d**

development [dɪˈvɛləpmənt] n. 發展

例: After working for hours, I developed a headache.
(工作幾個鐘頭之後，我頭開始痛了。)

356. diary [ˈdaɪərɪ] n. 日記　　**d**

keep a diary　　寫日記

例: I'm in the habit of keeping a diary.
(我有寫日記的習慣。)

357. dictionary [ˈdɪkʃənˌɛrɪ] n. 字典　　**d**

consult the dictionary　　查字典

例: If you don't know a word, consult the dictionary.
= If you don't know a word, look it up in the dictionary.
(你若不懂某個字，就查字典吧。)

358. die [daɪ] vi. 死去　　**d**

die of + 疾病　　死於某疾病

例: The young man died of AIDS.
(這個年輕人死於愛滋病。)

Old habits die hard.
(老習慣難死——積習難改。諺語)

359. **dying** [ˈdaɪɪŋ] a. 渴望的

be dying for + N　　渴望得到……

= be eager for + N

例: I'm dying for her love.
(我渴望得到她的愛。)

360. **different** [ˈdɪfərənt] a. 不同的

be different from...　　與……不同

= differ from...

differ [ˈdɪfɚ] vi. 不同

例: Mina is very different from her sister Gina in personality.
(米娜與她妹妹吉娜個性很不相同。)

361. **difficult** [ˈdɪfɪkəlt] a. 困難的

= hard [hɑrd]

= tough [tʌf]

例: It is difficult for me to answer the question.
(這個問題我很難回答。)

362. **dig** [dɪg] vt. 挖掘 (三態為: dig、dug、dug)

例: Let's dig a hole and plant the tree.
(咱們挖個洞把樹栽種下去。)

363. **dim** [dɪm] a. 微弱的

bright [braɪt] a. 明亮的

例: Studying in the dim light will harm your eyes.
(在黯淡的燈光下讀書會傷眼睛。)

364. dining room [ˈdaɪnɪŋ ˌrum] n. (家裏的) 餐室　**d**

例: Every night we have dinner in the dining room.
（我們每晚都在自家餐廳用餐。）

365. direction [dəˈrɛkʃən] n. 方向; (藥物、機器等的) 使用說明 (恆用複數)　**d**

ask for directions　　問路

例: If you are lost, ask a policeman for directions.
（你若迷路時，找警察問路。）
　　Read the directions carefully before taking the pills.
（服藥之前要細心看一下使用說明。）

366. dirty [ˈdɝtɪ] a. 髒的　**d**

a dirty old man　　色鬼

例: All of my clothes are dirty and have to be washed.
（我所有的衣服都髒了，須要洗了。）

367. discover [dɪˈskʌvɚ] vt. 發現　**d**

discovery [dɪsˈkʌvərɪ] n. 發現
make an important discovery　　有重大的發現

例: Columbus discovered America in 1492.
（哥倫布於一四九二年發現美洲。）

368. dish [dɪʃ] n. 碟子; 菜　**d**

do the dishes　　洗碗盤
= wash the dishes

例: It's your turn to do the dishes.
（輪到你洗碗了。）

369. discuss [dɪˈskʌs] vt. 討論　**d**

discussion [dɪˈskʌʃən] n. 討論
discuss sth with sb　　和某人討論某事

be under discussion　在討論中

例: I won't decide for you. You'll have to discuss it with your father.

(我不會為你做決定。你得跟你爸爸討論這件事。)

370. **distance** [ˈdɪstəns] n. 距離

in the distance　在遙遠的地方

keep sb at a distance　與某人保持距離

例: I see a girl in the distance.

(我看到遠處有個女孩。)

He isn't very nice. Keep him at a distance.

(他非善類。跟他保持距離。)

371. **dive** [daɪv] vi. 潛水 (三態為: dive、dived/dove、dived/dove)

go diving　潛水

例: I went diving in the sea during my last vacation.

(上次渡假時我到大海潛水。)

372. **doctor** [ˈdɑktɚ] n. 醫生; 博士

例: The doctor is not available to see you today.

(今天醫生沒空為你看診。)

373. **doll** [dɑl] n. 洋娃娃

例: In general, girls love dolls while boys like toy cars.

(一般而言，女孩喜歡洋娃娃，而男孩喜歡玩具車。)

374. **dollar** [dɑlɚ] n. 美元

例: During my trip to the States, I spent about seven hundred dollars.

(我此次美國之行花了約七百美元。)

375. double [ˈdʌbl̩] a. 二倍的 & vt. 加倍　　　　d

例: I paid double the price for the ticket.
(這張票我花了兩倍的價錢買的。)

376. downstairs [ˌdaʊnˈstɛrz] adv. 樓下　　　d

upstairs [ˌʌpˈstɛrz] adv. 樓上

go downstairs/upstairs　下樓/上樓

例: We went downstairs to see our friends off.
(我們下樓送朋友。)
＊see sb off　送別某人

377. download [ˌdaʊnˈlod] vt. 下載　　　d

例: Do you know how to download things from the Internet?
(你知道如何從網際網路下載東西嗎？)

378. dozen [ˈdʌzn̩] n. 一打 (十二個)　一打的……; 十幾個……　　d

a dozen + 複數名詞　一打的……

a/two/three...dozen eggs　一打/兩打/三打……蛋

dozens of + 複數名詞　幾十個……

例: There were a dozen policemen standing outside the building.
(有十幾名警察站在大樓外。)

379. draw [drɔ] vt. 畫 (三態為: draw、drew、drawn)　　d

draw a picture　畫畫

例: I'm drawing a picture of a dog, not a pig.
(我畫的是一隻狗，不是豬。)
＊draw 亦可作不及物動詞, 有下列重要用法:
　be drawing near　即將來臨
= be around the corner
= be coming soon

例: Christmas is drawing near.
(聖誕節就要到了。)

380. **drawer** ['drɔɚ] n. 抽屜

例: Your socks are in the top drawer.
(你的襪子在上層抽屜裏。)

381. **dream** [drim] n. & vi. 夢

dream of...　　夢想/夢到……
例: The girl dreams of meeting Tom Cruise one day.
(這女孩夢想有一天能見到阿湯哥。)
＊dream 亦可作及物動詞, 但須以 a dream 作受詞。
例: I dreamed a sweet dream last night.
(我昨晚作了個甜美的夢。)

382. **dress** [drɛs] n. 洋裝 & vt. 使穿衣 (常用於被動)

get dressed　　穿好衣服
be dressed in ＋ 顏色　　穿了一身……顏色的衣服
例: You should get dressed now or we'll be late.
(你現在應穿好衣服, 否則我們會遲到。)
She is dressed in red.
(她穿了一身紅色的衣服。)

383. **drink** [drɪŋk] vt. 喝 (三態為: drink、drank、drunk)

例: I'm thirsty. I need something to drink.
(我口渴, 需要喝點東西。)

384. **drive** [draɪv] vt. & vi. 駕駛 (三態為: drive、drove、driven)

driver ['draɪvɚ] n. 駕駛員
drunken driving　　酒醉駕駛
= drunk driving

例: I drive my son to school every day.
(我每天開車送兒子上學。)

Drunk driving is illegal all over the world.
(全球各地酒醉駕駛都是違法的。)

＊illegal [ɪˈligl̩] a. 違法的

385. **drop** [drɑp] vt. 丟棄 & vi. 順道來訪 (與 by 並用)

drop sb a line 　　給某人寫個短信

drop in on sb 　　順道探訪某人

drop by 　　順道來訪

例: Be careful. Don't drop it.
(小心。別讓它掉下來。)

Drop me a line if you can.
(可以的話，寫個隻字片語給我。)

I dropped in on John on my way home.
(我回家途中順便去看約翰。)

Drop by if you have time.
(你如果有時間就順便過來一下嘛。)

386. **drown** [draʊn] vi. 溺水 & vt. 將……淹死

例: He saved the boy from drowning.
(他救了那男孩使他免於溺死。)

387. **drug** [drʌg] n. 藥; 毒品

take drugs 　　吸毒

drugstore [ˈdrʌgstɔr] n. 雜貨店

例: Taking drugs can ruin your health.
(吸毒會毀了你的健康。)

＊ruin [ˈruɪn] vt. 破壞

388. **drum** [drʌm] n. 鼓

drummer ['drʌmɚ] n. 鼓手

例: Can you play the drums?

(你會打鼓嗎?)

389. **dry** [draɪ] a. 乾燥的 & vt. 使……乾

keep sth dry 將……保持乾燥

例: Dry your hair after you wash it, or you'll catch (a) cold.

(洗頭之後要把頭髮擦乾,否則會著涼的。)

390. **duck** [dʌk] n. 鴨子

例: The ducks were swimming in the pond.

(鴨子在池塘裏游泳。)

391. **dumpling** ['dʌmplɪŋ] n. 包餡的麵食

dumpling 水餃

rice dumpling 湯圓; 粽子

例: My favorite food is dumplings.

(我最愛的食物就是水餃。)

392. **during** ['djʊrɪŋ] prep. 在……期間

例: Will you keep an eye on my house during my absence?

(我不在的時候,你可否替我看門?)

＊keep an eye on... 好好看守……

393. **dust** [dʌst] n. 灰塵

dusty ['dʌstɪ] a. 多灰塵的

duster ['dʌstɚ] n. 雞毛撣子

例: The table is dusty and needs to be cleaned.

(桌子有灰塵需要清乾淨。)

394. **duty** [ˈdjutɪ] n. 責任　　　　　　　　　　d

　　be on duty　　值日

例: It's my duty to walk the dog after dinner.
（飯後遛狗是我的責任。）

Dad is on duty today, so he won't be back for dinner.
（今天爸爸值班，所以不會回來吃晚飯。）

395. **each** [itʃ] a. & pron. 每一個

each and every...　　每一個……

例: Each of the students should bring their own lunch.

= Each and every student should bring their own lunch.

（每一個學生都應自備午餐。）

396. **ear** [ɪr] n. 耳朵

turn a deaf ear to...　　對……充耳不聞

例: The boy turned a deaf ear to his father's advice.

（男孩對他爸爸的忠告充耳不聞。）

397. **earn** [ɝn] vt. 賺

earn a/one's living　　謀生

= make a/one's living

例: He earns his living by teaching.

（他靠教書維生。）

398. **early** ['ɝlɪ] adv. 早 & a. 早的

例: He gets up early and goes to bed late.

（他早起晚睡。）

The early bird catches the worm.

（早起的鳥有蟲吃。——諺語）

399. **earth** [ɝθ] n. 土地

the Earth　　地球

on earth　　在世上

= in the world

例: Everyone should do their part to protect the Earth.

（每個人都應盡本份保護地球。）

It's not too much to say that Mary is the most beautiful girl on earth.

（瑪麗是世上最美的女孩子，這個說法並不過份。）

* on earth 或 in the world 亦可置於疑問詞 (What、Where、
How、Why、Who...等)之後,表『究竟』、『到底』之意。

例: Who on earth is he?
（他到底是誰？）
How in the world are you going to do it?
（你究竟要怎麼做這件事？）

400. **earthquake** ['ɝθkwek] n. 地震

例: The earthquake caused a lot of damage to the island.
（地震對該島造成很大的損害。）

401. **east** [ist] n. & adv. 東方

south [sauθ] n. & adv. 南方
west [wɛst] n. & adv. 西方
north [norθ] n. & adv. 北方
go east 往東走 (east 是副詞)
= go to the east (east 是名詞)

例: The sun rises in the east and sets in the west.
（太陽東邊昇起西方落下。）

402. **easy** ['izɪ] a. 容易的; 輕鬆的

take it easy 不要緊張

例: Easy come, easy go.
（容易得到的東西也容易消失──尤指金錢。──諺語）
Take it easy. It's not that serious.
（別緊張。沒那麼嚴重。）

403. **effort** ['ɛfət] n. 努力

in an effort to V 為了要……
= in order to V
make an effort to V 努力設法……
= try very hard to V

例: Tom made an effort to please his girlfriend.
（湯姆努力設法討好他的女友。）

I've been studying hard in an effort to pass the test tomorrow.
（我一直很用功為了要考過明天的考試。）

404. **egg** [εg] n. 蛋   e

get a goose egg   得了個大鵝蛋 (比喻得零分)

例: Mary got a goose egg on her math test because she didn't
study.
（瑪麗因為沒讀書，數學考了零分。）

Don't put all your eggs in one basket.
（別孤注一擲。————諺語）

＊basket [ˈbæskɪt] n. 籃子

405. **either** [ˈiðɚ] pron. & a. 兩者之一 (的) & adv. 也 (不) (與 not 並用)   e

either...or...   不是……就是……
not...either   也不……

例: Either you or he is wrong.
（不是你就是他的錯。）

He can't sing, and he can't dance, too. (✕, too 只用於肯定句中)

→ He can't sing, and he can't dance, either. (○)
（他不會唱歌，也不會跳舞。）

406. **electricity** [ˌɪlɛkˈtrɪsətɪ] n. 電   e

例: The car runs on electricity.
（這輛車是電動的。）

＊run on...   靠……驅動

407. **elementary** [ˌɛləˈmɛntərɪ] a. 初步的, 基礎的   e

an elementary school   小學

例: Most elementary school students go on to junior high school.
（大多數小學生會繼續唸國中。）

408. **else** [εls] a. 其他的

＊本字只置於 no、some、every、any 之後：

someone else　　別人
no one else　　沒別的人
anyone else　　任何其他的人
everyone else　　所有其他的人
something else　　別的事
nothing else　　沒別的事
anything else　　任何其他的事
everything else　　所有其他的事

例: No one else can answer the question except for Larry.
（除了賴瑞以外，沒別的人能回答這個問題。）
There is something else I want to let you know.
（我還有一件事要讓你知道。）

409. **email** [ˈimel] n. 電子郵件 & vt. 對……發送電子郵件

例: Email me as soon as you get this message.
（你一收到這個訊息就發電子郵件給我。）

410. **embarrass** [ɪmˈbærəs] vt. 使尷尬

embarrassed [ɪmˈbærəst] a. 感到尷尬的
embarrassing [ɪmˈbærəsɪŋ] a. 令人尷尬的

例: I felt embarrassed when I found that my fly was open.
（發現褲襠是開著的時候，我感到很尷尬。）

411. **employ** [ɪmˈplɔɪ] vt. 雇用 (= hire)

employee [ɪmˈplɔɪi] n. 雇員
employer [ɪmˈplɔɪɚ] n. 雇主

例: I felt happy when the boss decided to employ me.
（老闆決定雇用我時，我高興極了。）
My father is a government employee
（我爸爸是公務員。）

412. **empty** [ˈɛmptɪ] a. 空的

例: My stomach is empty. I'm so hungry I could eat a horse.
(我的胃空空的。我餓得連一匹馬都可吃下去。)

413. **end** [ɛnd] vt. & vi. 終止, 結束 & n. 結束

come to an end　　結束
= end

例: It seems that my schoolwork will never end.
= It seems that my schoolwork will never come to an end.
(我的功課似乎永遠做不完。)

414. **enemy** [ˈɛnəmɪ] n. 敵人

例: Laziness is your own worst enemy.
(懶惰是你最大的敵人——諺語)

415. **engine** [ˈɛndʒɪn] n. 引擎

engineer [ˌɛndʒəˈnɪr] n. 工程師
例: The engine in my car needs to be repaired.
(我車子的引擎需要修理了。)

416. **enjoy** [ɪnˈdʒɔɪ] vt. 欣賞, 喜歡 (以名詞或動名詞作受詞)

enjoy oneself　　玩得愉快
= have a good time
例: Young children enjoy to watch cartoons. (✗)
→ Young children enjoy watching cartoons. (○)
(小孩子喜歡看卡通片。)
Did you enjoy yourself at the party?
(派對上你玩得愉快嗎?)

417. **enough** [ɪˈnʌf] a. 足夠的 & adv. 足以

enough 作形容詞時, 可置於名詞前, 但若作副詞時, 則置於形容詞或副

詞之後, 即:

adj./adv. + enough + to V/for N

例: We don't have enough time to finish the work.
(我們時間不夠，無法把工作做完。)

He isn't enough good for the job. (✗)
→ He isn't good enough for the job. (○)
(這份工作他不能勝任。)

418. **enter** [ˈɛntɚ] vt. 進入

entrance [ˈɛntrəns] n. 入口

exit [ˈɛgzɪt] n. 出口

例: Mark just entered the room.
(馬克剛剛進入房間。)

My brother is going to take the college entrance examination next year.
(我哥哥明年就要參加大學入學考試。)

419. **envelope** [ˈɛnvəlop] n. 信封

例: This envelope is addressed to you.
(這信封的地址是寫給你的。)

420. **equal** [ˈikwəl] a. 平等的 & vt. 等於

be equal (adj.) to...   等於……
= equal (vt.)...

例: Men are born equal.
(人生而平等。)

Four plus four equals eight.
= Four plus four is equal to eight.
(四加四等於八。)

421. escalator ['ɛskəˌletɚ] n. 電扶梯

elevator ['ɛləˌvetɚ] n. 電梯

例: The escalator is out of order. You'll have to use the stairs.
(電扶梯壞了。你得使用樓梯間了。)

422. especially [ɪsˈpɛʃəlɪ] adv. 特別地

例: Everyone should study for the test, especially those who missed the last class.
(每個人都應唸書準備考試,尤其是那些錯過上一堂課的人。)

423. etc. [ɛtˈsɛtrə] adv. 及其他……等等

= and so on

= and the like

例: We ate mangoes, peaches, strawberries, etc.
(我們吃了芒果、桃子、草莓等等。)

424. eve [iv] n. 前夕

on the eve of...　　在……的前夕

例: On the eve of her wedding, Jenny changed her mind.
(珍妮在婚禮前夕改變心意。)

425. even ['ivən] adv. 甚至

例: He can't even write his own name, not to mention a letter.
(他甚至連自己的名字都不會寫,更別提一封信了。)

426. evening ['ivnɪŋ] n. 夜晚

in the evening　　晚上

= at night

例: I'm busy during the day, but I'll be free in the evening.
(我白天忙,不過晚上會有空。)

427. **event** [ɪ'vɛnt] n. 事件

in the event of...　　萬一……

= in case of...

例: The horrible event took place on September 11, 2001.
(這椿可怕的事件發生在二〇〇一年九月十一日。)

Never get nervous in the event of an earthquake.
(萬一有地震，千萬不要緊張。)

428. **eventually** [ɪ'vɛntʃuəlɪ] adv. 最後地

例: Jessica will eventually marry her boyfriend.
(潔西卡終究會嫁給她男友。)

429. **ever** ['ɛvɚ] adv. 曾經

本字不要隨意用在肯定句中。

例: I have ever seen him before. (✗)

→ I have seen him before. (○)
(我曾經見過他。)

＊ ever 通常用於下列情況中：

a. 問句

例: Have you (ever) seen him before?
(你以前曾見過他嗎？)

Did he (ever) call?
(他曾打過電話來嗎？)

b. if 子句

例: If you (ever) do that again, I'll punish you.
(你如果再做這樣的事，我就會處罰你。)

否定句 (與 not 並用)

例: I will not ever do that again.

= I will never do that again.
(我永遠不會再做那樣的事。)

430. **everybody** ['ɛvrɪ,bɑdɪ] pron. 每個人

= everyone

例: Everybody should obey the law.

(每個人都應守法。)

*obey [ə'be] vt. 遵守

431. **everything** ['ɛvrɪ,θɪŋ] pron. 一切事物; 最重要者

nothing ['nʌθɪŋ] n. 沒什麼事物

anything ['ɛnɪθɪŋ] n. 任何事務

例: Money is something, but not everything.

(錢固然重要,但並非萬能。──諺語)

Is everything all right?

(一切還好嗎?)

432. **everywhere** ['ɛvrɪ,wɛr] adv. 每個地方

nowhere ['no,wɛr] adv. 沒有任何地方

somewhere ['sʌm,wɛr] adv. 某處

anywhere ['ɛnɪ,wɛr] adv. 任何地方

例: Randy looked everywhere for his missing shoe.

(藍迪到處找他失蹤的鞋子。)

433. **examination** [ɪg,zæmə'neʃən] n. 考試

(常縮寫為 exam [ɪg'zæm])

do well on the exam/test　　考試考得很好

例: The examination has been put off for another week.

(考試已再順延一個禮拜。)

He did quite well on the exam.

(他考試考得很好。)

434. **exactly** [ɪg'zæktlɪ] adv. 正是, 沒錯

*本字多置於疑問詞 what、where、how 之前, 作強調用法。

例: A hot bath is exactly what I need after a long day at work.
(上班一整天之後，洗個熱水澡正是我所需要的。)

　That's exactly where I live.
(那正是我住的地方。)

435. **example** [ɪgˈzæmp!] n. 例子　　　　　　　　　　ⓔ

For example, ...　　舉例而言,……
set a good example　　樹立好榜樣

例: I have a lot of work to do. For example, I have to clean my room.
(我有很多工作要做。比如說，我必須打掃我的房間。)

　John set a good example for us to follow by studying hard.
(約翰很用功為我們樹立好榜樣。)

436. **except** [ɪkˈsɛpt] prep. 除了……之外　　　　　　ⓔ

except...　　除了……之外 (與 all、every、any、no 四字並用)
= except for...

例: Everyone except (for) Mike is invited to the party.
(除了麥克以外，每個人都受邀參加派對。)

　No one can do it except (for) Peter.
(除了彼得以外，沒有人能做這件事。)

437. **excite** [ɪkˈsaɪt] vt. 使興奮　　　　　　　　　　ⓔ

exciting [ɪkˈsaɪtɪŋ] a. 令人興奮的
excited [ɪkˈsaɪtɪd] a. 感到興奮的
be excited about...　　對……感到興奮

例: It was really exciting to hear that my son had passed the entrance exam.
(聽到兒子入學考通過了，這真令人興奮。)

　I was very excited about the good news.
(這個好消息令我興奮。)

438. excuse [ɪk'skjuz] vt. 原諒 & [ɪk'skjus] n. 藉口

make an excuse   找藉口

例: Excuse me. Do you know where the restroom is?
(對不起，您知道廁所在哪兒嗎？)

John always makes excuses for being late to class.
(約翰總為上課遲到找藉口。)

439. exercise ['ɛksɚˌsaɪz] n. & vi. 運動

例: Running is very good exercise.
(跑步是很好的運動。)

To stay healthy, you should exercise on a daily basis.
(要保持健康，你應每天運動。)

440. exit ['ɛgzɪt] n. 出口

例: The exit of the building is on the right hand side.
(大樓的出口就在右手邊。)

441. expect [ɪk'spɛkt] vt. 期望

例: I didn't expect to bump into you again.
(我沒料到會再次碰到你。)

442. expensive [ɪk'spɛnsɪv] a. 昂貴的

inexpensive [ˌɪnɪk'spɛnsɪv] a. 不貴的 (品質不錯)

cheap [tʃip] a. 便宜的 (品質可能較差)

例: Those shoes are too expensive. I can't afford them.
(這鞋太貴。我買不起。)

443. experience [ɪk'spɪrɪəns] n. 經驗

experienced [ɪk'spɪrɪənst] a. 有經驗的

be experienced in...   在……方面有經驗

例: Traveling to a foreign country is a great experience.

(到外國去旅遊是個很棒的經驗。)
John is well experienced in writing.
(約翰寫作經驗豐富。)

444. **expert** [ˈɛkspɚt] n. 專家

例: He is an expert in Chinese history.
(他是中國歷史專家。)

445. **explain** [ɪkˈsplen] vt. 說明, 解釋

explanation [ˌɛkspləˈneʃən] n. 解釋

例: Please explain to me why you were late again.
(請向我解釋你為何又遲到了。)

446. **explore** [ɪkˈsplɔr] vt. 探測

例: I will explore the other side of the mountain and see what
there is.
(我去勘察山的另一邊，看看那裏有什麼。)

447. **extra** [ˈɛkstrə] a. 額外的

例: There was a lot of extra food left over after the picnic.
(野餐後有好多菜剩下來。)

448. **eye** [aɪ] n. 眼睛

be the apple of one's eye   是某人最愛的人 (注意 eye 為單數)
keep an eye on...   好好盯著……

例: My daughter is the apple of my eye.
(我的女兒是我的掌上明珠。)

Keep an eye on that thief lest he should run away.
(好好看著那賊以免他跑了。)

449. face [fes] n. 臉

    in the face of...   面臨……

    lose face   丟臉

    例: David lost face when his friends found out he had lied.

        (大衛在他朋友發現他說謊時感到很沒面子。)

        What would you do in the face of such a problem?

        (面臨這樣的問題時,你會怎麼辦?)

450. factory [ˈfæktərɪ] n. 工廠

    例: The shoe factory was shut down last year.

        (這家製鞋工廠去年關門了。)

451. fail [fel] vi. 失敗 & vt. 未通過 (考試)

    fail the test   考試不及格

    fail to V   未能……

    failure [ˈfeljɚ] n. 失敗

    例: If you don't study, you are sure to fail the test.

        (你若不讀書,一定會考不及格。)

        He failed to keep his word.

        (他未能守信。)

        Failure is the mother of success.

        (失敗為成功之母。——諺語)

452. fair [fɛr] a. 美麗的; 晴朗的 (天氣); 公平的 & n. 展覽會

    a fair-weather friend   酒肉朋友

    例: It isn't fair that I can't stay out late and my brother can.

        (我不能晚歸,我弟弟卻可以,這不公平。)

        There is going to be a book fair next month.

        (下個月將有一場書展。)

453. **fairy** ['fɛrɪ] n. 小仙女

a fairy tale　　童話故事

例: In the fairy tale, the witch tries to eat the children.
(這則童話故事中，女巫想吃掉孩子。)

454. **fall** [fɔl] vi. 跌倒; 變成 & n. 秋天 (= autumn ['ɔtəm])

三態為: fall、fell、fallen。

*fall 作『變成』解時, 之後接少數幾個固定的形容詞, 常用的如下:

fall asleep　　睡著了 (變成睡著的)

fall ill　　生病了 (變成生病的)

例: The old woman fell down and injured her leg.
(老婆婆跌倒, 傷了腿。)

He fell asleep during class.
(上課時他睡著了。)

Last fall I went to visit my aunt in Spain.
(去年秋天, 我到西班牙看阿姨。)

455. **family** ['fæməlɪ] n. 家庭, 家人

例: How many member are there in your family?
(你家裏有多少人?)

456. **famous** ['feməs] a. 有名的

be famous for...　　因……而出名

= be known for...

例: France is famous for its wine.
(法國因產葡萄酒而出名。)

457. **fan** [fæn] n. 扇子; 影迷

例: The famous actor waved at all of his fans.
(這位名演員向他所有的影迷揮手。)

458. **far** [fɑr] adv. 遙遠地 & a. 遙遠的

far away from...　　離……很遠
be far from + adj./n.　　一點也不……
= be not adj./n. at all
　例: I live far away from my school.
　　　(我住的地方離學校很遠。)
　　　He is far from good/a good boy.
= 　He is not good/a good boy at all.
　　　(他一點也不好/不是好孩子。)

459. **fare** [fɛr] n. (車、船、飛機等) 交通費

fee [fi] n. 手續費
tuition fee [tjuˈɪʃən ˌfi] n. 學費
　例: When you get on the bus, you must pay the fare first.
　　　(你上公車時,得先付車資。)

460. **farm** [fɑrm] n. 農場 & vi. 務農

on the farm　　在農場上
farmer [ˈfɑrmɚ] n. 農夫
　例: John was brought up on the farm.
　　　(約翰是在農場撫養長大的。)
　　　My family has been farming here for almost fifty years.
　　　(我家人在此務農幾近五十年。)

461. **fashion** [ˈfæʃən] n. 時裝; 流行

be in fashion　　流行起來
be out of fashion　　不再流行
fashionable [ˈfæʃənəbḷ] a. 時髦的 (= popular)
　例: These new boots are very fashionable.
　　　(這些新款靴子很時髦。)

Miniskirts are in fashion again.
(迷你裙又流行起來。)

462. fast [fæst] a. 快速的 & adv. 快速地

例: Taking the MRT is fast and easy.
(搭捷運既快又方便。)

＊ MRT 是 Mass Rapid Transit (大眾快速運輸) 的縮寫。

463. fasten [ˈfæsn̩] vt. 綁緊

fasten A to B　　將 A 綁在 B 上
= tie A to B

例: Fasten your seatbelt while (you are) seated.
(若坐著時要繫好安全帶。)

The bag was fastened to her back.
(她的背包繫在她背上。)

464. fat [fæt] n. 脂肪 & a. 胖的

例: Carol used to be fat, but now she's thin.
(卡蘿以前很胖，不過現在卻變瘦了。)

465. fate [fet] n. 命運

例: It was our fate to meet each other.
(我們注定會相遇。)

466. father [ˈfɑðɚ] n. 父親

mother [ˈmʌðɚ] n. 母親
father-in-law　　岳父; 公公
mother-in-law　　岳母; 婆婆
grandfather　　祖父; 阿公
grandmother　　祖母; 阿媽

例: My father used to be a pilot.
(我爸爸以前是個飛行員。)

467. **faucet** [ˈfɔsɪt] n. 水龍頭　　　　　　　　　　　　f

turn on the faucet　　打開水龍頭 (非 open the faucet 『將水龍頭拆開』)

turn off the faucet　　關掉水龍頭

例: Don't waste water! Turn off the faucet.

(別浪費水！把水龍頭關起來。)

468. **fault** [fɔlt] n. 缺點, 過失　　　　　　　　　　　f

be at fault　　有錯

= be wrong

find fault with...　　挑剔……

例: Do you know who was at fault?

(你知道誰有錯嗎？)

I hate people who like to find fault with others.

(我討厭那些喜歡找別人麻煩的人。)

469. **favor** [ˈfevɚ] n. 恩惠　　　　　　　　　　　　f

do sb a favor　　幫某人一個忙

ask a favor of sb　　請某人幫忙

例: Please do me a favor and close the door.

(請幫個忙把門關起來。)

May I ask a favor of you?

(我可以請你幫個忙嗎？)

470. **favorite** [ˈfevərɪt] a. 最喜愛的 & n. 最喜愛的人或物　f

例: My favorite color is blue.

(我最喜歡的顏色是藍色。)

Rock music is my favorite.

(搖滾樂是我的最愛。)

471. fax machine [ˈfæks məˌʃin] n. 傳真機

例: The fax machine is jammed.
（傳真機卡紙了。）

472. feed [fid] vt. 餵食 & vi. (動物) 進食

三態為: feed、fed、fed。
feed on...　　(動物) 吃……為食
live on...　　(人) 吃……為食
例: Don't forget to feed the baby.
（別忘了要餵小寶寶。）
Cattle feed on grass.
（牛吃草為生。）
Most Chinese live on rice.
（大多數中國人吃米飯為生。）

473. feel [fil] vt. 感受, 觸摸 (接名詞) & vi. 感覺起來 (接形容詞)

三態為: feel、felt、felt。
feel cold/hot　　感覺起來很冷/很熱
feel the pain　　感受到痛
feel like + 名詞　　感覺像……
例: I felt her hand in the darkness.
（在黑暗中我觸摸到她的手。）
I felt sad after hearing the story.
（聽完故事後我覺得很悲傷。）
I feel like a fool whenever I'm with her.
（每次跟她在一起，我覺得自己就像傻瓜一樣。）

474. feeling [ˈfilɪŋ] n. 感覺

feelings [ˈfilɪŋz] n. 感情
例: I have a feeling that he'll come.
（我有預感他會來。）

You've hurt my feeling. (✗)
→ You've hurt my feelings. (○)
(你傷了我的心。)

475. **fellow** [ˈfɛlo] n. 伙伴; 傢伙

例: Tom is a really nice fellow.
(湯姆真是個好伙伴。)

476. **fence** [fɛns] n. 圍牆; 欄杆

例: The fence is too high to get over.
(圍牆太高爬不過去。)

477. **festival** [ˈfɛstəvḷ] n. (傳統) 節日

the Lantern Festival　　元宵節
the Dragon Boat Festival　　端午節
the Mid-Autumn Festival　　中秋節
例: The Mid-Autumn Festival is around the corner.
(中秋節就要到了。)

478. **fever** [ˈfivɚ] n. 發燒

have a fever　　發燒
have a runny nose　　流鼻涕
例: You must have a fever because you feel very hot.
(你摸起來燙燙的，因此你一定發燒了。)

479. **few** [fju] a. 少數的

a few + 複數名詞　　一些……
quite a few + 複數名詞　　不少……(= many...)
few + 複數名詞　　沒幾個……
only a few + 複數名詞　　只有幾個……
例: I have a few friends, but John has quite a few friends.
(我有一些朋友，不過約翰卻有很多朋友。)

比較:

little [ˈlɪtl] a. 少量的

a little + 不可數名詞　　一些……

quite a little + 不可數名詞　　不少……

little + 不可數名詞　　沒多少……

only a little + 不可數名詞　　只有少量的……

例: I have a little money, but John has quite a little money.

(我有一些錢,不過約翰卻有很多錢。)

480. field [fild] n. 領域; 曠野

例: He is an expert in that field.

(他是那個領域的專家。)

There are ten cows in the field.

(原野上有十頭乳牛。)

481. fight [faɪt] vi. 打架; 吵架 (三態為: fight、fought、fought)

fight over...　　為……吵架

fight for...　　為……奮鬥

fight against...　　抵抗……

例: The two boys fought over a girl they both liked.

(這兩個男孩為共同愛上的女孩吵架。)

We should fight for freedom.

(我們應為自由而戰。)

482. fill [fɪl] vt. 充滿

be filled with...　　充滿……

fill out/in the form　　填寫表格

例: My heart was filled with joy when I saw her again.

(我再次見到她時,心中充滿喜悅。)

Fill out this form, and then give it back to me.

(把表格填好交給我。)

483. **film** [fɪlm] n. 影片 (可數); 底片 (不可數)

a film 　　一部影片 (= a movie)

a roll of film 　　一捲底片

例: They are making/shooting a film in Spain.
(他們正在西班牙拍電影。)

I'd like to buy two rolls of film.
(我想買兩捲底片。)

484. **final** [ˈfaɪn̩] a. 最後的

the final examinations 　　期末考 (因各科均有期末考, 故常用複數)

= the finals

例: John is busy preparing for the finals.
(約翰正忙著準備期末考。)

485. **finally** [ˈfaɪn̩lɪ] adv. 最後地

例: It's the weekend and I can finally relax.
(週末到了，我終於可以輕鬆了。)

486. **find** [faɪnd] vt. 發現 (三態為: find、found、found)

find out that... 　　了解……

例: Where can I find the library?
(我在哪兒可以找到圖書館？)

I finally found out that Mary had cheated on me.
(我終於發現瑪麗對我不忠。)

487. **fine** [faɪn] a. 美好的; 精緻的 & vt. 罰款

例: That was a fine meal you prepared.
(你弄的這一餐真棒。)

He was fined for speeding.
(他因為超速被罰款。)

488. finger ['fɪŋgɚ] n. 手指頭

keep one's fingers crossed　　(把中指及食指交叉成十字型) 祈求好運

例: I'll take a test tomorrow, so keep your fingers crossed for me.
(我明天要考試，因此替我祈福吧。)

489. finish ['fɪnɪʃ] vt. 結束

finish sth　　做完某事
= be finished with sth
= be done with sth

例: I have finished my homework.
= I'm finished with my homework.
(我功課做完了。)

490. fire ['faɪr] n. 火 & vt. 免職, 開除

set sth on fire　　放火燒某物
= set fire to sth

例: John was fired from his job last week.
(上星期約翰被免職了。)
The boys set the house on fire.
(這些孩子放火燒房子。)

491. firecracker ['faɪrˌkrækɚ] n. 爆竹 (常用複數)

firework ['faɪrˌwɝk] n. 煙火 (常用複數)

set off firecrackers/fireworks　　放鞭炮/煙火

例: We set off firecrackers every Chinese New Year.
(我們每逢農曆新年就放炮。)

比較:
They set off fireworks in celebration of National Day.
(他們放煙火慶祝國慶。)

492. fire engine [ˈfaɪr ˌɛndʒɪn] n. 消防車   **f**

= fire truck [ˈfaɪr ˌtrʌk]

例: The fire engines rushed to the fire in less than three minutes.
(消防車不到三分鐘就趕到火災現場。)

493. firm [fɝm] a. 堅定的 & n. 公司, 行號   **f**

例: You should stay firm and never give up.
(你應保持堅定絕不放棄。)

The law firm is on the fifth floor.
(這家法律事務所是在五樓。)

494. first [fɝst] a. 第一的   **f**

be the first...to V   是第一個……

例: Bill was the first person to answer the question correctly.
(比爾是第一個答對問題的人。)

495. fish [fɪʃ] n. 魚 (單複數同形) & vi. 釣魚, 捕魚   **f**

one/two/three...fish   一條/兩條/三條……魚

go fishing   去釣魚

fisherman [ˈfɪʃɚmən] n. 漁人

例: We went fishing soon after the exam was over.
(考試一完畢我們便釣魚去了。)

496. fit [fɪt] vt. & vi. 適合 & a. 適合的; 健康的 (= healthy)   **f**

stay fit   保持健康

= stay healthy

例: These pants no longer fit me. They're too tight.
(這條褲子不再合我身。它太緊了。)

To stay fit, you should exercise every day.
(要保持健康,每天就應該運動。)

497. fix [fɪks] vt. 修理 (= repair); 準備 (餐點)

    fix dinner/lunch/breakfast　　弄晚餐/午餐/早餐

= cook dinner...

= make dinner...

    例: When will you fix dinner?

      (妳什麼時候做飯呀?)

      Ed knows how to fix computers.

      (艾德懂得如何修電腦。)

498. flag [flæg] n. 旗

    例: The flag waved in the breeze.

      (旗子在微風中飄揚。)

499. flashlight [ˈflæʃˌlaɪt] n. 手電筒

    例: The flashlight doesn't work because the batteries are dead.

      (手電筒不起作用,因為電池沒電了。)

      ＊battery [ˈbætərɪ] n. 電池

500. flat [flæt] a. 平的

    have a flat tire　　爆胎

    例: We had a flat tire on our way to work.

      (上班途中,我們的車子爆胎了。)

501. flight [flaɪt] n. 班機; 飛行

    例: When does your flight leave?

      (你的班機何時起飛?)

      The flight to Tokyo is about three hours.

      (飛到東京大約三小時。)

502. float [flot] vi. 漂浮

例: Mary can float, but she doesn't know how to swim.
(瑪麗可以在水面上漂浮，但她不懂怎麼游泳。)

503. floor [flɔr] n. 地板; 樓層

＊表住第幾樓用 floor 一字, 表『幾層樓高的大樓』則用 story 一字。

例: I live on the fifth floor.
(我住在五樓。)

That's a five-floor building. (✗)

→ That's a five-story building. (○)
(那是一幢五層樓的建築。)

504. floppy disk [ˌflɑpɪ ˈdɪsk] n. 軟碟

hard disk [ˌhɑrd ˈdɪsk] n. 硬碟

例: Put all the information on a floppy disk.
(把所有資料存放在軟碟上。)

505. flour [flaʊɚ] n. 麵粉 (與 flower『花』同音)

例: Cakes are made from flour.
(蛋糕是用麵粉做的。)

506. flow [flo] vi. 流動

例: Water from the river flows into the sea.
(河水流入到大海裏。)

507. flower [ˈflaʊɚ] n. 花

例: The flowers in front of our house are blooming.
(我們家前面的花朵在綻放著。)

＊ bloom [blum] vi. (花朵) 開花

508. fly [flaɪ] vi. 飛 & vt. 駕駛 (飛機) & n. 蒼蠅

*fly 作動詞時, 三態為: fly、flew [flu]、flown [flon]。

例: I see a plane flying across the sky.
(我看到一架飛機飛過天空。)

Can you fly the plane?
(你會開飛機嗎？)

509. fog [fɑg] n. 霧

foggy ['fɑgɪ] a. 多霧的
sunny ['sʌnɪ] a. 出太陽的
windy ['wɪndɪ] a. 刮風的
rainy ['renɪ] a. 下雨的
cloudy ['klaʊdɪ] a. 多雲的, 陰天的

例: It was so foggy that I couldn't see anything in front of me.
(霧很大, 因此我看不到面前的任何東西。)

510. follow [fɑlo] vt. 跟隨, 聽從; 了解 (= understand)

例: Follow my orders, or you'll be sorry.
(聽從我的命令, 否則你會後悔。)

I don't quite follow you.
(我聽不太懂你的話。)

511. fond [fɑnd] a. 喜歡的

be fond of...　　喜愛……
= enjoy...

例: I'm fond of taking a walk after dinner.
(我喜歡晚餐後散個步。)

512. food [fud] n. 食物

例: My favorite food is French fries.
(我最喜愛的食物就是薯條。)

513. **fool** [ful] n. 呆子 & vi. 嬉戲

fool around　　閒蕩

例: Stop fooling around and do something.
（別再混了，做點事吧。）

Only a fool would do such a thing.
（只有傻子才會做這樣的事。）

514. **foolish** [ˈfulɪʃ] a. 愚蠢的

= stupid [ˈstjupɪd]
clever [ˈklɛvɚ] a. 聰明的

例: How did you come up with such a foolish idea?
（你怎麼想出這麼蠢的點子？）

515. **foot** [fʊt] n. 腳; 英尺 & vt. 付 (賬)

feet [fit] n. 腳; 英尺 (複數)
on foot　　走路
foot the bill　　付款
= pay the bill

例: H goes to school on foot.
（他步行上學。）

James is five feet five inches tall.
（阿詹身高五尺五寸。）

Don't worry. I'll foot the bill for dinner.
（別擔心。晚餐的賬我來付。）

516. **football** [ˈfʊtˌbɔl] n. 美式足球

例: Football is the most popular sport in the world.
（美式足球是世上最受歡迎的運動。）

517. **footprint** [ˈfʊtˌprɪnt] n. 足跡

例: There were hundreds of footprints on the sand.
(沙灘上有好幾百個腳印。)

518. **force** [fɔrs] n. 力氣 & vt. 施壓

force sb to V　　強迫某人……
例: Don't force me to do anything I don't want to do.
(不要強迫我做任何我不想做的事。)

519. **foreign** [ˈfɔrɪn] a. 外國的

foreigner [ˈfɔrɪnɚ] n. 外國人
例: It always pays to learn a foreign language.
(學外文永遠值得。)
　　*此處 pays 是不及物動詞, 表『值得』, 等於 is worthwhile。

520. **forest** [ˈfɔrɪst] n. 森林

jungle [ˈdʒʌŋgl] n. 熱帶叢林
woods [wʊdz] n. 樹林 (恆用複數)
例: He was lost in the forest.
(他在森林中迷路了。)

521. **forget** [fɚˈgɛt] vt. 忘記

三態為: forget、forgot、forgotten。
forget to V　　忘了要……
forget Ving　　忘了曾……
例: My mother forgot to wake me up this morning. That's why I
was late for class.
(媽媽今天忘了要叫醒我。那也是我上課遲到的原因。)
I forgot seeing him before. Now I remember.
(我忘了曾經見過他。現在我想起來了。)

522. **forgive** [fɚˈgɪv] vt. 原諒　　**f**

三態為: forgive、forgave、forgiven。

例: I couldn't forgive him for lying to me.
(他對我撒謊，這一點我不能原諒他。)

523. **fork** [fɔrk] n. 叉子　　**f**

knife [naɪf] n. 刀子 (複數為 knives [naɪvz])
chopstick [ˈtʃɑpstɪk] n. 筷子
a pair of chopsticks。　一雙筷子

例: We use chopsticks, but they use knives and forks.
(我們使用筷子，但他們使用刀叉。)

524. **form** [fɔrm] n. 形式; 表格 & vt. 形成　　**f**

例: Fill out the form, and then wait in line.
(填妥表格然後排隊等候。)

We formed a circle and danced around the campfire.
(我們圍成一個圓圈繞著營火跳舞。)

525. **forward** [ˈfɔrwɚd] adv. 向前地　　**f**

backward [ˈbækwɚd] adv. 向後地
look forward to + Ving　　期待……

例: I'm looking forward to seeing you again soon.
(我期待很快再見到你。)

526. **fox** [fɑks] n. 狐狸　　**f**

wolf [wʊlf] n. 狼
be as sly as a fox　　狡猾得跟狐狸一樣
be as angry as a bear　　氣得跟熊一樣
be as busy as a bee　　忙得跟蜜蜂一樣

例: George is as sly as a fox.
(喬治狡猾得要命。)

527. free [fri] a. 免費的; 自由的

freedom [ˈfridəm] n. 自由

free = for free = free of charge   免費的

＊charge [tʃardʒ] n. 收費

be free from/of...   免於……

例: I didn't have to pay for it because it was free/for free/free of charge.

(這個東西我不須要花錢買,因為是免費的。)

He is poor, but he is free from care.

(他很窮,但他無憂無慮。)

528. freeze [friz] vt. & vi. 冷凍; 站立不動

三態為: freeze、froze [froz]、frozen [frozn]。

frozen food   冷凍食品

be freezing cold   冷得發凍

例: It's freezing cold outside, so you should wear a coat.

(外頭冷得發凍,因此你應穿件外套。)

529. fresh [frɛʃ] a. 新鮮的

spoilt [spɔɪlt] a. 腐敗的, 不新鮮的

例: The market is the best place to buy fresh food.

(市場是買新鮮食品的最佳去處。)

530. friend [frɛnd] n. 朋友

make friends with...   與……交友

例: No one likes to make friends with a selfish person.

(誰都不喜歡與自私的人交朋友。)

531. friendly [ˈfrɛndlɪ] a. 友好的

be friendly with...   對……友善

例: I like David because he is friendly with everyone.
(我喜歡大衛因為他對大家都友善。)

532. **frighten** [ˈfraɪtn̩] vt. 使害怕, 驚嚇　　f

　　frightened [ˈfraɪtn̩d] a. 感到害怕
　　frightening [ˈfraɪtn̩ɪŋ] a. 令人害怕的
　　be frightened of...　　害怕……
　= be afraid of...
　　例: Don't frighten me. I have no guts.
　　　(別嚇我。我沒膽。)
　　　＊guts [gʌts] n. 膽量
　　　　例: I'm frightened of my father because he is always strict.
　　　　　(我怕我爸爸，因為他始終很嚴格。)

533. **front** [frʌnt] n. 前面　　f

　　in front of...　　在 (某物外部) 的前面
　　in the front of...　　在 (某物內部) 的前面
　　例: The old woman sat in the front of the bus.
　　　(老太太坐在公車內的前面。)
　　　A stupid guy stood in front of the bus.
　　　(一個蠢蛋站在公車的前面。)

534. **fruit** [frut] n. 水果　　f

　　例: Bananas are my favorite fruit.
　　　(香蕉是我最喜愛的水果。)

535. **fry** [fraɪ] vt. 油炸　　f

　　fried chicken　　炸雞
　　例: Mother fried the dumplings in hot oil.
　　　(媽媽用滾燙的熱油炸水餃。)

536. full [ful] a. 充滿的　　**f**

be full of...　　充滿……
= be filled with...
例: The whole room was full of reporters.
（整個房間擠滿了記者。）

537. fun [fʌn] n. 趣味 & a. 有趣的　　**f**

funny [ˈfʌnɪ] a. 滑稽的
a fun man　　有趣的人
a funny man　　滑稽的人
make fun of...　　取笑……
have fun + Ving　　從事……很愉快
= have a good time + Ving
例: Going to the beach can be a lot of fun.
（到海邊去會很好玩。）
We had lots of fun to chat last night. (✗)
→ We had lots of fun chatting last night. (○)
（我們昨晚聊天聊得很愉快。）

538. fur [fɝ] n. (動物的) 毛　　**f**

hair [hɛr] n. (人的) 毛髮
例: The cat licked its fur while it sat in the sun.
（貓咪坐在陽光下時舐著牠身上的毛。）

539. furniture [ˈfɝnɪtʃɚ] n. 傢俱 (不可數名詞)　　**f**

a furniture (✗)
two furnitures (✗)
a piece of furniture (○)　　一件傢俱
例: We bought some new furniture yesterday.
（我們昨天添購了一些新傢俱。）

540. **future** [ˈfjutʃɚ] n. 未來 & a. 未來的

  in the future　　未來
  in the near future　　最近的未來
  the future world　　未來世界

  例: What are you planning to do in the future?
  （你未來計劃要做什麼？）

541. **gain** [gen] vt. 得到

　　gain weight　　增重, 胖了
　= put on weight
　　lose weight　　減重, 瘦了
　　例: You've gained weight; you need to go on a diet.
　　　　(你胖了, 須要節食了。)

542. **game** [gem] n. 遊戲, 比賽

　　play games　　玩遊戲
　　Game Over!　　遊戲結束/輸了！(電玩術語)
　　例: The game was called off due to rain.
　　　　(由於下雨, 比賽取消了。)

543. **garage** [gəˋrɑʒ] n. 車庫, 修車廠

　　a garage sale　　清倉大拍賣
　(老美要搬家時會把家裡一些用不到的各類東西, 如衣服、玩具、書
　籍、餐具等清理出來, 放在車庫賤售, 此稱"a garage sale"。)
　　例: The car is parked in the garage.
　　　　(車子停在車庫裏。)

544. **garbage** [ˋgɑrbɪdʒ] n. 垃圾 (不可數)

　= trash [træʃ]
　　a garbage (✗)
　　a piece of garbage (○)　　一件垃圾
　　例: Can you take the garbage out when you leave?
　　　　(你離開時, 可以把垃圾帶走嗎？)

545. **garden** [ˋgɑrdn̩] n. 花園; 菜園 (= vegetable garden)

　　例: We grow vegetables in the garden.
　　　　(我們在菜園種了些蔬菜。)

546. gas [gæs] n. 瓦斯; 汽油 (是 gasolene/gasoline [ˌgæsl'in] 的縮寫) **g**

a gas station　　加油站

例: You should pull over before you run out of gas.

(趁著汽油還沒用光前,你應把車停到路邊。)

＊ pull over　　將車停到路邊

547. gate [get] n. 大門 **g**

door [dor] n. 房間的門

例: The gate is guarded 24 hours a day.

(大門廿四小時都有警衛看守。)

548. generally [ˈdʒɛnərəlɪ] adv. 一般而言 **g**

Generally speaking,...　　一般而言,……

＝ In general,...

例: Generally speaking, the more you have, the more you want.

(一般而言,你擁有的愈多,想要的亦愈多。)

549. gentle [ˈdʒɛntl̩] a. 溫和的, 柔和的 **g**

gentleman [ˈdʒɛntl̩mən] n. 紳士, 君子

例: There was a gentle breeze blowing through the window.

(一陣柔和的微風從窗戶吹進來。)

550. geography [dʒɪˈɑgrəfɪ] n. 地理 **g**

例: I majored in geography while in college.

(我唸大學時主修地理。)

551. get [gɛt] vt. 買; 得到 (以名詞作受詞) & vi. 變成 (以形容詞作受詞) **g**

(三態為: get、got、gotten/got)

get 表『變成』時, 多接表『生氣的』形容詞。

get mad/angry　　生氣了

get 亦可表『受到』或『被』,之後接過去分詞。

get hurt/injured/killed　　受傷/受傷/死亡; 喪生

get 亦可表『陷入』,之後接 in 形成的片語。

get in trouble　　陷入困境

例: I got mad when Mary decided to break up with me.

(瑪麗決定要和我分手時,我火大了。)

　John got hurt in a car accident.

(約翰在車禍中受傷。)

　If you get in trouble, give me a call.

(你碰到麻煩時,打電話給我。)

　Where did you get that watch?

(那只錶你在哪兒買的?)

---

552. **ghost** [gost] n. 鬼　　**g**

例: Do you believe in ghosts?

(你相信有鬼嗎?)

＊believe in...　　相信……的存在

---

553. **giant** [ˈdʒaɪənt] a. 巨大的 & n. 巨人　　**g**

例: There was a giant cockroach crawling on my bed.

(有隻大蟑螂在我床上爬。)

＊cockroach [ˈkɑkrotʃ] n. 蟑螂

　crawl [krɔl] vi. 爬行

---

554. **gift** [gɪft] n. 禮品; 天賦的才能　　**g**

gifted [ˈgɪftɪd] a. 有天賦的

have a gift for...　　有……的天賦

= be gifted in...

例: Thank you for the gift for my birthday.

(謝謝你送我的生日禮物。)

　John has a gift for music.

(約翰有音樂的天賦。)

555. giraffe [dʒəˈræf] n. 長頸鹿　　**g**

例: In Taiwan, you can only see giraffes in a zoo.
(在台灣只有在動物園裏才可以看到長頸鹿。)

556. give [gɪv] vt. 給 (三態為: give, gave [gev], given [ˈgɪvn])　　**g**

give sb a hand　　幫助某人
give sb a ride　　開車送某人
例: Please give me a hand with these heavy boxes.
= 　Please help me with these heavy boxes.
(請幫我提這些重箱子。)

557. glad [glæd] a. 高興的　　**g**

be glad to V　　樂意⋯⋯
例: "(I'm) Glad to meet you." "Same here." (=Me, too.)
(『幸會。』『彼此彼此/我也一樣。』)

558. glass [glæs] n. 玻璃 (不可數); 玻璃杯 (可數); 眼鏡 (複數)　　**g**

a piece of glass　　一塊玻璃
a glass/two glasses　　一只杯子/兩只杯子
a pair of glasses　　一付眼鏡
例: The table is made of glass.
(這桌子是玻璃做的。)
　　Fetch me a glass of water.
= 　Get me a glass of water.
(拿杯水給我。)

559. glove [glʌv] n. 手套　　**g**

a pair of gloves　　一副手套
例: In the winter, it's so cold that one must wear gloves.
(冬天天氣冷，因此要戴手套。)

560. glue [glu] n. 膠水 & vt. 用膠黏住　　　　　　　　　　　g

例: Help me glue this picture back together.
(幫我把這張照片用膠水黏起來。)

561. go [go] vi. 去　　　　　　　　　　　　　　　　　　　g

go on + Ving　　繼續做……
= continue + Ving/to V
go + Ving　　從事休閒活動
go dancing/swimming/hiking/skating/shopping/camping/bowling/golfing...
去跳舞/游泳/健行/滑冰/購物/露營/打保齡球/打高爾夫球……
go + 表『生氣的』的形容詞
go mad/crazy　　生起氣來

例: We can't go swimming today because it's too cold.
(今天天氣太冷，我們不能去游泳。)
He went on writing while he talked to me.
(他跟我說話時繼續寫東西。)

562. goal [gol] n. 目標　　　　　　　　　　　　　　　　g

achieve a goal　　達成目標

例: Mary's goal is to get a Master's degree.
(瑪麗的目標就是要得到碩士學位。)
To achieve the goal, Mary must work hard.
(要達到目標，瑪麗就得努力。)

563. golden [ˈgoldn̩] a. 金黃色的; 珍貴的　　　　　　　g

a golden opportunity　　千載難逢的好機會

例: A golden watch is not necessarily a gold watch.
(金黃色的錶未必是金錶。)
Don't miss that golden opportunity.
(不要錯過那個好機會。)

564. **goat** [got] n. 山羊　　　　　　　　　　　　　**g**

sheep [ʃip] n. 綿羊 (單複數同形)
one goat/two goats/three goats...　　一隻/兩隻/三隻……山羊
one sheep/two sheep/three sheep...　　一隻/兩隻/三隻……綿羊
例: Goats feed on grass.
（山羊吃草為生。）

565. **good** [gʊd] a. 好的　　　　　　　　　　　　　**g**

for good　　永遠
be good for nothing　　一無是處
be good at...　　擅長……
例: I'll love you for good/forever.
（我會永遠愛妳。）
　　John is good for nothing.
（約翰是個窩囊廢。）
　　Peter is good at dancing.
（彼得跳舞很行。）

566. **goods** [gʊdz] n. 貨物 (恆用複數, 不可數)　　**g**

例: All the goods should be put in the warehouse.
（所有的貨物應當放到倉庫裏。）
　　＊warehouse [ˈwɛrhaʊs] n. 倉庫

567. **goodbye** [gʊdˈbaɪ] int. 再見　　　　　　　　**g**

say goodbye to...　　向……道別
say hello to...　　向……問好
例: He said goodbye to his parents before getting on the train.
（他向父母道別後便上了火車。）

568. **goose** [gus] n. 鵝 (單數)　　　　　　　　　　**g**

geese [gis] n. 鵝 (複數)

goose bump [ˈgus ˌbʌmp] n. 雞皮疙瘩

get goose bumps　　起雞皮疙瘩

例: I got goose bumps when I heard the bad news.

(我聽到這壞消息時全身起雞皮疙瘩。)

569. government [ˈgʌvɚnmənt] n. 政府　　**g**

例: The city government should do something about the traffic.

(市政府對交通應有所作為。)

570. grade [gred] n. 年級; 等級; 成績 (恆用複數)　　**g**

例: What grade are you in?

(你唸幾年級?)

　My grades have improved by leaps and bounds.

(我的成績突飛猛進。)

＊by leaps and bounds　　大躍進, 突飛猛進

571. graduate [ˈgrædʒʊet] vi. 畢業　　**g**

graduate from...　　從……畢業

例: Soon after Lisa graduated from college, she went on to law school.

(麗莎大學一畢業, 便接著唸法律研究所。)

572. grandparents [ˈgrændˌpærənts] n. 祖父母　　**g**

grandfather [ˈgrændˌfɑðɚ] n. 祖父; 爺爺

grandmother [ˈgrændˌmʌðɚ] n. 祖母; 奶奶

grandchild [ˈgrændtʃaɪld] n. 孫子女

(grandson 孫子; granddaughter 孫女)

great grandfather　　n. 曾祖父

great grandmother　　n. 曾祖母

573. grape [grep] n. 葡萄 ⓖ

例: There are a bunch of grapes on the table.

(桌上有一串葡萄。)

574. grass [græs] n. 草 ⓖ

a blade of grass　　一根草 (非 a grass)

例: The grass is always greener on the other side of the fence.

(外國的月亮比較圓；外來的和尚會唸經。——諺語)

fence [fɛns] n. 圍牆, 竹籬巴

＊ 站在自家看自己的草坪時, 總認為不夠綠, 而看看圍牆另一邊別人家的草坪, 總覺得別人家的草坪比較綠。本諺語即源自此一概念。

575. grateful [ˈgretfəl] a. 感激的 ⓖ

be grateful to sb for sth　　因某事而感激某人

= be thankful to sb for sth

例: You should be grateful to John for what he has done for you.

(你應感激約翰為你做的一切。)

576. gray [gre] a. 灰色的 ⓖ

例: The sky is gray and cloudy. It may rain soon.

(天空灰灰陰陰的。可能很快就要下雨了。)

577. great [gret] a. 極好的 ⓖ

(=cool [kul] =wonderful [ˈwʌndɚfl] a. 大的; 偉大的)

例: I felt great after I finished doing all of my homework.

(做完功課後, 我覺得好爽。)

578. greedy [ˈgridɪ] a. 貪心的 ⓖ

be greedy for sth　　貪求某物

例: Tom is greedy for fame and money.

(湯姆貪求名利。)

579. **green** [grin] a. 綠的 & n. 綠色　　　g

be green with envy　　羨慕得要死

envy [ˈɛnvɪ] n. 羨慕

例: Steve was green with envy when his brother won the prize.
(史提夫的哥哥得獎時，史提夫羨慕極了。)

580. **greet** [grit] vt. 問候; 迎接　　　g

greeting [ˈgritɪŋ] n. 問候, 致意

例: Please give my greetings to John when you see him.
(見到約翰時，請代我向他問好。)

Mary greeted everyone at the party.
(瑪莉向每個來參加宴會的人問候。)

581. **groceries** [ˈgrosərɪz] n. 雜貨 (尤指蔬菜類, 恆用複數)　　　g

grocery store [ˈgrosərɪ ˌstor] n. 有賣蔬菜的雜貨店

drugstore [ˈdrʌgstor] n. (便利商店類的) 雜貨店

例: I went to the supermarket to buy groceries.
(我到超市買雜貨。)

582. **group** [grup] n. 團體　　　g

a group of...　　一群……

例: A small group of students lined up at the bus stop.
(一小群學生在公車站排排隊。)

583. **grow** [gro] vi. 成長 & vt. 種植　　　g

(三態為: grow、grew [gru]、grown [gron])

grow up　　長大

例: The farmer grows all type of crops.
(這位農夫什麼農作物都種。)

＊crop [krɑp] n. 農作物

Peter grew up in the country, while Mary was brought up in the city.

(彼得是在鄉下長大的，而瑪麗則是在城市被拉拔大的。)

584. **grownup** [ˈgronˌʌp] n. 成人

= adult [əˈdʌlt]

例: You're a grownup now, so you shouldn't be childish anymore.

(你現在是大人了，因此不能再孩子氣。)

*childish [ˈtʃaɪldɪʃ] a. 幼稚的

585. **guess** [gɛs] vt. & n. 猜測

make a guess　　猜一猜

例: I don't know the answer, but I'll make a guess at it.

(我不知道答案，但我會猜一猜。)

586. **guest** [gɛst] n. 客人

例: Be my guest. Let me pay for dinner.

(我請客。晚餐我出錢。)

587. **guide** [gaɪd] n. 嚮導 & vt. 指導, 引導

a tour guide　　導遊

例: He used to work as a tour guide.

(他以前做過導遊。)

I don't know much about the work, so you'll have to guide me.

(這工作我不太熟，因此你得指導我。)

588. **gum** [gʌm] n. 口香糖 (不可數, =chewing gum [ˈtʃuɪŋˌgʌm])

a stick of gum　　一片口香糖

= a piece of gum

a pack of gum　　一包口香糖

例: I don't like chewing gum because it's sticky.
(我不喜歡嚼口香糖，因為它很黏。)
＊chew [tʃu] vt. 咀嚼
　sticky [ˈstɪkɪ] a. 黏黏的

589. **gun** [gʌn] n. 槍　　　　　　　　　　　　　　**g**

例: The policeman aimed his gun at the bad guy.
(警察把槍瞄準那個壞蛋。)

590. **gym** [dʒɪm] n. 健身房　　　　　　　　　　　**g**

work out at the gym　　在健身房健身
例: Peter spends most of his time working out at the gym.
(彼得大部份時間都在健身房內健身。)

591. habit [ˈhæbɪt] n. 習慣

    be in the habit of...   有……的習慣

    例: John is in the habit of getting up early.

    （約翰有早起的習慣。）

592. hair [hɛr] n. 頭髮

    comb one's hair   梳頭髮

  * comb [kom] n. 梳子 & vt. 用梳子梳

    have one's hair cut   理髮

    例: Mary's hair comes down to her waist.

      （瑪麗的頭髮長到腰部。）

      You need to have your hair cut; it's too long.

    （你須要理髮了；它太長了。）

593. half [hæf] n. 一半 & adv. 一半地

    half an hour   半小時 (非 a half hour)

    an hour and a half   一個半小時

 = one and a half hours

    two and a half hours   兩個半小時

    例: Well begun is half done.

      （好的開始是成功的一半。——諺語。）

      Half of the work is finished.

    （工作已完成了一半。）

594. hall [hɔl] n. 大廳

    例: Take your hat off when you enter the hall.

    （進入大廳時要脫帽。）

595. hamburger [ˈhæmbɝɡɚ] n. 漢堡 (= burger [bɝɡɚ])

    例: Let's order some hamburgers and French fries.

    （咱們叫些漢堡及薯條吧。）

596. **hammer** ['hæmɚ] n. 鎚子　　h

例: The carpenter used a hammer to drive the nails into the wood.
（木匠用鎚子把釘子釘到木頭裏。）
＊carpenter ['kɑrpəntɚ] n. 木工, 木匠

597. **hand** [hænd] n. 手 & vt. 交出　　h

have...on hand　　手頭上有……
shake hands with sb　　和某人握手
on the other hand　　另一方面
be near at hand　　即將來臨
= be coming soon
hand in...　　交出……
= turn in...

例: I have about NT$5,000 on hand.
（我手頭上大約有五千元台幣。）
Hand in your paper after class.
（下課後把報告交出來。）
The exam is near at hand.
（考試就要到了。）
John is good at singing. On the other hand, he can't dance.
（約翰很會唱歌。另一方面，他卻不會跳舞。）

598. **handkerchief** ['hæŋkɚtʃɪf] n. 手帕　　h

例: The old man blew his nose on a handkerchief.
（老先生用手帕擤鼻涕。）
＊blow one's nose　　擤鼻涕

599. **handsome** ['hænsəm] a. 英俊的　　h

例: He is very handsome, but he isn't very bright.
（他很帥，但腦袋卻不靈光。）

600. **hang** [hæŋ] vt. & vi. 懸掛; 吊死   h

    hang 作『懸掛』時, 三態為: hang、hung、hung。

    hang 作『吊死』時, 三態為: hang、hanged、hanged。

    例: They hung the painting upside down.

        (他們把這張畫掛反了。)

        The man was hanged for robbing a bank.

        (這男子因搶劫銀行被吊死。)

601. **happen** [ˈhæpən] vi. 發生   h

    happen to + N   發生於……

    happen to + V   碰巧……

    例: What happened to your left eye?

  =   What's the matter with your left eye?

        (你的左眼怎麼了?)

        I happen to have $100 with me.

        (我正巧身上有一百元。)

602. **harbor** [ˈhɑrbɚ] n. 港口   h

    例: The old man waited for the boat at the harbor.

        (老先生在港口等船。)

603. **hardly** [ˈhɑrdlɪ] adv. 幾乎不   h

  = almost not

    例: Don't marry him because you hardly know him.

        (別嫁給他, 因為妳幾乎不了解他。)

604. **hardware** [ˈhɑrdˌwɛr] n. 硬體 (不可數)   h

    software [ˈsɑftˌwɛr] n. 軟體 (不可數)

    例: The price of computer hardware has gone down recently.

        (電腦硬體的價格最近下滑。)

605. **hardworking** [ˈhɑrdwɝkɪŋ] a. 用功的, 努力的

= diligent [ˈdɪlədʒənt]

例: Almost all teachers like hardworking students.
(幾乎所有的老師都喜歡用功的學生。)

606. **harm** [hɑrm] n. 傷害 (不可數) & vt. 傷害

do harm to sb　　對某人有害
= do sb harm
do sb good　　對某人有益 (無"do good to sb"用法)

例: As we all know, smoking does harm to us.
= As we all know, smoking does us harm.
(我們都知道，抽煙對我們有害。)

607. **hat** [hæt] n. 帽子

例: He put on his hat and went out.
(他戴上帽子後便走了出去。)

608. **hate** [het] vt. 恨

hate Ving　　痛恨……
= hate to V

例: I hate people who lie to me.
(我痛恨說謊的人。)

I hate | to work | with him because he is never responsible.
　　　 | working |

(我不喜歡跟他共事因為他從不負責。)

609. **hatch** [hætʃ] vt. & vi. 孵 (蛋)

例: The eggs hatched after the hen sat on them for days.
(母雞在蛋上孵了好幾天之後，蛋就孵出來了。)

Don't count your chickens before they are hatched.
(蛋還沒孵出來前不要計算會孵出多少雞——不要打如意算盤。
　——諺語)

610. **head** [hɛd] n. 頭 & vi. 前往　　　h

head to/for + 地方　　前往某地

keep one's head　　保持冷靜

例: Let's head to the beach this weekend.
(這個週末咱們到海邊去吧。)

　　Keep your head. Don't be so nervous.
(保持冷靜。別那麼緊張。)

611. **health** [hɛlθ] n. 健康　　　h

healthy [ˈhɛlθɪ] a. 健康的

be in good/poor health　　健康很好/差

例: He is in good health because he exercises.

= He stays healthy because he exercises.
(他運動,所以很健康。)

612. **hear** [hɪr] vt. & vi. 聽到　　　h

hear from...　　收到……的訊息

hear of/about...　　聽說有關……的事

例: I haven't heard from you in a long time.
(我好久沒收到你的來信/音訊了。)

　　Have you heard about John's promotion?
(你有沒有聽說約翰升遷了?)

613. **heart** [hɑrt] n. 心　　　h

know...by heart　　默背……

a heart of gold　　善心

at heart　　心地

例: I know this poem by heart.
(這首詩我可以默背下來。)

　　Mrs. Brown has a heart of gold.
(布朗太太有著菩薩心腸。)

Mrs. Brown is kind at heart.

(布朗太太心地善良。)

614. **heat** [hit] n. 熱 & vt. 加熱　　h

例: If you can't stand the heat, get out of the kitchen.

(你若受不了熱，就離開廚房吧。)

Heat the food before eating it.

(食物熱過後再吃。)

615. **heaven** [ˈhɛvən] n. 天堂　　h

hell [hɛl] n. 地獄

go to heaven　　上天堂

go to hell　　下地獄

例: Heaven helps those who help themselves.

(自助者天助。——諺語)

616. **heavy** [ˈhɛvɪ] a. 重的　　h

light [laɪt] a. 輕的

例: Help me lift this heavy box.

(幫我抬這重箱子。)

617. **helicopter** [ˈhɛlɪˌkɑptɚ] n. 直升機　　h

例: The helicopter landed on the roof of the building.

(直升機降落在那棟建築物的屋頂上。)

＊land [lænd] vi. 降落

roof [ruf] n. 屋頂

618. **hello** [hɛˈlo] int. 喂, 你好 (打招呼用語)　　h

say hello to sb　　向某人問好

例: Hello, Mark. It's been a long time.

(哈囉，馬克。好久不見了。)

Say hello to John when you see him.
(見到約翰時，向他問好。)

619. **height** [haɪt] n. 高度　　　　　　　　　　h

high [haɪ] a. 高的
in height (= high)　　高
例: The wall is 5 feet 5 inches │ in height.
　　　　　　　　　　　　　　　 │ high.

(這道牆高五呎五吋。)

620. **help** [hɛlp] vt. & n. 幫忙　　　　　　　　h

help sb (to) + V　　幫某人從事……
cannot help + Ving　　忍不住……
= cannot help but + V
例: Will you help me solve this math problem?
(幫我解這道數學題，好嗎？)
　　I couldn't help laughing when I heard the joke.
= I couldn't help but laugh when I heard the joke.
(聽到這消息時，我忍不住笑。)

621. **hide** [haɪd] vt. & vi. 躲藏 (三態為: hide、hid、hidden)　h

play hide-and-seek　　玩捉迷藏
例: We often played hide-and-seek when we were kids.
(我們小時候常玩捉迷藏。)
　　Where was the cat hiding?
(貓躲到哪裏去了？)

622. **high** [haɪ] a. 高的　　　　　　　　　　h

low [lo] a. 低的
be high in...　　含有豐富的……
例: He is high in position, but he is friendly.
(他職位高卻很和善。)

This fruit is high in Vitamin C.
(這個水果含有豐富的維他命 C。)

623. **hike** [haɪk] vi. & n. (在山中或鄉間) 健行　　h

go hiking　　去健行
例: On Sundays, we often go hiking in the mountains.
(星期天的時候，我們常在山中健行。)

624. **hill** [hɪl] n. 山丘　　h

例: The hills are filled with butterflies in all shapes and colors.
(山間裏盡是各式各樣色彩繽紛的蝴蝶。)

625. **history** [ˈhɪstrɪ] n. 歷史　　h

in history　　史上
例: To me, Koxinga is the greatest hero in Chinese history.
(對我而言，鄭成功是中國歷史上最偉大的英雄。)

626. **hit** [hɪt] vt. 打 (三態同形)　　h

hit sb on the + 部位　　打中某人身上的部位
例: The ball hit me on the head.
(這球打中我的頭。)

627. **hobby** [ˈhɑbɪ] n. 嗜好　　h

例: One of my hobbies is stamp collecting.
(我的嗜好之一便是集郵。)
＊stamp [stæmp] n. 郵票
collect [kəˈlɛkt] vt. 蒐集

628. **hold** [hold] vt. 握住 (三態為 hold, held [hɛld], held)　　h

hold sb by the + 部位　　抓住某人身上的部位
例: He | held | me by the hand and said, "I love you."
　　 | took |

(他握住我的手說：『我愛妳。』)

629. **holiday** [ˈhɑləˌde] n. 假日

be on holiday　　渡假 (英式)
= be on vacation　　渡假 (美式)
例: On holidays, I like to stay at home and listen to music.
（每逢假日我喜歡待在家裡聽音樂。）

630. **hole** [hol] n. 洞

例: I stepped into a hole and hurt my ankle.
（我踏進洞裏傷到腳踝。）
＊ankle [ˈæŋkḷ] n. 腳踝

631. **home** [hom] n. 家

make oneself at home　　不要拘束
例: Come on! Make yourself at home.
（別這樣嘛！不要拘束。）

632. **homework** [ˈhomˌwɝk] n. 家庭作業 (不可數)

a homework　　　（✗）
a piece of homework (○)　　一份作業
a lot of homework (○)　　許多作業
例: Your homework should be turned in by Friday.
（你的作業星期五以前要交。）

633. **honest** [ˈɑnɪst] a. 誠實的

honesty [ˈɑnəstɪ] n. 誠實
例: Be honest with me and tell me everything.
（對我要老實，把一切都告訴我。）
Honesty is the best policy.
（誠實為上策。──諺語）
＊policy [ˈpɑləsɪ] n. 政策

634. **honey** [ˈhʌnɪ] n. 蜂蜜; 親愛的 (暱稱)　　　h

例: I don't care for honey. I prefer sugar in my tea.

(我不喜歡蜂蜜。我比較喜歡茶裏放糖。)

＊prefer [prɪˈfɝ] vt. 比較喜歡

sugar [ˈʃʊgɚ] n. 糖

635. **honor** [ˈɑnɚ] n. 光榮　　　h

in honor of sb　　祝賀某人; 為某人

例: Ladies and gentlemen, it's an honor to deliver a speech to you.

(諸位女士,諸位先生,很榮幸能與大家說話。)

There is a party tonight in honor of our new principal.

(今晚要為我們新到任的校長舉行派對。)

636. **hook** [hʊk] n. & vt. 鉤　　　h

be hooked on...　　迷上……

例: You can't catch a fish without a hook.

(沒釣鉤你釣不到魚。)

David is hooked on the girl he met on the train.

(大衛迷上了他在火車上認識的女孩子。)

637. **hope** [hop] n. & vt. 希望　　　h

hopeful [ˈhopfḷ] a. 充滿希望的

hopeless [ˈhoplɪs] a. 沒希望的, 絕望的

give up hope　　放棄希望

be hopeful about...　　對……抱希望

例: No matter what happens, never give up hope.

(不管發生什麼事,千萬不要放棄希望。)

We should be hopeful about the future.

(我們應對未來保持希望。)

638. **horn** [hɔrn] n. 角; 號角

    blow one's own horn   自誇

    例: I don't like him because he likes to blow his own horn.
    (我不喜歡他因為他喜歡自吹自擂。)

639. **horse** [hɔrs] n. 馬

    例: Mary rode the horse around the field.
    (瑪麗在田野騎著馬到處走。)

640. **horror** [ˈhɔrɚ] n. 恐怖

    horrible [ˈhɔrəbḷ] a. 可怕的; 糟透的
    a horror movie   恐怖片
    a horrible movie   爛片
  = a terrible movie

    例: To my horror, a typhoon is coming.
    (令我害怕的是，颱風就要來了。)
    *typhoon [taɪˈfun] n. 颱風

641. **hospital** [ˈhɑspɪtḷ] n. 醫院

    例: Mary went to the hospital to have her baby.
    (瑪麗到醫院去生產。)

642. **host** [host] n. 男主人; 廣播電視男主持人 & vt. 主辦, 主持

    hostess [ˈhostɪs] n. 女主人; 廣播電視女主持人

    例: Good morning, everyone, this is your host Pete Lai.
    (大家早，我是節目主持人賴皮。)
    Which country just hosted the Asian Games?
    (哪個國家剛剛主辦了亞運？)

643. **hot** [hɑt] a. 熱的

    a hot potato   燙手山芋, 棘手的問題

例: This hot weather makes it difficult to fall asleep.
(炎熱的天氣使人難入眠。)

644. **hotel** [hoˈtɛl] n. 旅館, 飯店　　h

例: It is getting late. We'd better stay at a hotel for the night.
(天色漸晚。我們最好待在飯店過夜。)

645. **hour** [aʊr] n. 小時　　h

keep good hours　　早睡早起規律生活
= keep early hours
hour after hour　　連續好幾個鐘頭
例: The boy waited hour after hour for his father to pick him up.
(小男孩等他爸爸來接他,等了好幾個小時。)

646. **house** [haʊs] n. 房子　　h

be on the house　　主人請客
例: Are you going to buy a house?
(你將買一棟房子?)
Ladies and gentlemen, everything here is on the house. Enjoy yourselves!
(各位女士,各位先生,這裏的一切由主人請客。痛快玩吧!)

647. **housewife** [ˈhaʊsˌwaɪf] n. 家庭主婦　　h

(複數形為 housewives [ˈhaʊsˌwaɪvz])
例: Many housewives today have to work to help raise the family.
(今天許多家庭主婦必須工作以協助家庭生計。)

648. **housework** [ˈhaʊsˌwɝk] n. 家事 (不可數)　　h

例: I help Mom with her housework on weekends.
(週末時我會幫媽媽做家事。)

649. how [haʊ] adv. 如何　　h

例: Do you know how to cook?
(你知道怎麼煮飯嗎？)

I have no idea how well the girl sings.
(我不知道這女孩子唱得有多棒。)

650. however [haʊˈɛvɚ] conj. 無論多麼地 & adv. 然而　　h

*however 作連接詞時, 等於 no matter how; 若作副詞時, 則表『然而』,
在句中出現時, 之前置句點或分號, 之後置逗點。

例: However nice he is, I don't like him.
= No matter how nice he is, I don't like him.
(不管他多麼好, 我都不喜歡他。)

You can come with me. However, you have to pay your own
way.
= You can come with me; however, you have to pay your own
way.
(你可以跟我來; 不過, 你得自費。)

651. huge [hjudʒ] a. 巨大的　　h

例: I'm so full because I had a huge breakfast this morning.
(我吃得太飽了, 因為我今早吃了一頓特別豐盛的早餐。)

652. human [ˈhjumən] a. 人性的; 凡人的 & n. 人類　　h

(=human being [ˌhjumən ˈbiɪŋ])
human nature　　人性

例: Tom is only human. He does things wrong from time to time.
(湯姆只不過是凡人, 有時他也會犯錯。)

653. humble [ˈhʌmbḷ] a. 謙虛的; 簡陋的　　h

例: You should always be humble in dealing with people.
(你始終應謙虛待人。)

John was born into a humble family.
(約翰出自寒門。)

654. **hunger** [ˈhʌŋɚ] n. 飢餓 　　h

hungry [ˈhʌŋgrɪ] a. 飢餓的
be hungry for...　　　渴望得到……
= be eager for...

例: If you're hungry, you should grab a bite to eat.
(你要是肚子餓，就去買點東西吃吧。)

655. **hurry** [ˈhɝɪ] n. 匆匆忙忙 & vi. 快 　　h

be in a hurry　　匆忙
hurry up　　動作快一點

例: Hurry up, or we'll be late.
(快一點，否則我們會遲到了。)

　　Why are you always in such a hurry?
(你幹嘛一直那麼匆忙？)

656. **hurt** [hɝt] vt. 傷害 & vi. 疼痛 (三態同形) 　　h

例: What you said hurt my feelings.
(你的話刺傷了我的心。)

　　My finger hurts.
(我的手指頭好痛喲。)

657. **husband** [ˈhʌzbənd] n. 丈夫 　　h

wife [waɪf] n. 妻子

例: A good husband should remain true to his wife.
(好丈夫始終應對妻子忠實。)

658. **ice cream** ['aɪsˌkrim] n. 冰淇淋

例: I'd like two scoops of chocolate ice cream.
(我想要兩球巧克力冰淇淋。)
scoop [skup] n. 一杓

659. **idea** [aɪˈdiə] n. 想法

have no idea + 疑問詞 (如 what, when, how, why, who 等) 引導的名
詞子句 不知道……
例: I have no idea where he lives.
= I don't know where he lives.
(我不知道他住哪裏。)

660. **ideal** [aɪˈdɪəl] a. 理想的 & n. 理想

例: Tell me what an ideal husband is like.
(告訴我理想的丈夫是什麼樣子。)

661. **idle** ['aɪdḷ] a. 懶散的 & vi. 閒混

idle around 鬼混
= fool around
例: An idle youth, a needy age.
(少小不努力,老大徒傷悲。——諺語)
＊needy ['nidɪ] a. 窮困的
age [edʒ] n. 此處指『老年』

662. **ill** [ɪl] a. 生病的

illness ['ɪlnɪs] n. 病
fall ill 生病了
例: John fell ill and had to ask for leave.
(約翰生病了所以得請假。)

663. illegal [ɪˈligḷ] a. 非法的

legal [ˈligḷ] a. 合法的

例: It is illegal to park your car here.
(在這停車是違法的。)

664. imagine [ɪmˈædʒɪn] vt. & vi. 想像

imagination [ɪˌmædʒəˈneʃən] n. 想像力
imaginative [ɪˈmædʒənetɪv] a. 有想像力的

例: I just can't imagine what life would be like without you.
(生命中沒有妳，我無法想像是什麼樣子。)

665. important [ɪmˈpɔrtṇt] a. 重要的

importance [ɪmˈpɔrtṇs] n. 重要

例: What he's just said is really important.
(他剛才所說的真的很重要。)

666. impossible [ɪmˈpɑsəbḷ] a. 不可能的

possible [ˈpɑsəbḷ] a. 可能的

例: I'm busy now, so it's impossible for me to go out with you.
(我現在很忙，因此不可能跟你一塊兒外出。)

667. improve [ɪmˈpruv] vt. & vi. 改善; 進步

例: To improve your English, you should read more.
(要使英文進步就要多看書。)

668. inch [ɪntʃ] n. 英寸

be every inch + a/an...　　十足是個……

例: He is every inch a hero.
(他是個不折不扣的英雄。)

669. include [ɪn'klud] vt. 包括

例: The money includes the tip.
(這些錢包括小費在內。)

670. including [ɪn'kludɪŋ] prep. 包括

例: All my friends love music, including John.
(我朋友都喜歡音樂,包括約翰在內。)

671. indoors [,ɪn'dɔrz] adv. 在室內 (置於動詞之後)

indoor ['ɪndɔr] a. 室內的 (之後置名詞)
outdoors [,aut'dɔrz] adv. 在戶外 (置於動詞之後)
outdoor ['autdɔr] a. 戶外的 (之後置名詞)

例: I enjoy many outdoor activities, including jogging and swimming.
(我喜歡許多戶外活動,包括慢跑和游泳。)

Tennis can be played either outdoors or indoors.
(網球可以在戶外打,亦可以在室內打。)

672. infect [ɪn'fɛkt] vt. 使感染

be infected with...　　感染了……
例: They say John is infected with AIDS.
(據說約翰感染了愛滋病。)

673. injure ['ɪndʒɚ] vt. 使受傷

injury ['ɪndʒərɪ] n. 受傷
例: David had a car accident; luckily, however, he was not injured.
(大衛出了車禍;不過,所幸的是,他沒受傷。)

674. **ink** [ɪŋk] n. 墨水

例: Without ink, the fountain pen doesn't work.
(沒墨水的話，鋼筆是寫不出字的。)

675. **information** [ˌɪnfɚˈmeʃən] n. 消息, 資料 (不可數)

例: Thank you for giving me so much information about John.
(謝謝你給我那麼多有關約翰的資訊。)

676. **insect** [ˈɪnsɛkt] n. 昆蟲

例: Not all insects do us harm. Some do us a lot of good.
(並非所有的昆蟲都對我們有害。有些對我們頗有好處。)

677. **inside** [ɪnˈsaɪd] n. 內部 & prep. 在……之內 & adv. 在內部

outside [aʊtˈsaɪd] n. 外部 & prep. 在……的外面 & adv. 在外部

例: It is said that there is a monster inside the building.
(inside 是介詞)
(據說大樓裏有隻怪物。)
＊monster [ˈmɑnstɚ] n. 怪物
Don't stay inside too long. Get out and exercise for a while.
(inside 是副詞)
(別在裏面待太久。出去運動一下。)
The door is locked from the inside. (inside 是名詞)
(這扇門被反鎖了。)

678. **instead** [ɪnˈstɛd] adv. 代替; 相反地

instead of...　　非但不……反而……
例: Instead of working hard, John plays around all day.
(約翰不用功，反而整天混。)
He isn't good. Instead, he is bad.
(他不好。相反地，他很壞。)

679. **interest** [ˈɪntrɪst] vt. 使……感興趣 & n. 興趣

interesting [ˈɪntrɪstɪŋ] a. 令人有趣的
interested [ˈɪntrɪstɪd] a. 感到有趣的
be interested in...　　對……感興趣
= show an interest in...
例: Strange to say, the music teacher isn't interested in music.
(說來也怪，這位音樂老師對音樂不感興趣。)

680. **international** [ˌɪntɚˈnæʃən!̩] a. 國際的

national [ˈnæʃən!̩] a. 國家的; 國立的
international affairs [əˈfɛrz] n. 國際事務
例: A diplomat should master international affairs.
(外交官應精通國際事務。)
＊diplomat [ˈdɪpləmæt] n. 外交官
master [ˈmæstɚ] vt. 精通

681. **Internet** [ˈɪntɚˌnɛt] n. 網際網路 (與 the 並用, 常簡寫成 the Net)

surf the Internet　　上網
例: By surfing the Internet, you can find the information you want.
(藉由上網，你可以找到你需要的資料。)

682. **interrupt** [ˌɪntəˈrʌpt] vt. 打斷

例: Sorry for interrupting your talk, but I have something important to tell you.
(抱歉打斷諸位的談話，不過我有重要的事要告訴諸位。)

683. **intersection** [ˌɪntəˈsɛkʃən] n. 十字路口

= crossroads [ˈkrɔsrodz] n. (單複數同形)
one intersection = one crossroads　　一個十字路口
two intersections = two crossroads　　兩個十字路口

例: Go straight ahead and turn right at the first intersection.
(直走,在第一個十字路口右轉。)

684. **introduce** [ˌɪntrə'djus] vt. 介紹

introduction [ˌɪntrə'dʌkʃən] n. 介紹
introduce A to B　　將 A 介紹給 B

例: May I have the honor of introducing John to you, Mary?
(瑪麗,我有這個榮幸把約翰介紹給妳嗎?)

685. **invent** [ɪn'vɛnt] vt. 發明

invention [ɪn'vɛnʃən] n. 發明 (不可數); 發明物 (可數)

例: Tell me who invented the plane.
(告訴我飛機是誰發明的。)

　　Necessity is the mother of invention.
(需求是發明之母。——諺語)

686. **invite** [ɪn'vaɪt] vt. 邀請

invitation [ɪnvə'teʃən] n. 邀請
at the invitation of...　　應……之邀請

例: Thank you for inviting me to dinner.
(謝謝你邀我吃晚餐。)

　　I sang an English song at John's invitation.
(應約翰的邀請我唱了一首英文歌。)

687. **involve** [ɪn'vɑlv] vt. 使涉入

get/be involved in...　　涉入……

例: I was shocked when I learned that Peter was involved in that case.
(當我知道彼得涉入那個案件時,我很震驚。)

688. **island** [ˈaɪlənd] n. 島嶼　　　　　　　　　　　　　　i

　　on the island　　在島上 (非 in the island)

　　around the island　　環島

例: I'm planning to bike around the island.

　　(我計劃要騎腳踏車環島旅行。)

　　＊bike [baɪk] n. 腳踏車 (= bicycle [ˈbaɪsɪkḷ]) & vi. 騎腳踏車

689. jacket ['dʒækɪt] n. 夾克　　j

例: Put on your jacket, or you may catch (a) cold.
（穿上夾克，否則你可能會感冒。）

690. jam [dʒæm] n. 果醬　　j

a traffic jam　　交通阻塞
traffic ['træfɪk] n. 交通 & a. 交通的
例: I was late because I was caught in a traffic jam.
（我因為碰到塞車，所以遲到了。）
I prefer using jam on my toast instead of butter.
（我比較喜歡用果醬抹土司，而不是奶油。）
＊prefer [prɪ'fɝ] vt. 比較喜歡

691. jar [dʒɑr] n. 玻璃罐　　j

例: The lid of this jar is stuck. Can you open it for me?
（這個玻璃罐的蓋子卡死了。請你幫我打開，好嗎？）
＊lid [lɪd] n. 蓋子
stuck [stʌk] a. 被卡住的

692. jeans [dʒinz] n. 牛仔褲　　j

a pair of jeans　　一條牛仔褲
例: You look great in blue jeans.
（你穿藍色牛仔褲很好看。）

693. jelly ['dʒɛlɪ] n. 果凍　　j

例: The girl's face was covered with jelly.
（這女孩子的臉沾滿果凍。）

694. job [dʒɑb] n. 工作　　j

例: Mary lost her job when she was caught stealing.
（瑪麗偷竊被逮個正著，立刻丟了飯碗。）

695. jog [dʒɑg] vi. & n. 慢跑 **j**

go jogging　　慢跑去

= go for a jog

例: Let's go jogging in the park now.
（咱們現在到公園慢跑去。）

696. join [ˈdʒɔɪn] vt. 參與, 加入 **j**

join sb in Ving　　加入某人的行列一起……

例: Can I join you in singing?
（我可以加入你們一塊兒唱歌嗎？）

697. joke [dʒok] n. 玩笑; 笑話 **j**

play a joke on sb　　對某人開玩笑

例: I was only playing a joke on you. I wasn't serious.
（我只是對你開個玩笑罷了。我不是認真的。）

Paul told a joke and everyone burst into laughter.
（保羅說了個笑話，讓所有人哄堂大笑。）

＊serious [ˈsɪrɪəs] a. 認真的

698. journey [ˈdʒɝnɪ] n. 旅行 (特別指長途旅行, 等於 a long trip) **j**

take sb on a journey　　帶某人旅行

例: Father took us on a train journey around Taiwan last year.
（去年爸爸帶我們坐火車環遊台灣。）

699. joy [dʒɔɪ] n. 歡樂 **j**

例: Seeing her smile fills my heart with joy.
（看到她微笑讓我心中充滿歡喜。）

700. jump [dʒʌmp] vi. 跳 **j**

jump to one's feet　　跳起來

例: I jumped to my feet when he patted me on the back.

(他拍我的背時，我跳了起來。)

701. **juice** [dʒus] n. 果汁 j

例: The orange juice is fresh because I squeezed it myself.
(這柳橙汁是新鮮的，因為是我自己榨的。)
* squeeze [skwiz] vt. 擠壓; 榨 (汁)

702. **jungle** [ˈdʒʌŋgḷ] n. 熱帶叢林 j

例: Rumor has it that there are tigers in the jungle.
(謠傳這片叢林裏有老虎。)
* rumor [ˈrumɚ] n. 謠傳
 Rumor has it that... 謠傳……; 據說……
= It is said that...
= They say that...

703. **junior** [ˈdʒunɪɚ] a. 年紀較小的; 地位較低的 & n. 年幼者 j

senior [ˈsinɪɚ] a. 年紀較長的; 地位較高的 & n. 年長者
junior high school   國中
a senior high school   高中
be junior/senior to...   比……年幼/年長
例: He is five years junior to me.
= He is five years my junior.
(他比我小五歲。)

704. **just** [dʒʌst] adv. 僅僅 (=only); 剛才; 正是 j

例: Don't be so hard on him. After all, he's just a child.
(不要對他那麼兇。畢竟他只是個小孩子。)
* be hard on...   對……很兇
I just arrived, so I'm a little tired.
(我剛剛到，因此有點累。)
He is just the man I want to marry.
(他正是我要嫁的人。)

705. **keep** [kip] vt. 持有 (以名詞或代名詞作受詞) & k

 vi. 保持……的狀況 (接形容詞作補語); 繼續 (接現在分詞, 表示進行的狀態)

 三態為: keep、kept [kɛpt]、kept。

 例: Keep the change, please.
  (零錢免找。)

  Keep quiet, please.
  (請安靜。)

  Keep (on) working hard, and you'll be successful some day.
  (不斷努力,那麼有一天你就會成功。)

706. **key** [ki] n. 鑰匙 k

 be the key to + N 是開啟……的鑰匙

 例: Hard work is the key to success.
  (努力是成功之鑰。)

707. **keyboard** [ˈkibɔrd] n. 鍵盤 k

 例: This keyboard makes too much noise.
  (這個鍵盤發出的聲音太吵。)

708. **kick** [kɪk] vt. 踢 k

 例: The soccer player kicked the ball into the goal.
  (球員把球踢進球門。)

  ＊goal [gol] n. 原指『目標』,此處指『球門』

709. **kid** [kɪd] n. 孩子 (是 child 的俚語說法) & vi. 開玩笑 (多用於進行式) k

 例: Who's that kid by the window?
  (窗邊的那個孩子是誰呀?)

  I was just kidding with you. I'm not getting married.
= I was just joking with you. I'm not getting married.
  (我剛才只是跟你開玩笑。我還沒打算結婚。)

710. **kill** [kɪl] vt. & vi. 殺死

kill time by Ving　　藉……打發時間

例: The dog was killed when a car hit it.
(車把狗狗撞死了。)

We killed time until dinner by watching TV.
(晚飯前我們看電視打發時間。)

711. **kilogram** [ˈkɪloˌɡræm] n. 公斤 (常縮寫成 kilo [ˈkilo])

例: I weigh 80 kilograms.
(我重八十公斤。)
＊weigh [we] vi. 重達

712. **kilometer** [kɪˈlɑmɪtɚ] n. 公里

例: The next store is seven kilometers away.
(下個商店離這兒有七公里遠。)

713. **kind** [kaɪnd] a. 仁慈的 & n. 種類

be kind to sb　　對某人心腸很好
a kind of...　　一種……
the kind of...　　那種……

例: Tom is kind to everyone he knows.
(湯姆對每個他認識的人都很好。)

He's the kind of a man you can trust. (✕)
→ He's the kind of man you can trust. (○)
(他是那種你可以信任的人。)

714. **king** [kɪŋ] n. 國王

queen [kwin] n. 王后; 女王

例: The king made the poor girl his queen.
(國王娶這位窮姑娘為后。)

715. kitchen [ˈkɪtʃən] n. 廚房　　k

例: Mother is busy making dinner in the kitchen.
(媽媽正在廚房忙著做晚飯。)

716. kite [kaɪt] n. 風箏　　k

fly a kite　　放風箏
例: On weekends, we go to the riverside to fly kites.
(週末時，我們到河邊放風箏。)

717. knee [kni] n. 膝　　k

leg [lɛg] n. 腿
thigh [θaɪ] n. 大腿
ankle [ˈæŋkḷ] n. 腳踝
foot [fʊt] n. 腳
例: On your knees!
(跪下！)

718. kneel [nil] vi. 跪 (三態為 kneel、knelt [nɛlt]、knelt)　　k

例: He knelt down and asked her to forgive him.
(他跪下來，要求她原諒他。)

719. knife [naɪf] n. 刀子 (複數形為 knives [naɪvz])　　k

例: That knife is very sharp, so you should be careful when using
it.
(那刀子很利，因此使用時要小心。)

720. knit [nɪt] vt. 編織　　k

例: Sue knitted a sweater for her father's birthday.
(小蘇編織了一件毛衣當做她爸爸的生日禮物。)
＊sweater [ˈswɛtɚ] n. 毛衣

721. knock [nɑk] vt. & vi. 敲擊　　k

　　knock on the door　　敲門 (非 knock the door)
　　knock sb down　　將某人擊倒
　　knock sb out　　將某人擊昏
　　例: Knock on the door before you enter.
　　　　(進門前先敲門。)

722. knot [nɑt] n. 繩結　　k

　　tie the knot　　結婚; 結為連理
　＝get married
　　例: Mary and Tom tied the knot last week.
　　　　(瑪麗和湯姆上星期完婚。)

723. know [no] vt. 知道 (三態為: know、knew、known)　　k

　　knowledge [ˈnɑlədʒ] n. 知識
　　have a good knowledge of...　　很懂……
　　knowledgeable [ˈnɑlədʒəb!] a. 很有知識的
　　例: Did you know that Paul is running for class leader?
　　　　(你知道保羅要選班長嗎？)
　　　＊run for...　　競選……
　　　John has a good knowledge of Chinese history.
　　　(約翰很懂中國史。)
　　　I respect David because he is knowledgeable.
　　　(我尊敬大衛因為他很有學問。)

724. laboratory [ˈlæbrətɔrɪ] n. 實驗室 (常使用縮寫形 lab [læb])

例: They're doing experiments in the laboratory.
(他們正在實驗室做實驗。)
＊experiment [ɪkˈspɛrɪmənt] n. 實驗

725. lack [læk] vt. & n. 缺乏

例: This soup lacks salt. Maybe you should add some.
(這碗湯缺鹽。也許你應加一些。)

726. ladder [ˈlædɚ] n. 梯子

例: John climbed the ladder to change the light bulb.
(約翰爬梯子要換燈泡。)
＊light bulb [ˈlaɪt ˌbʌlb] n. 電燈泡

727. lady [ˈledɪ] n. 小姐, 女士

gentleman [ˈdʒɛntḷmən] n. 先生, 紳士
例: That lady over there happens to be my mother.
(那邊那位女士正巧是我媽媽。)

728. lake [lek] n. 湖

pond [pɑnd] n. 池
sea [si] n. 海
ocean [ˈoʃən] n. 洋
river [ˈrɪvɚ] n. 河
stream [strim] n. 小溪
例: Do not swim in the lake alone.
(不要單獨在湖裏游泳。)

729. lamp [læmp] n. 燈

例: I need a lamp on the desk.
(我需要一盞燈在桌上。)

730. **land** [lænd] n. 土地 (不可數) & vi. (飛機) 著陸

　　a piece of land 　　一塊土地

　　例: This piece of land is used for farming.
　　（這塊地供農作用。）

　　　　The plane landed on the runway.
　　　　（飛機降落在跑道上。）

731. **lantern** [ˈlæntən] n. 燈籠

　　the Lantern Festival [ˈfɛstəvl] n. 元宵節

　　例: During the Lantern Festival, children carry colorful lanterns.
　　（元宵節那一天，孩子們會提著花花綠綠的燈籠。）

732. **language** [ˈlæŋgwɪdʒ] n. 語言 (可數); 用字 (不可數)

　　dirty language 　　髒話 (非 a dirty language)

　　a language 　　某種語言

　　例: How many different languages do you speak?
　　（你能說多少種語言？）

　　　　Do not use dirty language in any situation.
　　　　（任何情況下都不要說髒話。）

　　　　＊situation [ˌsɪtʃʊˈeʃən] n. 情況

733. **late** [let] a. 遲到的 (多置於 be 動詞之後) &

　　adv. 遲; 晚 (多置於句尾, 修飾之前的動詞)

　　例: He was late for the meeting.
　　＝ He arrived at the meeting late.
　　　　（他開會遲到了。）

734. **lately** [ˈletlɪ] adv. 最近 (與現在完成式或完成進行式並用)

　　＝ recently [ˈrisntlɪ]

　　＝ of late

例: He has been quite busy lately.
(他最近很忙。)

735. later [ˈletɚ] adv. 稍後

例: I'll tell you the story later.
(我稍後會把這件事告訴你。)
He went to Japan in 1970. Three years later, he died there.
(他於一九七○年赴日。三年後,死在該地。)

736. latest [ˈletɪst] a. 最新的; 最近的 (與 the 並用)

例: Have you heard the latest news about that singer?
(有沒有聽說這位歌手最新的消息?)

737. large [lɑrdʒ] a. 大的

by and large   一般而言
例: This meal is too large for me to eat by myself.
(這頓飯量太多,我一個人吃不完。)
By and large, girls are more shy than boys.
= In general, girls are more shy than boys.
(一般而言,女孩子要比男孩子害羞。)

738. last [læst] a. 最後的

例: The last person in the room should turn off the lights.
(房間裏最後的一個人要把所有的燈關掉。)

739. laugh [læf] vi. 笑 & n. 笑 (可數, 唯常用單數, 與 a 並用)

laugh at...   取笑……
give a laugh   笑出聲來
例: I laughed when I heard the joke.
(我聽到這笑話便笑了。)
Don't laugh at him just because he is fat.
(不要因為他肥就取笑他。)

When she saw him, she gave a laugh and hugged him.
(她見到他來，便笑著擁抱他。)

740. laughter [ˈlæftɚ] n. 笑 (不可數)

burst into laughter   突然大笑
= burst out laughing
burst into tears   突然大哭
= burst out crying

例: Laughter is the best medicine.
(笑是良藥。——諺語)
He burst into laughter when he heard the joke.
(他聽到這笑話時爆笑出來。)

741. lay [le] vt. 放置 (= put); 產 (卵) (三態為: lay、laid、laid)

lay an egg   生產; 產卵
例: Don't lay anything on the table.
(桌上不要放任何東西。)
The hen just laid an egg.
(母雞剛剛下蛋。)
＊hen [hɛn] n. 母雞
cock [kɑk] n. 公雞

742. lazy [ˈlezɪ] a. 懶惰的

laziness [ˈlezɪnɪs] n. 懶惰
例: John does poorly in school because he's so lazy.
(約翰太懶，因此在校功課表現不佳。)
Laziness will get you nowhere.
(懶惰會使你沒出息。)

743. laundry [ˈlɔndrɪ] n. (待洗或洗好的) 衣服 (不可數)

do the laundry   洗衣服

例: Do the laundry first, and then wash the dishes.
（先洗衣服再洗碗盤。）

744. lead [lid] vt. 帶領 & vi. 導致 (三態為: lead、led [lɛd]、led)

lead to...　　導致……

= bring about...

例: Our teacher led us into the classroom.
（老師帶著我們進入教室。）

His carelessness led to a car accident.
（他的粗心導致一起車禍。）

745. leader [ˈlidə] n. 領袖, 領導者

a class leader　　班長

例: Mary is a good leader because everyone listens to her.
（瑪麗是個好領導, 因為大家都聽她的。）

746. leaf [lif] n. 樹葉 (複數形為 leaves [livz])

turn over a new leaf　　重新做人

例: In the fall, most leaves turn brown, orange and gold.
（秋天時, 大多樹葉會變成棕色、橙色還有金黃色。）

I'm going to turn over a new leaf and study every night.
（我要重新做人, 因此每晚用功讀書。）

747. lean [lin] vi. 傾斜

例: John leaned against the wall talking on the phone.
（約翰靠著牆講電話。）

748. learn [lɜn] vt. & vi. 學習

learn a lesson　　學到教訓

例: You should learn from your mistakes.
（你應從錯誤中學習。）

Tom learned his lesson and will never lie to his mother again.
(湯姆學到教訓，再也不對媽媽說謊了。)

749. **least** [list] a. 最少的 (是 little 的最高級) & adv. 最少地

less [lɛs] a. 較少的 (是 little 的比較級) & adv. 較少地

例: I have little money, Peter has less (money), and Mary has the least (money).

(我錢很少，彼得更少，而瑪麗最少。)

Mary is the least beautiful of the three girls.
(三個女孩中，瑪麗是最不漂亮的一位。)

750. **leather** [ˈlɛðɚ] n. 皮革

例: This jacket is made of leather.
(這夾克是皮做的。)

＊be made of...　　由……製做而成

751. **leave** [liv] vi. 離開 & vt. 留下 (三態為: leave、left [lɛft]、left)

leave for + 地方　　動身前往某地

例: John left for Hong Kong yesterday.
(約翰昨天到香港去了。)

752. **leg** [lɛg] n. 腿

例: Sue hurt her leg when she went jogging.
(小蘇慢跑時傷到腿。)

753. **lend** [lɛnd] vt. 借給 (某人) (三態為: lend、lent、lent)

borrow [ˈbaro] vt. 向……借

lend sb sth = lend sth to sb　　借某物給某人

borrow sth from sb　　向某人借某物

例: Can you lend $500 to me?

＝　Can you lend me $500?

(你能否借五百元給我？)

Can you borrow me $500? (✗)

→ Can I borrow $500 from you? (○)

(我可以向你借五百元嗎?)

754. length [lɛŋθ] n. 長度

long [lɔŋ] a. 長的

例: The river is 300 kilometers in length.

= The river is 300 kilometers long.

(這條河長三百公里。)

755. lesson [ˈlɛsn̩] n. 課文; 教訓

teach sb a lesson   教訓某人

learn one's lesson   學到教訓

例: "Tomorrow's lesson will be about frogs," said the teacher.

(老師說:『明天的課要談的是青蛙。』)

"I hope you've learned your lesson," said Tom's mother.

(湯姆的媽媽說:『我希望你已學到教訓。』)

756. let [lɛt] vt. 讓, 允許 (三態均為 let)

例: Why don't you let him try it again?

(你何不讓他再試一次呢?)

Let's go to the movies tonight.

(咱們今晚看電影去吧。)

757. letter [ˈlɛtɚ] n. 信

mail/send a letter to sb   寄信給某人

例: I mailed a letter to John last month, but so far there hasn't been any answer yet.

(上個月我寄了一封信給約翰,但迄今仍無回音。)

758. level [ˈlɛvl] n. 程度, 水準

at the level of...　　在……的程度

do one's level best to V　　盡全力

= do one's best to V

例: Tom's English is at the highest level in his class.

（湯姆的英文程度是班上最高的。）

　　You should do your (level) best to help him.

（你應盡全力幫助他。）

759. library [ˈlaɪbrɛrɪ] n. 圖書館

例: The library is a good place to study.

（圖書館是讀書的好地方。）

760. license [ˈlaɪsəns] n. 執照

例: You can't drive without a driver's license.

（無駕照就不能開車。）

761. lick [lɪk] vt. 舐

例: The dog licked the boy's face.

（狗狗舐小男孩的臉。）

762. lie [laɪ] vi. 說謊

（三態為: lie、lied、lied) & n. 謊言; 躺, 位於 (三態為: lie、lay [le]、

lain [len])

* lie 不論作『說謊』或『躺』解, 其動名詞或現在分詞的形態均為

lying。

tell a lie　　說謊

a white lie　　善意的謊言

例: I was punished for lying.

（我因說謊而受罰。）

　　Don't tell lies, not even a white lie.

（不要說謊，甚至連善意的謊言都不行。）

He has lain in bed for five hours.
(他在床上已躺了五個小時。)

Our school lies in the countryside.
(我們學校座落在鄉間。)

763. **life** [laɪf] n. 生活 (可數); 生命 (不可數); 人命 (可數)

　　live a/an...life　　過……的生活

　　例: He lived a carefree life.

　　　(他過著無憂無慮的生活。)

　　　　＊carefree [ˈkɛrˌfri] a. 無憂無慮的

　　例: Without the sun, there would be no life on earth.

　　　(沒有太陽，世上就不會有生命。)

　　　The flood claimed more than 20 lives.

　　　(這次的水災奪走了二十條人命。)

　　　　＊flood [flʌd] n. 洪水

　　　　claim [klem] vt. 奪走 (人命)

764. **lift** [lɪft] vt. 舉起 & n. 搭便車 (= ride)

　　例: That box is too heavy to lift.

　　　(那箱子太重而提不動。)

　　　I need a lift to the grocery store.

　= I need a ride to the grocery store.

　　　(我需要搭個便車到雜貨店。)

765. **light** [laɪt] a. 輕的; 明亮的 & n. 光亮; 電燈 & vt. 點燃

　　(三態為: light、lit/lighted、lit/lighted)

　　例: The box isn't heavy; it's light.

　　　(這箱子不重，很輕。)

　　　It gets light at five in summer.

　　　(夏天五點鐘天就亮了。)

　　　Turn on the light; it's too dark in here.

　　　(把電燈打開，這裡面太暗了。)

Light the cigarette for me, son.
(小子，替我點煙。)

766. **likely** ['laɪklɪ] a. 可能的

＊本字只用於下列兩個情況:

　It is likely + that 子句　　很可能……

＝主詞 + be likely to V

　例: It is likely that John and Mary will get married.

＝　John and Mary are likely to get married.
　　(約翰和瑪麗可能會結婚。)

767. **limit** ['lɪmɪt] n. & vt. 限制

within limits　　　在限度內

be limited to...　　被侷限於……

例: I can help you but within limits.
　　(我可幫你忙，不過在限度內。)

　　Her hobbies are limited to singing and dancing.
　　(她的嗜好僅限於唱歌跳舞而已。)

768. **line** [laɪn] n. 線, 線條 & vi. 排成線狀

line up　　　排隊

例: Please stand behind the yellow line.
　　(請站在黃線後。)

　　Line up! Don't cut in.
　　(排隊！不要插隊。)

769. **link** [lɪŋk] vt. 連接; 產生關聯 & n. 關係

例: The two families are linked by marriage.
　　(這兩個家庭因通婚而有連繫。)

　　John has cut off links with all his friends.
　　(約翰切斷了他與所有朋友的關係。)

770. **lion** [ˈlaɪən] n. 獅子

例: The lion roared at the people from inside the cage.
(獅子從籠裏對那些人發出吼聲。)
 ＊roar [rɔr] vi. 發出吼聲
 　cage [kedʒ] n. 籠子

771. **lip** [lɪp] n. 嘴唇 (因有兩片, 故常用複數)

例: Give me a kiss on the lips.
(親我的嘴唇嘛！)

772. **list** [lɪst] n. 列表; 名單 & vt. 將……列出

例: List the names of all of your classmates on this paper.
(把你班上所有同學的名字列在這張紙上。)
 Make a list of all the things you want to buy.
(把你要買的所有東西一一列表。)

773. **listen** [ˈlɪsən] vi. 聆聽

listen to...　　聆聽……
例: I enjoy listening to music at night.
(我喜歡在晚上聽音樂。)

774. **litter** [ˈlɪtɚ] vi. 亂丟東西 (如紙屑、垃圾等)

& n. (紙屑、垃圾等) 廢棄物 (集合名詞, 不可數)
例: If you litter in the park, you might have to pay a fine.
(你若在公園亂丟東西, 可能要付罰款。)
 There was litter all over the street after the gathering.
(集會後, 街上都是垃圾。)

775. **little** [ˈlɪtl] a. 小的; 少量的 (接不可數名詞) & adv. 少許

little by little　　漸漸地
a little (bit)　　有點兒

例: His English is improving little by little.

(他的英文漸漸在進步中。)

I'm a little tired , so I need to take a rest.

(我有點兒累，因此我需要休息一下。)

The little boy is not my son, but my nephew.

(小男孩不是我兒子，而是我姪子。)

＊nephew [ˈnɛfju] n. 姪子; 外甥

776. live [lɪv] vi. 生活; 住 & vt. 過……的生活 (以 life 作受詞)

& [laɪv] a. 現場的 & [laɪv] adv. 現場

live a/an...life　　過……的生活

例: I live in Taipei. Where do yo live?

(我住在台北。你住哪兒？)

They lived a happy life in the small town.

(他們在一個小鎮上過著幸福的生活。)

That's a live show; in other words, it is broadcast live.

(那是現場節目。換言之，它是現場播出。)

＊第一個 live 是形容詞, 修飾 show; 第二個 live 是副詞, 修飾
broadcast。

broadcast [ˈbrɔdkæst] vt. 播出 (三態同形)

777. living [ˈlɪvɪŋ] n. 生計 & a. 存活的

make a/one's living/earn a/one's living　　謀生

例: He makes a living (by) teaching English.

(他靠教英文維生。)

We found two living people in the car accident.

(車禍中我們發現兩名生還者。)

778. lobster [ˈlɑbstɚ] n. 龍蝦

shrimp [ʃrɪmp] n. 小蝦

例: Do you know the difference between a lobster and a shrimp?

(你知道龍蝦與小蝦的區別嗎？)

779. local ['lokl] a. 當地的

例: I went to the local post office to mail the letter.
(我到當地郵局去寄信。)

780. locate ['loket] vt. 找到⋯⋯的位置

本字多用於被動語態, 形成下列句構:
be located in/at/on...　　座落於⋯⋯

例: I couldn't locate the post office.
(我找不到郵局。)

Our school is located in Taipei/at the top of the hill/on the other side of the city.
(我們學校位於台北市/山頂上/城市的另外一邊。)

781. lock [lɑk] n. 鎖 & vt. 將⋯⋯鎖起來

lock...up　　　將⋯⋯鎖好
lock sb out　　將⋯⋯鎖在門外

例: Lock the door (up) when you leave the house.
(離家時把門鎖好。)

I was locked out of my house when I left the keys inside.
(我把鑰匙留在屋內，把自己反鎖在外。)

782. long [lɔŋ] a. 長的 & adv. 長期 & vi. 渴望

long 作動詞時有兩個用法:
long to V　　渴望⋯⋯
long for N　　渴望得到⋯⋯

例: Your hair is too long; you need to have it cut.
(你頭髮太長，需要理了。)

How long will you stay here?
(你會待在這裏多久？)

I long to see her again.
(我渴望再次見到她。)

I long for a chance to talk to her.
(我渴望有機會跟她說話。)

783. **lose** [luz] vt. 失去 (三態為: lose、lost [lɔst]、lost)

be lost　　迷路

例: You are too fat, Peter. If you don't lose weight, I won't marry you.
(彼得，你太胖了。若不減肥，我就不嫁給你。)

I was lost in town yesterday.
(我昨天在城裏迷路了。)

784. **loss** [lɔs] n. 損失

例: The company suffered a big loss when the manager died.
(經理過世，對公司是一大折損。)

＊suffer [ˈsʌfɚ] vt. 遭受

785. **lot** [lɑt] n. 大量; 一塊空地

a lot of...　　許多 (之後置可數複數名詞或不可數名詞)
＝lots of...

a parking lot　　停車場

例: Don't worry. I still have lots of money left.
(別擔心。我剩下的錢還很多。)

786. **lottery** [ˈlɑtərɪ] n. 彩券制度

a lottery ticket [ˈtɪkɪt] n. 一張彩券

例: I bought a lottery yesterday. (✗)
→ I bought a lottery ticket yesterday. (○)
(我昨天買了一張彩券。)

787. **loud** [laʊd] a. 大聲的

例: Turn down the music because it's too loud.
(把音樂關小聲一點，太吵了。)

＊turn down...　　將 (收音機、電視) 音量關小
turn up...　　將 (收音機、電視) 音量開大
turn on...　　將 (收音機、電視、電燈等電器) 打開
turn off...　　將 (收音機、電視、電燈等電器) 關掉

---

788. **lousy** [ˈlaʊzɪ] a. 差勁的 (= terrible [ˈtɛrəbḷ])

例: The CD I bought was really lousy.
(我買的 CD 有夠爛。)

---

789. **love** [lʌv] n. & vt. 愛

loving [ˈlʌvɪŋ] a. 慈愛的
lovely [ˈlʌvlɪ] a. 好看的
love at first sight　　一見鍾情

例: Peter was crazy about Mary the first time he met her. It was really love at first sight.
(彼得與瑪麗初識便為她瘋狂。這真是一見鍾情。)
Mary is a kind and loving mother.
(瑪麗是個心地好又慈愛的母親。)
You look lovely in your new hat.
(妳戴上新帽子很好看。)

---

790. **low** [lo] a. 低的; 低沈的; 消沈的

例: The price of the watch is low.
(這手錶的價格很便宜。)
Paul has a low voice.
(保羅聲音很低沈。)
Mary is feeling really low today. Let's do something to cheer her up.
(瑪麗今天心情低落。咱們設法讓她振作起來。)
＊cheer sb up　　使某人振作起來
cheer [tʃɪr] vt. 鼓勵

791. **luck** [lʌk] n. 幸運

lucky ['lʌkɪ] a. 幸運的

wish sb good luck　　祝某人好運

例: I wish you good luck.

(祝你好運。)

You should feel lucky that you have such a good wife.

(你有這麼好的太太應感到幸運才是。)

792. **luggage** ['lʌgɪdʒ] n. 行李 (集合名詞, 不可數)

= baggage ['bægɪdʒ] (不可數)

a luggage (✗)

→ a piece of luggage/baggage　　一件行李 (○)

例: How many pieces of luggage do you have with you?

(你隨身攜帶多少件行李?)

793. **lunch** [lʌntʃ] n. (個人吃的) 午餐

luncheon ['lʌntʃən] n. 午餐餐會

例: What did you have for lunch yesterday?

(你昨天午餐吃些什麼?)

There will be a luncheon for the teachers tomorrow.

(明天老師們有個午餐餐敘。)

794. **lung** [lʌŋ] n. 肺 (因肺葉有兩片, 故本字常用複數)

例: Paul's father has lung cancer.

(保羅的父親得了肺癌。)

795. madam [ˈmædəm] n. 夫人 (尊稱) m

例: "Madam, may I help you?" asked the salesman.
(銷售員,『夫人,可以為您效勞嗎?』)

796. machine [məˈʃin] n. 機器 m

by machine　　機器製造
by hand　　手工製造
例: The machine doesn't work. Get it repaired.
(這機器故障了。拿去送修吧。)
　Things made by machine are cheaper than things made by hand.
(機器做的東西要比手工做的東西便宜。)

797. magazine [ˌmæɡəˈzin] n. 雜誌 m

例: Our magazine sells thousands of copies a month.
(我們雜誌每個月賣好幾千本。)

798. magic [ˈmædʒɪk] n. 魔術; 魔力 m

magician [məˈdʒɪʃən] n. 魔術師
do magic tricks　　變魔術, 耍把戲
例: The clown did magic tricks for the children.
(小丑耍把戲給孩子們看。)

799. main [men] a. 主要的 m

main point　　重點
main idea　　主旨
例: What were the main points of his speech?
(他演講的重點是什麼?)

800. make [mek] vt. 製造; 泡 (茶、咖啡等飲料); 做 (飯) m

make tea/coffee/dinner　　泡茶/泡咖啡/做晚飯

= fix tea/coffee/dinner

= prepare tea/coffee/dinner

例: Will you make me a cup of tea?

(泡杯茶給我,好嗎?)

It's time to make dinner now.

(現在是做晚飯的時候了。)

801. **man** [mæn] n. 男人 (可數); 人類 (不可數, 之前不置任何冠詞)　　m

men [mɛn] n. 男人 (複數)

例: The man over there is my father.

(那邊的那位男士是我爸爸。)

Man is different from animals because he can laugh.

(人與動物不同,因為他會笑。)

802. **manner** [ˈmænɚ] n. 方法 (等於 way, 與 in 並用)　　m

manners [ˈmænɚz] n. 禮貌, 舉止 (恆用複數)

例: You should do it in the usual manner.

(你應該用平常的方式做這件事。)

Watch your manners.

(注意你的禮貌。)

803. **map** [mæp] n. 地圖　　m

例: Follow the map and you'll find the post office.

(按照地圖的指示,你就可以找到郵局。)

804. **mark** [mɑrk] n. 標記 & vt. 標示　　m

例: Mark the correct answer on your test paper.

(把正確的答案標示在測驗卷上。)

805. **market** [ˈmɑrkɪt] n. 市場　　m

supermarket [ˈsupɚˌmɑrkɪt] n. 超市

in the market　　在市場裏

be on the market　　上市 (出售)

例: The market is open every morning until twelve.
(市場每天早上營業到十二點。)

　　This new product will soon be on the market.
(這個新產品很快就會上市。)

806. **marry** [ˈmærɪ] vt. 與……結婚 (非 marry with...)　**m**

married [ˈmærɪd] a. 結婚的
get married　　完婚
be married to sb　　與某人結婚
= marry sb

例: I married with Paula ten years ago. (✗)
→　I married Paula ten years ago. (○)
=　Paula and I got married ten years ago.
=　I was married to Paula ten years ago.
(我十年前與寶拉結婚。)

807. **mask** [ˈmæsk] n. 面具　**m**

例: The children wore masks at the Halloween party.
(孩子們在萬聖節派對上帶面具。)
＊Halloween [ˌhæloˈin] n. 萬聖節前夕

808. **mate** [met] n. 伴侶　**m**

例: Finding the right mate is a difficult job.
(找到合適的伴侶不是件容易的事。)

809. **match** [mætʃ] n. & vi. 相配　**m**

例: These two socks don't match.
(這兩隻襪子不相配。)

　　That couple are a perfect match.
(那對情侶是天作之合。)

810. **mathematics** [ˌmæθə'mætɪks] n. 數學 m

(常縮寫成 math [mæθ])

例: Mathematics is my best subject in school.

(數學是我在學校最拿手的一科。)

＊subject ['sʌbdʒɪkt] n. 科目, 學科

811. **matter** ['mætɚ] n. 事情 & vi. 重要 m

(通常用於"it doesn't matter + 疑問詞引導的名詞子句")

例: What's the matter with him?

= What's wrong with him?

(他發生了什麼事/他怎麼了？)

It doesn't matter when he'll come.

(他何時來並不重要。)

812. **may** [me] aux. 可能; 可以 m

例: Clean up the room. Dad may be back anytime.

(把房間整乾淨。爸爸可能隨時會回來。)

May I help you?

(我可以幫您什麼忙嗎？)

813. **maybe** ['mebi] adv. 也許 (等於 perhaps, 使用時置於句首) m

例: I maybe can help you with the work. (✗)

→ Maybe I can help you with the work. (○)

(也許我可以幫你做這工作。)

814. **meal** [mil] n. 一餐, 一頓飯 m

eat between meals　吃零食

例: Do not eat between meals, or you'll easily put on weight.

(不要吃零食，否則你很容易變胖。)

815. **mean** [min] vt. 意思是(之後接名詞, 動名詞或 that 子句); m

有意要……(之後接"to + V")

三態為: mean、meant [mɛnt]、meant。

例: What do you mean by this word? (by 表『藉由……』)

= What does this word mean?

(這個字是什麼意思?)

By laughing at you, I mean that you are a fool.

(我笑你的意思是說你是個大傻瓜。)

He meant to help me, but I turned him down.

(他有意要幫我忙,不過我回絕了。)

816. **means** [minz] n. 方法 (尤用於下列介語中) m

by means of...　　藉由……

by no means　　絕不

例: We finished the job by means of teamwork.

(我們團結合作把工作做完了。)

＊teamwork [ˈtimˌwɝk] n. 團結合作; 團隊精神

By no means is he a good teacher.

(他絕不是個好老師。)

817. **measure** [mɛʒɚ] vt. 量 (長、寬、高) m

& n. 行動措施 (與動詞 take 並用)

例: Help me measure the length of this table.

(幫我量桌子的長度。)

We should | take measures | before it's too late.
　　　　　| take action |

(我們應採取措施,以免太遲。)

818. **meat** [mit] n. 肉類 (不可數) m

例: Tom doesn't eat meat.

(湯姆不吃肉。)

One man's meat is another man's poison.
(某人的良藥是他人的毒藥——對某甲有益的東西對某乙卻可能有害。諺語)

＊poison [ˈpɔɪzn̩] n. 毒藥

---

819. **medicine** [ˈmɛdəsn̩] n. 藥　　　　　　　　　**m**

　　eat medicine (✗)
→ take medicine (○)　　吃藥

例: Don't take medicine unless the doctor tells you to do so.
　　(除非醫生要你吃藥，否則不要亂吃藥。)

---

820. **medium** [ˈmidɪəm] n. 媒介 (單數) & a. 中號的　　　**m**

　　media [ˈmidɪə] n. 媒介 (複數)
　　the mass media　　大眾媒介，傳媒

例: The shirt comes in three sizes: small, medium and large.
　　(這件襯衫有三種尺寸：小、中、大。)

　　The mass media includes newspapers, radio and television.
　　(傳媒包括報紙、廣播及電視。)

---

821. **meet** [mit] vt. & vi. 會面　　　　　　　　　**m**

　　(三態為: meet、met [mɛt]、met) & vt. 滿足 (需求); 符合 (條件)
　　meet one's requirements　　滿足某人的要求
　　meet one's expectations　　符合某人的期望

例: Let's meet for lunch after class.
　　(咱們下課後碰面吃午飯。)

　　I will meet you at the airport at noon.
　　(中午我會在機場跟你會面。)

　　He passed the test and met his father's expectations.
　　(他考及格，沒辜負他父親的期望。)

822. **meeting** ['mitɪŋ] n. 會議　　　　m

例: I missed the meeting because of the rain.
(因為下雨，我錯過了會議。)

823. **melt** [mɛlt] vt. & vi. 融化　　　　m

例: The snow melted when the sun came out.
(太陽出來時，雪就融化了。)

824. **member** ['mɛmbɚ] n. 份子, 成員　　　　m

例: How many members are there in your family?
(你家裏有多少人？)

825. **memory** ['mɛmərɪ] n. 回憶, 記憶　　　　m

memorize ['mɛmə,raɪz] vt. 記憶
in memory of...　　以紀念……

例: I have good memories about my childhood.
(我對小時候的事記得很清楚。)
　　＊childhood ['tʃaɪld,hʊd] n. 孩提時期
　　We set up this fund in memory of the late principal.
(我們設立這個基金紀念已故的校長。)
　　＊fund [fʌnd] n. 基金
　　　principal ['prɪnsəpḷ] n. (中小學) 校長
　　　president ['prɛzədənt] n. 大學校長; 總統; 董事長

826. **menu** ['mɛnju] n. 菜單　　　　m

例: "Here is your menu. Let me know when you're ready to
order," said the waitress.
(女服務生說：『這是您的菜單。您準備點菜時請告訴我。』)

827. **merchant** ['mɝtʃənt] n. 從事一般買賣的商人　　　　m

businessman ['bɪznɪz,mæn] n. (在公司任職的) 商人; 企業家

例: The merchant cheated me at the night market.
（夜市的商人騙了我。）

828. **metal** ['mɛtḷ] n. 金屬　　**m**

例: Iron is a very useful metal.
（鐵是很有用的金屬。）
iron ['aɪɚn] n. 鐵

829. **meter** ['mitɚ] n. 公尺; (計程車) 里程表　　**m**

例: Tom lives only twenty meters away from me.
（湯姆住的地方與我相隔僅廿公尺。）

830. **middle** ['mɪdḷ] n. 中間　　**m**

in the middle of...　　在……中間
例: There's a dog in the middle of the road.
（馬路中間有隻狗。）
Peter fell asleep in the middle of the meeting.
（會議開到一半彼得便睡著了。）

831. **midnight** ['mɪdnaɪt] n. 午夜　　**m**

until midnight　　直到午夜
at midnight　　午夜時分
at noon　　中午時分
例: I stayed up until midnight studying.
（我熬夜讀書直到午夜。）

832. **might** [maɪt] aux. 也許 (可能性較小)　　**m**

may [me] aux. 很可能 (可能性較大)
例: Tony might call me later tonight.
（東尼說不定今晚稍侯會打電話給我。）

833. milk [mɪlk] n. 牛奶 m

例: Milk is good for your bones.
（牛奶對骨骼很好。）

It's no use crying over spilled milk.
（為濺灑出來的牛奶哭鬧是沒用的──覆水難收。諺語）

＊spill [spɪl] vt. 濺灑

834. million [ˈmɪljən] n. 百萬 m

例: Over one/a million people felt the earthquake.
（一百多萬人感受到這次的地震。）

835. mind [maɪnd] n. 心靈 & vt. 在意; 看護 m

make up one's mind to V　　下定決心……
in one's mind　　在某人心中
on one's mind　　令人煩心
To one's mind,...　　某人認為……

例: I've made up my mind to study hard from now on.
（我已下定決心從現在起用功讀書。）

Mary is the most beautiful girl in my mind.
（瑪麗是我心中最美的女孩子。）

To my mind, Mary is the most beautiful girl in the world.
= I think that Mary is the most beautiful girl in the world.
（我認為瑪麗是世上最美的女孩子。）

You don't look happy. What's on your mind?
（你不太高興的樣子。什麼讓你煩心？）

Mind your own business.
（少管閒事。）

Would you mind if I opened the window?
（你介意我把窗戶打開嗎？）

836. **mine** [maɪn] pron. 我的 (= my + 名詞)

yours　pron.　你/妳 (們) 的 (= your + 名詞)

his　　pron.　他的 (= his + 名詞)

hers　pron.　她的 (= her + 名詞)

theirs　pron.　他們的 (= their + 名詞)

ours　pron.　我們的 (= our + 名詞)

例: This book isn't yours; it's mine.

(這本書不是你的，是我的。)

837. **minute** [ˈmɪnɪt] n. 分鐘

second [ˈsɛkənd] n. 秒鐘

hour [aʊr] n. 小時

hold a minute　　稍侯

= wait a minute

= wait a second

= wait a moment

in a minute　　待會兒

= in a second

= in a moment

例: "Is John there, please?" "Hold a minute. I'll get him."

(『請問約翰在嗎？』『請稍侯。我去叫他。』)

　I'll be back in a minute.

(我待會兒就回來。)

838. **mirror** [ˈmɪrɚ] n. 鏡子

look into/in the mirror　　照鏡子

(以看著鏡內的東西, 非 look at the mirror)

例: He looked into the mirror and saw some gray hairs on his head.

(他照鏡子看見頭上有幾根白髮。)

839. miss [mɪs] n. 小姐 (冠於姓氏之前) & vt. 錯過; 想念

例: Miss Chen missed the bus by five seconds.
(陳小姐以五秒之差錯過公車。)

I really miss you so much.
(人家真的好想你嘛。)

840. mistake [mɪˋstek] n. 錯誤 & vt. 誤認

三態為: mistake、mistook、mistaken。

make a mistake　　犯錯

mistake A for B　　誤將 A 當做 B

例: We all learn by making mistakes.
(我們都是從錯誤中學習。)

Peter has long hair and is often mistaken for a girl.
(彼得留長髮,常被誤認為女人。)

841. mix [mɪks] vt. 混合

mix A with B　　將 A 與 B 混合

例: If you mix yellow with blue, you'll get green.
(黃與藍混在一起就會變成綠色。)

842. model [ˋmɑdḷ] n. 模特兒; 模型

a role model　　模範 (生)

a model plane　　模型飛機

例: Mary is a famous fashion model.
(瑪麗是知名的時裝模特兒。)

Peter is our role model in many ways.
(在許多方面,彼得堪稱我們的模範。)

843. moment [ˋmomənt] n. 時刻

in a moment　　片刻後, 稍後

at the moment　　當時; 此刻

例: I believe we'll get the truth in a moment.
(我相信片刻後我們就會知道真相。)
What are you doing at the moment?
(此刻你正在做什麼？)

844. **money** ['mʌnɪ] n. 錢 m

例: Money is something, but not everything.
(錢固然重要，但並非萬能。──諺語)
Money makes the world go around.
(有錢能使鬼推磨。──諺語)

845. **monkey** ['mʌŋkɪ] n. 猴子 & vi. 鬼混 (與 around 並用) m

monkey around 鬼混
= fool around
例: The monkey swung in the trees.
(這猴子在樹間盪來盪去。)
＊swing [swɪŋ] vi. 擺盪
三態為: swing、swung [swʌŋ]、swung。
Never monkey around with those bad guys.
(千萬不要與那些壞傢伙鬼混。)

846. **month** ['mʌnθ] n. 月份 m

例: My favorite month of the year is June.
(一年中我最喜歡的月份就是六月。)

847. **monster** ['mɑnstɚ] n. 怪物 m

例: The magician turned the boy into a monster.
(魔術師把男孩變成了怪物。)
＊magician [məˈdʒɪʃən] n. 魔術師

848. **monument** ['mɑnjʊmənt] n. 紀念碑

例: We built this monument in honor of the great hero.
(我們建立這座紀念碑紀念這位偉大的英雄。)

849. **moon** [mun] n. 月亮

sun [sʌn] n. 太陽
star [stɑr] n. 星星; 恆星
planet ['plænɪt] n. 行星
moonlight ['munlaɪt] n. 月光
once in a blue moon　　長期間偶爾才一次
例: I go to the movies once in a blue moon.
(我很久才會看一次電影。)

850. **mop** [mɑp] vt. (用拖把) 拖 & n. 拖把

mop the floor　　拖地板
mop sth up　　用拖把把某物清除
例: Mop the milk up off the floor.
(把地板上的牛奶拖乾淨。)

851. **more** [mɔr] a. 更多的 & adv. 更加 (之後可接副詞或形容詞)

＊more 作形容詞用時, 是 much 或 many 的比較級, 故之後可接不可數
名詞或可數的複數名詞。
more and more...　　愈來愈……
例: You have more money than I (do), but I'm happier than you.
(你比我有錢, 但我比你更快樂。)
　Mary is getting more and more beautiful.
(瑪麗變得愈來愈美。)

852. **morning** ['mɔrnɪŋ] n. 早上

in the morning　　清晨
this morning　　今天早上 (非 today morning)

this afternoon　　今天下午 (非 today afternoon)

this evening　　今晚 (非 today evening)

tomorrow morning/afternoon/evening (night)

明天早上/下午/晚上

first thing in the morning　　一大早要做的第一件事

例: I'll call you first thing in the morning.

(我一早要做的第一件事就是打電話給你。)

853. **most** [most] adv. 最……& a. 最多的 & pro. 大部份　　m

例: She is the most beautiful girl in our school.

(她是本校最美的女孩子。)

You have much money, I have more (money), but Mary has the most (money).

(你錢很多，我更多，不過瑪麗卻最多。)

854. **motor** [ˈmotɚ] n. 馬達　　m

例: Without a motor, a car can't run.

(沒馬達車子就不能跑。)

855. **motorcycle** [ˈmotɚ͵saɪkḷ] n. 摩托車　　m

motorcyclist [ˈmotɚ͵saɪklɪst] n. 機車騎士

例: In Taiwan, you have to be 18 and above to ride a motorcycle.

(在台灣，你必須年滿十八歲以上才能騎機車。)

856. **mountain** [ˈmaʊntṇ] n. 山 (指高山)　　m

hill [hɪl] n. 山丘 (指小丘陵)

mountain climbing　　爬山 (指用設備，如繩索等登山)

mountain hiking　　爬山 (指在山中沿著柏油馬路或小徑走)

例: Mountain climbing is one of my favorite pastimes.

(登山是我最喜愛的消遣之一。)

*pastime [ˈpæstaɪm] n. 消遣

Don't make a mountain out of a molehill.
(不要小題大做。——諺語)
＊molehill [ˈmolˌhɪl] n. 鼠丘

---

857. **mouse** [maʊs] n. 老鼠 (複數形為 mice [maɪs]; (電腦) 滑鼠   m

　　be as poor as a church mouse　　窮得一文都沒有
　　(教堂裏總是維持得乾乾淨淨, 沒食物留下來, 這裏的老鼠連吃的都沒
　　有, 故用本諺語喻某人窮透了。)
　　例: I'm as poor as a church mouse, so I don't have any money to
　　　　lend you.
　　(我窮透了, 所以沒錢借給你。)

---

858. **mouth** [maʊθ] n. 嘴   m

　　have a big mouth　　大嘴巴 (不能守密)
　＝ be a big mouth
　　例: John has a big mouth, so don't tell him any secrets.
　　(約翰是個大嘴巴, 因此不要把任何祕密告訴他。)

---

859. **move** [muv] vt. 移動 & vi. 移動; 搬家 & n. 移動   m

　　be on the move　　忙得馬不停蹄
　＝ be busy
　　例: Next week we are moving to a new apartment.
　　(下星期我們就要搬到新公寓。)
　　　　You've been on the move recently. What are you busy with?
　　(你最近很忙。在忙什麼呀?)

---

860. **movie** [ˈmuvɪ] n. 電影   m

　　shoot a movie　　拍電影
　　go to the movies　　看電影
　　例: That movie was a huge blockbuster.
　　(那部電影很賣座。)

＊blockbuster ['blɑkˏbʌstə] n. 賣座的電影
（影片太好，前往的觀眾都把街道"block"擠爆了）
I go to the movies on weekends to relax.
（週末我會看電影輕鬆一下。）

861. **mount** [maʊnt] n. 山 (通常縮寫成 Mt.，冠於山名之前)　m

　例: Mt. Ali is perhaps the most famous mountain in Taiwan.
　（阿里山也許是台灣最有名的山。）

862. **MRT**　　捷運　m

　例: The MRT stands for the Mass Rapid Transit system.
　（捷運是大眾快速運輸系統的縮寫。）
　　＊mass [mæs] a. 大眾的, 集體的
　　　rapid ['ræpɪd] a. 迅速的
　　　transit ['trænsɪt] n. 運輸
　　　system ['sɪstəm] n. 系統
　　　stand for...　　代表……

863. **mud** [mʌd] n. 爛泥巴　m

　例: The car got stuck in the mud.
　（車子陷入在爛泥裏動彈不得。）
　　＊get stuck in...　　卡在……之內

864. **muscle** ['mʌsl̩] n. 肌肉　m

　例: Your muscles will become strong if you work out every day.
　（你每天健身，肌肉就會強壯。）
　　＊work out　　健身, 運動

865. **museum** [mju'ziəm] n. 博物館　m

　例: There are many museums to visit in that city.
　（那個城市有很多博物館可以參觀。）

866. **music** ['mjuzɪk] n. 音樂

musical ['mjuzɪkḷ] a. 音樂的

a musical instrument ['ɪnstrəmənt] n. 樂器

例: The music is too loud; I can't hear anything.

(音樂太大聲，我什麼都聽不到。)

867. **must** [mʌst] aux. 必須, 一定 & n. 必要物, 必要條件

be a must　　非要不可的東西

例: All of us must do our part to help.

(我們都必須盡本份提供協助。)

This is not the right phone number; you must be wrong.

(這個電話號碼不對；你一定弄錯了。)

A good dictionary is a must if you want to learn English well.

(英文要學好，就非要有一本好字典不可。)

868. **mutton** ['mʌtn̩] n. 羊肉

例: Mother used mutton to make the soup.

(媽媽煮羊肉湯。)

869. **nail** [nel] n. 釘子 & vt. 用釘子釘　　**n**

　　fingernail [ˈfɪŋgɚˌnel] n. 手指甲

　　例: The nail is rusty; it cannot be used.
　　（釘子生鏽了，不能再用了。）
　　　＊rusty [ˈrʌstɪ] a. 生鏽的
　　　Nail that picture to the wall.
　　（把那幅畫釘在牆上。）

870. **name** [nem] n. 名字　　**n**

　　one's family name　　某人的姓
　＝ one's last name
　＝ one's surname [ˈsɚˌnem]
　　one's given name　　某人的名
　＝ one's first name
　　by the name of...　　名叫……
　＝ called...

　　例: My family name is Lai, and my given name is Shih-hsiung.
　　（我姓賴，名世雄。）
　　　I know a guy by the name of Wang Ba-dan.
　　（我認識一個名叫汪拔彈的傢伙。）

871. **narrow** [ˈnæro] a. 狹窄的　　**n**

　　wide [waɪd] a. 寬的

　　例: The road was too narrow for the big truck.
　　（馬路太窄，大卡車開不進來。）

872. **nasty** [ˈnæstɪ] a. 壞的, 不厚道的 (= unkind)　　**n**

　　例: Peter has a nasty personality.
　　（彼得為人不厚道。）
　　　personality [ˌpɚsəˈnælətɪ] n. 個性, 人格

873. **nation** [ˈneʃən] n. 國家 (= country)

national [ˈnæʃənəl] a. 國家的; 國立的

international [ˌɪntɚˈnæʃənəl] a. 國際的

例: That nation is one of the richest in the world.

(該國是世上最富有的國家之一。)

How many national parks do you have in your country?
(你們國家有多少國家公園？)

874. **nature** [ˈnetʃɚ] n. 大自然

(不可數, 不可與 the 並用); 本質 (可數, 多用單數, 且可與 the 並用, 如 the nature of the work『這個工作的性質』)

natural [ˈnætʃərəl] a. 自然的

例: I love nature, which is why I enjoy country life.

(我喜歡大自然，這也是我為何喜歡鄉村生活的原因。)

Just act natural when you give the speech.

(演講時放自然就好。)

This drink is all natural and good for your body.

(這個飲料全都是天然成份，對身體很好。)

875. **native** [ˈnetɪv] a. 土生土長的; 本土的 & n. 本地人, 原住民

one's native tongue   某人的母語

例: My native tongue is Chinese.

(我的母語是中文。)

My father is a native of New York.

(我爸爸是土生土長的紐約人。)

876. **napkin** [ˈnæpkɪn] n. 餐巾

例: Wipe your face with a napkin.

(用餐巾擦把臉吧。)

877. **naughty** ['nɔtɪ] a. 調皮的　　　　**n**

　　例: The naughty boys set fire to the house.
　　　　(這些頑童放火燒房子。)
　　＊ set fire to sth　　放火燒某物
　　＝ set sth on fire

878. **near** [nɪr] prep. 在……的附近　　　　**n**

　　例: The post office is located near the bank.
　　　　(郵局就座落在銀行附近。)

879. **nearby** ['nɪrˌbaɪ] adv. 在附近 (置於動詞後) & a. 附近的 (置於名詞前) **n**

　　例: I walk to school because I live nearby.
　　　　(我住在附近，所以我都是走路上學。)
　　　　The nearby restaurant serves good food.
　　　　(附近的那家餐廳菜色不錯。)
　　　＊serve [sɝv] vt. 上 (菜); 提供 (菜)

880. **nearly** ['nɪrlɪ] adv. 幾乎, 差一點　　　　**n**

　　例: Mike was nearly hit by a car when he ran across the street.
　　　　(麥克跑過街時差一點被車撞到。)

881. **necessary** ['nɛsəˌsɛrɪ] a. 必要的　　　　**n**

　　necessity [nə'sɛsətɪ] n. 需要 (不可數); 必需品 (恆用複數)
　　daily necessities　　日用品 (恆用複數)
　　It is necessary that 主詞＋(should)＋原形動詞　　……是有必要的
　　例: It is necessary that he study every night for this test.
　　　　(他有必要夜夜讀書準備考試。)

882. **neck** [nɛk] n. 頸部, 脖子　　　　**n**

　　a pain in the neck　　眼中釘, 討厭的傢伙
　　例: My neck is killing me.

(我的脖子痛得讓我受不了。)

Paul is a pain in the neck.

(保羅是個討厭鬼。)

883. **necktie** ['nɛktaɪ] n. 領帶

例: That necktie really looks nice on you.

(那條領帶繫在你身上真好看。)

884. **need** [nid] vt. 需要 & n. 需求

need to V　　需要……

be in need of + N　　需要……

need not + V　　不必…… (此時 need 視為助動詞, 不論主詞為第幾
人稱, 均用 need; 換言之, 無 needs not、needed not 的用法)

例: I need your help.

= I'm in need of your help.

(我需要你的協助。)

You need to report to me before leaving.

(你需要向我報到才能離開。)

He need not do it.

= He doesn't need to do it.

(他不必做這件事。)

885. **needle** ['nidl̩] n. 針

be like looking for a needle in a haystack

就像大海撈針一樣困難

例: Looking for a perfect girl to marry is like looking for a needle
in a haystack.

(找一位可以結婚的完美女孩就像大海撈針一樣困難。)

＊haystack ['hestæk] n. 乾草堆

Do you have a needle and thread I can use?

(你有沒有針線讓我用？)

＊thread [θrɛd] n. 線

886. **neighbor** [ˈnebɚ] n. 鄰居

　　neighborhood [ˈnebɚˌhʊd] n. 居家附近
　　in one's neighborhood　　某人居家附近
　　例: There's a good library in my neighborhood.
　　　　(我家附近有一座像樣的圖書館。)
　　　　Be nice to your neighbors.
　　　　(敦親睦鄰。)

887. **neither** [ˈniðɚ] adv. 既不 (與 nor 並用) & pron. 兩者皆不

　　neither...nor...　　既不……也不…… (連接對等的單字或片語)
　　neither of the two　　兩者皆不
　　例: Neither you nor I am wrong. (動詞按最近的主詞變化)
　　　　(你沒錯，我也沒錯。)
　　　　Neither of the two boys is wrong.
　　　　(這兩個男孩都沒錯。)

888. **nervous** [ˈnɝvəs] a. 緊張的

　　be nervous about...　　對……感到緊張
　　例: Don't be nervous about speaking to pretty girls.
　　　　(跟美女說話不要緊張。)

889. **net** [nɛt] n. 網子

　　例: Fishermen use nets to catch fish.
　　　　(漁夫用網捕魚。)
　　　　fisherman [ˈfɪʃɚmən] n. 漁夫

890. **never** [ˈnɛvɚ] adv. 永不, 絕對不

　　例: We will never finish the work if we don't hurry.
　　　　(如果我們不趕快的話，這工作永遠做不完。)
　　　　＊hurry [ˈhɝɪ] vi. 匆忙, 加快腳步

891. new [nju] a. 新的; 剛到的

brand-new [ˌbrænd'nju] a. 全新的

old [old] a. 老的; 舊的 (= used [juzd])

例: Is that coat new or old?

(那件外套是新的還是舊的?)

I'm new here. Can you show me the way to the train station?

(我初來本地。能否告訴我火車站怎麼走?)

Peter just bought a brand-new car.

(彼得剛買了一輛全新的車。)

892. news [njuz] n. 新聞; 消息 (不可數)

a news report   一則新聞報導

a good news (✗)

→ a good piece of news (○)   一則好消息

例: We get news from newspapers.

(我們從報紙獲得新聞。)

893. newspaper ['njuzpepɚ] n. 報紙

例: Go get me a newspaper.

(去給我買份報紙來。)

894. next [nɛkst] a. & adv. 下一個

next to...   緊鄰……; 在……之旁

next door to...   在……的隔壁

例: I'll be back next week.

(我下星期回來。)

He sat next to Mary.

(他緊靠著瑪麗而坐。)

I live next door to the bank.

(我就住在銀行隔壁。)

895. **nice** [naɪs] a. 好的; 善良的   n

be nice to...   對……很好

例: Bill is nice to everyone.
（比爾對每個人都很好。）

896. **night** [naɪt] n. 夜晚   n

例: I sleep by day and work by night.
= I sleep during the day and work at night.
（我白天睡覺，晚上工作。）

897. **no** [no] adv. 不 & a. 全無的 & n. 不   n

say no to...   向……說『不』; 拒絕……

例: Say no to smoking.
（拒絕抽煙吧。）

There's no one I know in the room.
（房間裏沒有一個人是我認識的。）

898. **noise** [ˈnɔɪz] n. 噪音   n

make (a) noise   發出噪音

noisy [ˈnɔɪzy] a. 吵鬧的

例: Stop making noise! I'm studying.
（別吵！我在唸書。）

I don't like John because he's too noisy.
（我不喜歡約翰因為他太吵。）

899. **none** [nʌn] pron. 無一人; 無一物   n

例: None of my friends can sing. (此處 None 等於 No one)
（我的朋友沒有一個會唱歌。）

He wanted to borrow money from me, and I told him I had
none. (此處 none 等於 no money)
（他想要向我借錢，但我告訴他我沒錢。）

900. noon [nun] n. 中午　　　　　　　　　ⓝ

at noon　　中午

例: The meeting ended at noon.

(會議在中午結束。)

901. noodle ['nudḷ] n. 麵條　　　　　　　ⓝ

例: Can I have a bowl of beef noodles, please?

(給我來一碗牛肉麵，好嗎？)

＊bowl [bol] n. 碗

a bowl of...　　一碗……

902. normal ['nɔrmḷ] a. 正常的　　　　　ⓝ

例: Everything was normal until the fire started.

(火災發生前一切都很正常。)

903. north [nɔrθ] adv. & n. 北方　　　　　ⓝ

south [sauθ] adv. & n. 南方

east [ist] adv. & n. 東方

west [wɛst] adv. & n. 西方

＊以上單字作名詞用時, 之前應置冠詞 the, 若無 the, 則視為副詞。

例: I live in the north. (north 是名詞, 之前有 the)

(我住在北方。)

Taoyuan is about 25 kilometers south of Taipei.

(south 是副詞, 之前無 the)

(桃園位於台北南方大約廿五公里處。)

904. nose [noz] n. 鼻子　　　　　　　　ⓝ

keep one's nose to the grindstone　　孜孜不息地努力工作

＊grindstone ['graɪndston] n. 磨石

例: I love John because he keeps his nose to the grindstone at all times.

(我喜歡約翰，因為他始終都在不斷的努力工作。)

905. **notebook** ['notˌbʊk] n. 筆記本

例: Take out your notebook and jot down what I wrote.
(把你的筆記本拿出來，抄下我寫的東西。)
jot [dʒɑt] down...　　抄下……
= write down...

906. **notice** ['notɪs] vt. & n. 注意

take notice of...　　注意……
= pay attention to...
例: Take notice of every word I'm going to say.
(注意我要說的每個字。)
Did you notice the girl over there? She's my girlfriend.
(你有沒有注意到那邊那個女孩子？她是我馬子。)

907. **novel** ['nɑvl̩] n. 小說

例: I enjoy the novel I bought last week.
(我很喜歡看上星期買的小說。)

908. **number** ['nʌmbɚ] n. 數量 (與複數名詞並用)

amount [ə'maʊnt] n. 量 (與不可數名詞並用)
a large number of...　　眾多的……
a large amount of...　　大量的……
例: He has collected a large number of foreign stamps.
(他蒐集了為數不少的外國郵票。)
He has made a large amount of money.
(他賺了不少錢。)

909. **nurse** [nɝs] n. 護士

例: The nurse took my temperature.
(護士量我的體溫。)
＊temperature ['tɛmprətʃɚ] n. 體溫; 溫度

910. obey [ə'be; o'be] vt. 服從

obedient [ə'bidɪənt] a. 服從的, 乖的

例: We should all obey the law.

(我們人人皆應守法。)

911. object ['ɑbdʒɪkt] n. 東西 (= thing); 目的; 目標 &

[əb'dʒɛkt] vi. 反對 (與介詞 to 並用)

object to N/Ving　　反對……

例: What's that object in the bag?

(袋子裏是什麼東西?)

The object of this lesson is to teach students how to write.

(本課的目的就是教學生如何寫作。)

I object to what you just said.

(我反對你剛才說的話。)

912. observe [əb'zɝv] vt. 觀察

例: If you want to be a teacher, you should first observe how I teach.

(如果你想當老師, 首先就應觀察我怎麼教。)

913. occasion [ə'keʒən] n. 場合; 大事

on occasion　　偶爾 (= sometimes)

例: Watch your manners on formal occasions.

(在正式的場合要注意禮儀。)

I visit my grandparents on occasion.

(我偶爾會去看我爺爺奶奶。)

914. occur [ə'kɝ] vi. 發生; 舉行; 突然想起 (用於下列句型)

It occurred to sb that...　　某人突然想起……

例: A traffic accident occurred/happened/took place this morning.

（今天早上發生一起車禍。）

The meeting occurred/took place at two yesterday afternoon.
（這場會議是昨天下午兩點開的。）

It occurred to me that today is my birthday.
（我突然想到今天是我的生日。）

---

915. **ocean** [ˋoʃən] n. 海洋

例: Cheer up! Remember the saying, "There are other fish in the ocean."
（振作起來！記住這句諺語：『天涯何處無芳草。』）

---

916. **o'clock** [əˋklɑk] n. 點鐘

clock [klɑk] n. 鐘
例: It's two o'clock by my clock.
（我的鐘顯現在是兩點。）

---

917. **offer** [ˋɑfɚ] vt. 提供 (= give)

例: Could you offer me a hand?
（幫我一個忙，好嗎？）

---

918. **office** [ˋɑfɪs] n. 辦公室; 公司 (= company); 事務所

take office 就職
officer [ˋɑfɪsɚ] n. 武官 (如軍人、警察)
a police officer 警官
official [əˋfɪʃəl] a. 官方的 & n. 文官 (如政府官員)
例: Father works in a large office.
（爸爸在一家大公司任職。）

John took office as mayor of this city yesterday.
（約翰昨天就職為本市市長。）

919. **often** [ˈɔfən] adv. 經常

例: How often do you exercise?
(你多久運動一次？)

We often go out for dinner.
(我們常在外頭吃晚飯。)

920. **oil** [ɔɪl] n. 油; 石油

burn the midnight oil　　開夜車
例: I burned the midnight oil studying English last night.
(我昨晚開夜車唸英文。)

921. **old** [old] a. 老的, 年長的

young [jʌŋ] a. 年輕的
例: How old are you?
(你貴庚呀？)

My older brother and younger sister are coming today.
(我哥哥及妹妹今天要來。)

922. **once** [wʌns] adv. 曾經 (多置於句中或句首)

& conj. 一旦 (置於句首)
例: He once lived here.
= He used to live here.
(他以前曾住在這裡。)

Once you see him, tell him I miss him a lot.
(一旦你見到他，告訴他我很想他。)

I have seen him once.
(我曾見過他一次。)

923. **only** [ˈonlɪ] adv. 僅僅 (= just)

例: This shirt cost only $100.
(這件襯衫只花了一百元就買到了。)

924. open ['opən] a. 開的 & vt. 打開 & vi. 開放

close [kloz] vt. 關閉

例: That store opens at eight in the morning and closes at ten at night.

(那家店早上八點開始營業,晚上十點打烊。)

Come on in! The door is open.

(進來嘛!門是開著的。)

925. operation [ˌɑpə'reʃən] n. 手術; 作業; 操作

perform an operation on...　　對……做手術

operate ['ɑpəret] vt. 操作 & vi. 動手術

例: The doctor performed an operation on the patient.

(醫生對病人動手術。)

926. opinion [ə'pɪnɪən] n. 意見, 看法

In one's opinion,...　　依某人之見,……

例: In my opinion, we shouldn't allow him to do it.

(依我之見,我們不應允許他做這件事。)

927. opportunity [ˌɑpə'tjunətɪ] n. 機會 (= chance)

例: Studying abroad is a good opportunity to learn English.

(出國留學是學英文的好機會。)

928. orange ['ɔrəndʒ] n. 柳橙; 橙色 & a. 橙色的

例: The oranges are very juicy.

(這些柳橙多汁。)

＊ juicy ['dʒusɪ] a. 多汁的

929. order ['ɔrdə] n. & vt. 命令; 訂購; 點菜

例: I'd like to order some French fries and a Coke.

(我想點薯條和一杯可樂。)

Don't order me to do this or that.
(別命令我做這做那的。)

930. **ordinary** [ˈɔrdnɛrɪ] a. 普普通通的

be out of the ordinary　　很出眾; 非泛泛之輩

例: Paul is very ordinary. There's nothing different about him.
(保羅十分平凡。他並沒有什麼出眾之處。)

This book is out of the ordinary.
(這本書非一般書所能比。)

931. **orchard** [ˈɔrtʃəd] n. 果園

例: This orchard is well-known for its fruit.
(這家果園的水果很出名。)

932. **organ** [ˈɔrgən] n. 器官; 風琴

例: Your heart is the most important organ in your body.
(心臟是人體最重要的器官。)

The woman played the organ and sang a song.
(這女子邊彈風琴邊唱歌。)

933. **other** [ˈʌðəˈ] a. 其他的

others [ˈʌðəˈz] n. 其他的人/東西

例: Some students study hard, while other students/others play
around.
(有些學生很用功,有些則鬼混。)

934. **ought** [ɔt] aux. 應該

ought to V　　應該……
= should V

例: You ought to tell the truth.
(你應該說實話。)

935. outdoors [ˌautˈdɔrz] adv. 在戶外

outdoor [ˈautdɔr] a. 戶外的

outdoor activity　　戶外活動

例: We should go outdoors while it isn't so hot.

(天氣不熱的時候我們應到戶外走走。)

936. outside [ˈautsaɪd] adv. 在外面

例: The boys ran outside to play.

(男孩們跑到外面玩。)

937. oven [ˈʌvən] n. 烤箱

例: Turn on the oven and then put in the chicken.

(把烤箱的電源打開再將雞肉放進去。)

938. over [ˈovɚ] prep. 越過

go over...　　複習……

例: Be sure to go over every lesson I've taught.

(務必要複習我所教的每一課。)

939. overseas [ˈovɚsiz] a. 海外的 & adv. [ˌovɚˈsiz] adv. 往海外

an overseas student　　留學生

study overseas　　在海外唸書; 留學

例: About one-third of my classmates are overseas students.

(我的同學大約三分之一是留學生。)

940. owe [o] vt. 欠

owe sb sth　　欠某人某物

例: How much money do I owe you?

(我欠你多少錢?)

941. **owing** [ˈɔɪŋ] a. 由於 (與介詞 to 並用)　　　　　　　　**o**

owing to...　　　由於……

= because of...

例: Owing to the rain, the game was called off.

（由於下雨，比賽取消了。）

942. **own** [on] vt. 擁有 & a. 自己的　　　　　　　　　　**o**

owner [ˈonɚ] n. 擁有者

例: Do you own a car?

（你有自己的車嗎？）

Paul is the owner of that bike.

（保羅是那輛腳踏車的車主。）

John has his own car.

= John has a car of his own.

（約翰有自己的車子。）

943. package ['pækɪdʒ] n. 包裹

例: I got a package from my mother.
(我收到媽媽寄來的包裹。)

944. page [pedʒ] n. (書的) 一頁

例: Open your books to page 40, please.
(請把你們的書翻到第四十頁。)

945. pain [pen] n. 痛苦

painful ['penfḷ] a. 痛苦的
a pain in the neck　　眼中釘; 討厭鬼
例: The pain in my leg has gotten worse.
(我的腿痛惡化了。)
Tom is a real pain in the neck.
(湯姆真是個討厭鬼。)
Working with him is a painful experience.
(跟他共事是個痛苦的經驗。)

946. paint [pent] n. (作畫的) 顏料; 油漆 & vt. 漆; 粉刷

painting ['pentɪŋ] n. 畫作
例: We need to paint the living room.
(我們需要粉刷客廳。)
The painting on the wall is beautiful.
(牆上的畫很美。)

947. pair [pɛr] n. 雙; 對

a pair of...　　一雙……
例: I just bought a new pair of shoes.
(我剛剛買了一雙新鞋。)

948. palace [ˈpælɪs] n. 皇宮

例: The king and queen live in a beautiful palace.
(國王及皇后住在華麗的皇宮裏。)

949. pants [pænts] n. 長褲

(= trousers [ˈtrauzɚz], 因褲管有兩條, 故恆用複數)

a pant (✗)

→a pair of pants (○)   一條褲子 (美式)

= a pair of trousers   一條褲子 (英式)

a pair of shorts   一條短褲

例: Those pants are too short for you to wear.
(那條褲子太短你不能穿。)

950. paper [ˈpepɚ] n. 紙張 (不可數); 文件 (可數);

報紙 (可數, 等於 a newspaper)

a piece of paper   一張紙

a paper   一份文件/報告/報紙/論文

a term paper   學期論文/報告

例: "Fill out this paper and then wait for the doctor," said the nurse.
(護士說:『把此文件填妥,然後等醫生來。』)

951. parcel [ˈpɑrsl̩] n. 包裹 (= package)

例: Peter received a parcel from his grandparents.
(彼得收到他爺爺奶奶寄來的包裹。)

952. pardon [ˈpɑrdn̩] n. & vt. 原諒; 寬恕

I beg your pardon.   對不起。(尤其是在聽不清楚對方的話時使用)

= Pardon me.

例: "I beg your pardon. What did you say?" asked the woman.
(『對不起。您剛才說什麼?』這女子問道。)

"Pardon me, but do you know where the restroom is?" the man asked.
(『對不起，您知道廁所在哪兒嗎？』這男子問道。)

953. **parents** [ˈpærənts] n. 父母　　　　　p

a single parent　　單親 (父或母)

例: My parents have been married for twenty years.
(我爸媽結婚有廿年了。)

954. **park** [pɑrk] n. 公園 & vt. & vi. 停 (車)　　p

例: The park near my house is full of trees.
(我家附近的公園長滿了樹。)

You can't park your car next to a red line.
(你不可把車停在紅線旁。)

955. **parrot** [ˈpærət] n. 鸚鵡　　　　　　p

例: A large parrot sat on the man's shoulder.
(有隻大鸚鵡停在男子的肩膀上。)

957. **part** [pɑrt] n. 部份; 零件 (常用複數)　　p

take part in...　　參與……
=participate in...
spare parts　　備用零件

例: Many people took part in the protest.
(許多人參與這次的抗議行動。)

＊ protest [ˈprotɛst] n. 抗議

957. **part-time** [ˌpɑrt ˈtaɪm] a. 兼職的 (置於名詞前)　　p

& adv. 以兼職方式 (置於動詞後)

full-time [ˌfʊlˈtaɪm] a. 專職的 & adv. 以專職方式

例: John got a part-time job at a bookstore.
(約翰在書店兼差。)

John works part-time as an English teacher.

= John is a part-time English teacher.

(約翰是兼任英文老師。)

958. **party** [ˈpɑrtɪ] n. 派對; 聚會 & vi. 玩樂　　　p

例: Everyone had a good time at the party.

(派對上大家玩得都很盡興。)

Peter does nothing but party all day.

(彼得整天除了玩樂其他什麼都不做。)

959. **pass** [pæs] n. 通行證 & vt. 通過; 傳遞　　　p

(三態為: pass、passed、passed)

pass the test/exam　　考試及格

pass the time　　打發時間

pass the salt/pepper/sugar　　(餐桌上) 遞鹽罐/胡椒罐/糖罐

例: How do you pass the time?

(你時間是怎麼打發的?)

Will you please pass the salt?

(請您把鹽罐遞過來好嗎?)

960. **passenger** [ˈpæsəndʒɚ] n. 乘客　　　p

例: There are 120 passengers on the plane.

(機上有一百廿名乘客。)

961. **past** [pæst] prep. 經過 & n. 過去的時光　　　p

in the past　　過去

例: He walked past my house without stopping.

(他步行經過我家沒停下來。)

It's half past ten.

(現在是十點半。)

962. pastime [ˈpæstaɪm] n. 消遣 　p

例: My favorite pastime is riding my bike.
（我最愛的消遣就是騎腳踏車。）

963. path [pæθ] n. 小路, 小徑 　p

例: This path leads to the top of the mountain.
（這條小路直通山頂。）

964. patient [ˈpeʃənt] a. 有耐心的 & n. 病人 　p

be patient with...　　對……有耐心

例: A good teacher is patient with his or her students.
（好老師對學生都會有耐心。）

The doctor looked at the patient to find out what was wrong.
（醫生幫病人看病以了解毛病出在哪裏。）

965. pay [pe] n. 待遇 & vt. & vi. 付 (款) & vi. 值得 　p

例: Peter thought the pay wasn't good, so he quit.
（彼得認為待遇不好，因此辭職了。）

Let me pay for the meal.
（這頓飯讓我來付錢。）

It pays to study English.
= It is worthwhile to study English.
（學英文是值得的。）

＊ worthwhile [wɝθˈwaɪl] a. 值得的

966. peace [pis] n. 和平; 安寧 　p

peaceful [ˈpisfl] a. 和平的; 祥和的

例: All I want is a little peace and quiet.
（我要的只不過是一點平靜罷了。）

967. pedestrian [pə'dɛstrɪən] n. 行人　　**p**

例: A pedestrian was hit by a car yesterday.
(昨天有一名行人被車撞了。)

968. pen [pɛn] n. 筆　　**p**

a fountain pen　　鋼筆
a ball-point pen　　原子筆
a pen pal　　筆友
例: This pen is almost out of ink.
(這支筆的墨水幾乎用光了。)

969. pencil ['pɛnsḷ] n. 鉛筆　　**p**

例: I need a new pencil because this one is broken.
(我需要一支新的鉛筆,因為這支斷了。)

970. penny ['pɛnɪ] n. (英鎊的) 一便士 (= cent [sɛnt] n. 美金的一分)　　**p**

dime [daɪm] n. (美金的) 一角
quarter ['kwɑrtɚ] n. (美金的) 兩毛五
例: There are one hundred pennies in a pound.
(一英磅有一百便士。)

971. people ['pipḷ] n. 人們 (無單數用法); 民族 (有單數用法)　　**p**

＊本字表『人們』時,是複數形,不可說 a/one people, two peoples...; 而
應說 one person (一個人), two persons/people (兩個人)……
＊若本字表『民族』時,則可說 a people (一個民族)、two peoples (兩
個民族)……
例: The Chinese are a peace-loving people.
(中國人是一個愛好和平的民族。)

There were many people at the concert.
(演唱會現場有很多人。)

972. perhaps [pəˋhæps] adv. 也許, 大概 (使用時置於句首)   **p**

例: Perhaps I will call on you tonight.
(也許今晚我會來看你。)
* call on...   拜訪……
= visit...

973. perfect [ˋpɝfɪkt] a. 完美的   **p**

例: That dress looks perfect on you.
(那件洋裝穿在你身上棒透了。)
    Practice makes perfect.
(熟能生巧。——諺語)

974. person [ˋpɝsn̩] n. 人   **p**

in person   親自
personal [ˋpɝsən̩l] a. 個人的, 私人的
例: That person over there is my mother.
(那邊那個人是我媽媽。)
    Tell me the story in person, please.
(請親自告訴我這件事情。)

975. pet [pɛt] n. 寵物   **p**

keep...as a pet   養……當寵物
例: My brother keeps a turtle as a pet.
(我弟弟養了一隻烏龜當寵物。)

976. photograph [ˋfotəˏɡræf] n. 照片 (常縮寫成 photo [ˋfoto])   **p**

take a photo   拍照
= take a picture
例: May I take your photograph?
(我可以為你拍張照嗎?)

977. **piano** [pɪ'æno] n. 鋼琴　　　　　**p**

　例: I know how to play the piano.
　　（我會彈鋼琴。）

978. **pick** [pɪk] vt. 摘取; 挑選; 拾起　　　**p**

　pick...　　摘取……
　pick out...　　挑起……
　pick...up　　拾起/購買 (= buy)/開車接……
　例: Don't pick flowers from the garden.
　　（不要摘花園裏的花。）
　　Pick out the best dictionary for me.
　　（替我挑最好的字典。）
　　Pick up the garbage and throw it into the garbage can.
　　（把垃圾撿起來丟到垃圾桶裏。）
　　Pick me up at 10.
　　（十點來接我。）

979. **picnic** ['pɪknɪk] n. 野餐　　　　　**p**

　go on a picnic　　野餐去
　例: I'd like to go on a picnic with my friends this weekend.
　　（這個週末我想和朋友去野餐。）

980. **picture** ['pɪktʃɚ] n. 畫; 照片 (= photo)　**p**

　take a picture/photo of...　　拍……的照片
　例: The artist painted a picture of the woman with her baby.
　　（藝術家畫了一幅畫，畫中的女子抱著小寶寶。）
　　Mary took a picture of her classmates.
　　（瑪麗為同學拍了張照片。）

981. **pig** [pɪg] n. 豬　　　　　　**p**

　eat like a pig　　吃得跟豬一樣

例: Steve sometimes eats like a pig.
(史提夫有時吃相像隻豬。)

982. **pile** [paɪl] n. 一堆　　　　　　　　　　　　p

a pile of...　　一堆……

例: I have a pile of work to do.
(我有一堆工作要做。)

983. **pity** [ˈpɪtɪ] n. 遺憾; 憐憫　　　　　　　　p

take pity on...　　對……表示同情
It's a pity that...　　遺憾……

例: It's a pity that you can't come to the party.
(很遺憾你不能來參加派對。)

We took pity on the dog and fed it some of our food.
(我們很同情這隻狗,便把我們吃的東西拿一些餵牠。)

984. **place** [ples] n. 地方　　　　　　　　　　p

come in first/second...place　　得第一名/第二名……

例: This place is too noisy to study in.
(這地方吵得無法讓人看書。)

Paul came in first place in the speech contest.
(演講比賽中,保羅得第一名。)

985. **plan** [plæn] n. & vt. 計劃　　　　　　　　p

plan to V　　計劃……

例: What are your plans for the weekend?
(你週末有什麼計劃?)

I plan to do my homework tonight.
(我計劃今晚要做功課。)

986. **plane** [plen] n. 飛機 (= airplane [ˈɛrplen]) 🅟

例: The plane took off at 11:00 a.m. and landed at 5:00 p.m.
(飛機上午十一點起飛,下午五點降落。)

987. **planet** [ˈplænɪt] n. 行星 🅟

star [stɑr] n. 恆星
例: The Earth is a planet, while the sun is a star.
(地球是行星,而太陽是恆星。)

988. **plant** [plænt] n. 植物; 工廠 & vt. 種植 🅟

a power plant　　發電廠
例: This plant needs a lot of sunshine.
(這種植物需要很多陽光。)

989. **plastic** [ˈplæstɪk] n. 塑膠 & a. 塑膠的 🅟

例: Plastic bags should be used again and again.
(塑膠袋應重複使用。)

990. **plate** [plet] n. 盤子 🅟

例: Tom's plate was filled with food.
(湯姆的盤子裝滿了食物。)

991. **play** [ple] n. 遊戲 & vi. 玩耍 & vt. 演奏 (樂器); 扮演 (角色) 🅟

playground [ˈplegraʊnd] n. 操場
play around　　鬼混
play the piano/flute/drums...　　彈鋼琴/吹笛子/打鼓……(與 the 並用)
play basketball/baseball　　打籃球/棒球 (不與 the 並用)
play an important role in...　　在……方面扮演重要的角色
例: Hard work plays an important role in achieving success.
(努力在獲致成功方面扮演重要的角色。)

992. pleasant [ˈplɛzn̩t] a. 令人愉快的, 美好的　　　p

例: The weather is pleasant today.
(今天天氣很好。)

993. please [pliz] vt. 使……高興 & adv. 請　　　p

be pleased with...　　對……感到高興/滿意
= be satisfied with...

例: I'm pleased with my son's performance.
(我對兒子的表現很滿意。)

Sit down, please.
(請坐。)

994. pleasure [ˈplɛʒɚ] n. 快樂 (不可數); 樂事 (可數)　　　p

take pleasure in...　　樂於……
It's a/one's pleasure to V　　……是件樂事

例: I take pleasure in writing this letter for you.
(我樂於為你寫這封信。)

It's my pleasure to meet you.
(幸會。)

995. plenty [ˈplɛntɪ] n. 充份 (用於下列片語中)　　　p

plenty of...　　不少的…… (之後接複數名詞或不可數名詞)

例: Don't rush because we have plenty of time.
(我們有的是時間,因此別急。)

996. p.m.　　下午　　　p

a.m.　　上午

例: I'll give you a call at 6:00 p.m.
(我下午六點打電話給你。)

997. **pocket** [ˈpɑkɪt] n. 口袋　　p

例: I put the money into my pocket, but now it's gone.
(我把錢放在口袋裏，現在卻不見了。)

998. **poem** [ˈpoəm] n. 詩 (可數)　　p

poetry [ˈpoətrɪ] n. 詩 (集合名詞, 不可數)
poet [ˈpoət] n. 詩人
例: John is good at writing poems.
(約翰寫詩很拿手。)

999. **point** [pɔɪnt] n. 點, 重點 & vt. 指出 & vi. 指著　　p

point out...　　指出……
point at...　　指著……
例: What he said didn't have a point.
(他的話沒重點。)
He pointed out two grammar mistakes in my writing.
(他指出我文章裏的兩個文法錯誤。)
It's not nice to point at people.
(指著人是不禮貌的。)

1000. **police** [pəˈlis] n. 警方 (視為複數, 常與 the 並用)　　p

a policeman [pəˈlismən] n. 警察 (單數)
policemen [pəˈlismən] n. 警察 (複數)
a police officer　　警官
a police department/station　　警察局
例: Call the police if anything happens.
(有事發生的話，打電話給警察。)

1001. **polite** [pəˈlaɪt] a. 有禮的　　p

politeness [pəˈlaɪtnɪs] n. 禮貌

例: Peter is always polite to others.
(彼得待人總是彬彬有禮。)

1002. pollute [pə'lut] vt. 污染　　　　　　　　　**p**

pollution [pə'luʃən] n. 污染

例: Many of the rivers in Taiwan have already been polluted.
(台灣有許多河流已被污染了。)

Pollution is a big problem in many large cities.
(在許多大都市裏污染是個嚴重的問題。)

1003. pond [pɑnd] n. 池塘　　　　　　　　　　**p**

例: The pond is full of fish.
(池塘裏都是魚。)

1004. pool [pul] n. 水池　　　　　　　　　　　**p**

swimming pool　　游泳池

例: The swimming pool is open all year.
(這座游泳池全年開放。)

1005. poor [pʊr] a. 貧窮的; 可憐的; 差勁的　**p**

poverty ['pɑvɚtɪ] n. 貧窮

例: John was born into a poor family.
(約翰出自寒門。)

The poor old man has no one to take care of him.
(這位可憐的老先生乏人照顧。)

His English is so poor that I can hardly understand him.
(他的英文真爛，我幾乎聽不懂他的話。)

1006. popular ['pɑpjələ] a. 流行的; 受歡迎的　**p**

be popular with...　　受到……歡迎
popular music　　流行樂 (= pop music)

例: John is helpful, which is why he's so popular with us.
(約翰樂於助人，這也是他頗受我們歡迎的原因。)

1007. **population** [ˌpɑpjəˈleʃən] n. 人口 (集合名詞)　p

a large population 　　人口眾多
a small population 　　人口很少
例: Taipei has many populations. (✗)
→ Taipei has a large population. (○)
(台北的人口眾多。)

1008. **port** [pɔrt] n. 港; 港口　p

a port city 　　港口城市
come into port/leave port 　　進港/出港
例: Many boats came into port this morning.
(今天早上許多船進港了。)

1009. **position** [pəˈzɪʃən] n. 位置; 職位; 地位　p

例: This position pays a lot of money, but the work is hard.
(這個職務待遇不錯，不過工作挺辛苦。)
　　 Losing my job put me in a bad position.
(失業使我陷入困境。)

1010. **possible** [ˈpɑsəbl̩] a. 可能的　p

as + a./adv. + as possible 　　儘可能……
例: It isn't possible for me to see you tonight.
(今晚我不可能來見你。)

1011. **post** [post] vt. 張貼; 寄 & n. 崗位　p

poster [ˈpostɚ] n. 海報
post office [ˈpost ˌɑfɪs] n. 郵局
postcard [ˈpostkɑrd] n. 明信片

例: Please post this letter for me.
(請替我寄這封信。)

The soldier was standing at his post.
(這名士兵正在站崗。)

Post this letter for me.
= Mail this letter for me.
(替我寄這封信。)

1012. **pot** [pɑt] n. 鍋　　　　　　　　　p

teapot [ˈtipɑt] n. 茶壺

例: That restaurant has the best spicy hot pot.
(那家餐廳的麻辣火鍋是最棒的。)
＊spicy [ˈspaɪsɪ] a. 辛辣的
hot pot [ˈhɑt ˌpɑt] n. 火鍋

1013. **potato** [pəˈteto] n. 馬鈴薯 (複數形為 potatoes)　　p

a small potato　　小人物
a big shot　　　大人物

例: These French fries are made from potatoes.
(炸薯條是用馬鈴薯做的。)

I'm a small potato, while he's a big shot.
(我是小人物，他則是大人物。)

1014. **pound** [paʊnd] n. 磅 (重量單位); 英磅　　p

例: How many pounds do you weigh?
(你重多少磅？)

1015. **pour** [pɔr] vt. 傾倒 & vi. 下大雨　　p

例: Will you pour me a glass of milk?
(幫我倒一杯牛奶好嗎？)

When it rains, it pours.

(不下雨則已，一下就是傾盆大雨——屋漏偏逢連夜雨；禍不單行。——諺語)

It's pouring outside, so you'd better carry an umbrella.
(外面正下著大雨，因此你最好帶把傘。)

1016. power ['pauɚ] n. 權力; 電力　　　　p

a power failure　　停電

例: The poor man has no power in his family.
(這個可憐的傢伙在家裏沒權力。)

We had a power failure last night.
(我們昨晚停電了。)

1017. practice ['præktɪs] n. & vt. & vi. 練習　　p

practice + Ving　　練習……

practical ['prætɪkļ] a. 實際的, 務實的

例: Practice makes perfect.
(熟能生巧。——諺語)

John practices to play the piano three hours a day. (✗)

→ John practices playing the piano three hours a day. (○)
(約翰每天練習彈鋼琴三個小時。)

1018. praise [prez] n. & vt. 讚美　　　　p

in praise of...　　以讚美……

例: People praised him for his courage.
(人們讚美他的勇敢。)

We sang a song in praise of the courage of the boy.
(我們唱首歌，稱頌這孩子的勇氣。)

1019. pray [pre] vi. 祈禱　　　　　　　p

prayer [prɛr] n. 祈禱文

say prayers　　禱告

例: Let's pray for his success.
(咱們祈禱他成功吧。)

He says prayers before eating.
(他飯前都會禱告一番。)

1020. **prefer** [prɪˈfɝ] vt. 比較喜歡

prefer A to B　　喜歡 A 勝於喜歡 B
prefer to V rather than V　　比較喜歡……勝過……
= prefer N/Ving to N/Ving

例: I prefer music to movies.

= I prefer to listen to music rather than go to the movies.

= I prefer listening to music to going to the movies.
(我比較喜歡聽音樂勝過看電影。)

1021. **prepare** [prɪˈpɛr] vt. & vi. 準備

prepare for...　　為……做準備

| prepare | breakfast/lunch/dinner | 做早餐/午餐/晚餐 |
| make |
| cook |

例: I'm preparing for the test.
(我在準備考試。)

1022. **present** [prɪˈzɛnt] vt. 提出; 贈送

& [ˈprɛznt] n. 禮物 & [ˈprɛznt] a. 出席的; 在場的
present sb with sth　　頒贈/呈現某人某物
be present at the meeting　　出席會議
be absent [ˈæbsn̩t] from the meeting　　會議中缺席

例: He presented a good report at the meeting.
(會議中他提出了一份很好的報告。)

The principal presented John with an award.
(校長頒獎給約翰。)

1023. **press** [prɛs] vt. 壓, 按 & n. 新聞界 (不可數, 與 the 並用)

the press 　　新聞界

be pressed for time 　　時間不夠用

例: Press this button to stop the music.

(按此按鈕音樂就停止。)

The press speaks highly of the singer.

(新聞界給這位歌手很高的評價。)

We're pressed for time, so you'd better hurry.

(我們時間不夠用了，因此你最好快一點。)

1024. **pretty** [ˈprɪtɪ] a. 漂亮的 (= beautiful) & adv. 相當地

例: Mary is a pretty girl.

(瑪麗是個美少女。)

It's pretty hot today.

(今天挺熱的。)

1025. **price** [praɪs] n. 價格

at any price 　　不惜任何待價

例: The price of this coat is too high/low.

(這件外套的價格太貴/太便宜了。)

John wants to marry that girl at any price.

(約翰不惜任何代價都要娶到那女孩子。)

1026. **pride** [praɪd] n. 驕傲

take pride in... 　　以……為榮

= be proud of...

例: Pride goes before a fall.

(驕者必敗。——諺語)

I take pride in my son's performance.

(我兒子的表現我引以為榮。)

1027. prince [prɪns] n. 王子

princess ['prɪnsəs] n. 公主

be a prince among...　　在……之中的佼佼者

例: John thinks he's a prince among cooks.

（約翰自認自己是廚師中的佼佼者。）

1028. principal ['prɪnsəpl] n. (中小學) 校長

president ['prɛzədənt] n. 大學校長; 董事長; 總統

例: The students calmed down when they saw the principal.

（學生看到校長時便安靜下來。）

1029. principle ['prɪnsəpl] n. 原則

a man of principle　　有原則的人

例: You can trust him; he's a man of principle.

（你可以信任他；他是有原則的人。）

1030. print [prɪnt] vt. & n. 印刷

be out of print　　絕版

例: The book is now out of print.

（這本書現在已絕版了。）

1031. private ['praɪvɪt] a. 私人的, 私有的

例: That building is private and no one is allowed to get in.

（那棟建築物是私人的，任何人都不得進入。）

1032. prize [praɪz] n. 獎賞, 獎品

win first/second...prize　　得第一名/第二名……

(first、second...之前不可置 the)

例: Paul won first prize in the speech contest.

（保羅在演講比賽中得了第一名。）

1033. **produce** [prə'djus] vt. 生產

produce ['prodjus] n. 農產品 (集合名詞, 不可數)

production [prə'dʌkʃən] n. 生產

例: We produce bicycles and sell them to other countries.
(我們生產自行車行銷到其他國家。)

1034. **program** ['progræm] n. 節目; (電腦) 程式; 計劃

例: I don't like that TV program.
(我不喜歡那個電視節目。)

The government started a program to help the poor.
(政府展開一項拯救貧窮的計劃。)

1035. **progress** ['prɑgrɛs] n. 進步

make progress   有進步

例: He is making progress little by little.
(他漸漸在進步中。)

1036. **promise** ['prɑmɪs] n. & vt. 承諾

make a promise   許下諾言

keep one's promise   堅守諾言

break one's promise   食言

例: Once you make a promise, you should keep it.
(你一旦做了承諾，就不得失信。)

1037. **pronounce** [prə'naʊns] vt. 發音

pronunciation [prə,nʌnsɪ'eʃən] n. 發音

例: How do you pronounce this word?
(這個字怎麼發音？)

1038. protect [prə'tɛkt] vt. 保護

protect sb from...　　保護某人免於……

protection [prə'tɛkʃən] n. 保護

例: Parents always try to protect their children from being harmed.

（父母總會設法保護孩子免受傷害。）

1039. proud [praʊd] a. 驕傲的

be proud of...　　對……感到驕傲

= take pride in...

例: I'm really proud of my daughter.

（我真為我女兒感到驕傲。）

1040. prove [pruv] vt. 證明

proof [pruf] n. 證明; 證據 (不可數)

例: I can't prove that he's right.

（我不能證明他是對的。）

1041. provide [prə'vaɪd] vt. 提供

provide sb with sth　　提供某人某物

例: I'll provide you the money you need. (✗)

→ I'll provide you with the money you need. (○)

（我會提供你所需要的錢。）

1042. probably ['prɑbəblɪ] adv. 很可能 (比 perhaps 可能性大)

例: I'll probably call you tomorrow.

（我很可能明天會打電話給你。）

1043. problem ['prɑbləm] n. 問題

have problems + Ving　　從事……有困難

= have difficulty + Ving

solve a problem　　解決問題

例: We have problems to communicate with him. (✗)
→ We have problems communicating with him. (○)
(我們跟他溝通有困難。)

1044. **public** [ˈpʌblɪk] a. 公開的; 公共的 & n. 大眾 (之前置 the)

be open to the public　　開放給大眾

例: There are many public pools in this area.
(這個地方有許多公共游泳池。)
This pool is open to the public.
(本游泳池對外開放。)

1045. **pull** [pʊl] vt. 拉, 拖

push [pʊʃ] vt. 推
pull one's leg　　騙某人, 對某人開玩笑 (不可譯成『扯某人後腿』)

例: I was just pulling your leg. I didn't fail the test.
(我剛才是騙你的。我考及格了。)

1046. **punish** [ˈpʌnɪʃ] vt. 懲罰

punishment [ˈpʌnɪʃmənt] n. 懲罰

例: John was punished for lying.
(約翰因說謊受罰。)

1047. **puppy** [ˈpʌpɪ] n. 小狗

例: For my birthday, my parents gave me a little puppy.
(我爸媽送我一隻小狗當做生日禮物。)

1048. **purple** [ˈpɝpl̩] n. & a. 紫色 (的)

例: Purple is my favorite color.
(紫色是我最愛的顏色。)

1049. **purse** [pɝs] n. (女用) 錢包; 手提包

例: Mary left her purse on the bus.

（瑪麗把錢包遺忘在公車上。）

1050. **push** [puʃ] vt. & n. 推; 按 (鈕); 敦促 & vi. 推擠　　　p

　　push sb to V　　敦促某人……

　　例: Push the red button to close the door.

　　（按紅色的按鈕關門。）

　　　Don't push and shove when you get on the train.

　　（上火車時不要又推又擠。）

　　　＊shove [ʃʌv] vi. 推擠

1051. **put** [pʊt] vt. 放置　　　p

　　例: Don't put the book here. Put it on the bookshelf.

　　（不要把書放在這裏。把它放在書架上。）

1052. quality [ˈkwɑlətɪ] n. 品質

quantity [ˈkwɑntətɪ] n. 量

a large quantity of...　　大量的……(接不可數名詞)

=a large amount of...

例: That shirt is of high quality.

(那件襯衫品質不錯。)

1053. question [ˈkwɛstʃən] n. 問題

be out of the question　　是不可能的事

=be impossible

without question　　無疑

=without (a) doubt

例: I know the answer to the question.

(我知道這問題的答案。)

Lending you money is out of the question.

(借錢給你是不可能的事。)

He is without question the best student in the class.

(他無疑是班上最棒的學生。)

1054. quick [kwɪk] a. 快速的

quickly [ˈkwɪklɪ] adv. 快速地

slow [slo] a. 慢速的

slowly [ˈslolɪ] adv. 慢慢地

例: Don't speak so quickly, or I won't be able to understand you.

(別講那麼快,否則我聽不懂你的話。)

1055. quiet [ˈkwaɪət] a. 安靜的 & vi. 安靜 & n. 安靜

例: Be quiet, everybody!

=　Quiet down, everybody!

(各位,安靜下來!)

1056. **quit** [kwɪt] vi. & vt. 辭職 & vt. 戒除 (三態同型)　　**q**

quit smoking　　戒煙

例: You should quit smoking as soon as possible.

(你應儘快戒煙。)

　　Mary quit (her job) after her boss yelled at her.

(老闆罵了瑪麗之後,她便辭職了。)

1057. **quite** [kwaɪt] adv. 相當地　　**q**

例: Paul was quite sad after his dog died.

(保羅的狗狗死了之後,他相當難過。)

1058. **quiz** [kwɪz] n. 小考　　**q**

pop quiz [ˈpɑp ˌkwɪz] n. 抽考

test [tɛst] n. 平常考; 單科測驗

exam [ɪgˈzæm] n. 大考; 入學考

例: He did well on the quiz.

(他小考考得不錯。)

1059. rabbit [ˈræbɪt] n. 兔子

例: The rabbit eats nothing but carrots.
(兔子什麼都不吃，只吃胡蘿蔔。)
＊carrot [ˈkærət] n. 胡蘿蔔

1060. race [res] n. 賽跑; 種族

例: Mary won the race.
(瑪麗賽跑贏了。)
We are in a race against time to finish our work.
(我們在跟時間賽跑，要趕快完成工作。)

1061. radio [ˈredɪo] n. 收音機

例: Turn down the radio; it's too loud.
(把收音機關小聲一點；太吵了。)

1062. railway [ˈrelwe] n. 鐵路

= railroad [ˈrelˌrod]
例: The storm closed the railway for two days.
(暴風雨使鐵路關閉了兩天。)

1063. rainbow [ˈrenbo] n. 彩虹

例: After the rain, a beautiful rainbow appeared.
(雨過之後，彩虹出現了。)

1064. rain [ren] n. 雨 & vi. 下雨

rain cats and dogs 下大雨
rainy [ˈrenɪ] a. 下雨的
例: It's raining cats and dogs. What should we do now?
(正在下大雨。我們該怎麼辦？)
Today is a rainy day.
(今天是雨天。)

1065. raise [rez] vt. 舉起; 撫養 & n. 加薪　　　r

raise a family　　養家

例: Raise your hand if you know the answer.

(知道答案的請舉手。)

The man has a big family to raise.

(這個人有一大家子要養。)

If you don't give me a raise, I'll quit.

(你若不給我加薪,我就不幹了。)

1066. rapid [ˈræpɪd] a. 迅速的　　　r

例: The Mass Rapid Transit (MRT) system makes traveling convenient.

(捷運系統使交通往來方便多了。)

1067. rather [ˈræðɚ] adv. 相當, 頗為　　　r

would rather V than V　　寧願……也不願……

例: It's rather hot today.

(今天滿熱的。)

I would rather die than marry him.

(我寧死也不願嫁給他。)

1068. reach [ritʃ] vt. 到達 (= arrive at); 拿/取到　　　r

例: By the time we reached the station, the train had gone.

(等到我們到達車站時,火車已經開了。)

Can you help me get that book there? I can't reach it.

(你可以幫我拿那本書嗎?我搆不到。)

1069. react [rɪˈækt] vi. 反應　　　r

react to...　　對……反應/回應

例: He didn't react to my question.

(他對我的問題沒有反應。)

1070. **read** [rid] vt. & vi. 閱讀　　　　　　　　　　　　**r**

　　read one's mind　　看透某人的心思

　　例: I read newspapers whenever I have time.
　　（我有空就看報。）

　　　　My mother can read my father's mind and knows what he
　　　　wants.
　　（我媽媽可以看透我爸爸的心思，知道他要什麼。）

1071. **ready** [ˈrɛdɪ] a. 準備好的　　　　　　　　　　　**r**

　　be ready to V　　準備……

　　例: Are you ready to go?
　　（妳準備要走了嗎？）

1072. **real** [riəl] a. 真實的　　　　　　　　　　　　　**r**

　　really [ˈri(ə)lɪ] adv. 真正地

　　例: The story is real; it's not made up.
　　（這故事是真的，不是捏造的。）

　　　　He is really a nice man.
　　（他真是個好人。）

1073. **reason** [ˈrizn̩] n. 理由 (之後接 for 或 why)　　**r**

　　例: I know the reason for his anger.
　　=　I know the reason why he is angry.
　　（我知道他生氣的理由。）

1074. **recently** [ˈrisn̩tlɪ] adv. 最近　　　　　　　　　**r**

　　例: I've been quite busy recently.
　　（我最近蠻忙的。）

1075. **receive** [rɪˈsiv] vt. 收到; 接待　　　　　　　　**r**

　　reception [rɪˈsɛpʃən] n. 收到; 接待

例: Did you receive the letter I sent you?
(我寄給你的信，你收到了嗎？)

I was warmly received by them.
(他們熱情地接待我。)

1076. **record** [ˈrɛkɚd] n. 紀錄; 唱片 & vt. [rɪˈkɔrd] 記錄; 錄音

set a record　創下紀錄

break the record　破紀錄

例: Not only did he win the race, but he set a new record.
(他不僅贏了比賽，也創了新紀錄。)

Record everything I say.
(把我說的每句話錄下來。)

1077. **red** [rɛd] n. & a. 紅色 (的)

例: The red light means danger.
(紅燈表示危險。)

1078. **refuse** [rɪˈfjuz] vt. 拒絕

例: He refused to answer any questions.
(他拒絕回答任何問題。)

1079. **regular** [ˈrɛgjəlɚ] a. 規律的

例: John lives a regular life.
(約翰過著規律的生活。)

1080. **relation** [rɪˈleʃən] n. 關係

relative [ˈrɛlətɪv] n. 親戚

例: I have no relations with him.
(我跟他沒啥關係。)

He is a relative of mine. In fact, he's my cousin.
(他是我親戚。事實上，他是我表哥。)

1081. **relax** [rɪˋlæks] vi. 放輕鬆

relaxed [rɪˋlækst] a. 感到輕鬆的

relaxing [rɪˋlæksɪŋ] a. 令人輕鬆的

例: Relax! There's nothing to worry about.

(放輕鬆！沒什麼好擔心的。)

The music is relaxing. I feel relaxed whenever I hear it.

(這音樂令人輕鬆。我每次聽到這音樂便放鬆起來。)

1082. **remain** [rɪˋmen] vi. 留下來; 保持……

＊本字作『保持』解時, 之後多置形容詞, 作主詞補語。

例: None of the food remained when I came back.

(我回來時，沒有任何剩菜了。)

When I asked him why he was angry, he just remained silent.

(我問他為何生氣時，他只是保持緘默。)

1083. **remember** [rɪˋmɛmbɚ] vt. 記得; 想起

例: I can't remember his name.

(我記不得他的名字了。)

1084. **rent** [rɛnt] n. 房租; 租金 & vt. 租用

a house for rent　　房屋出租

例: Go and find if there's a house for rent.

(去找找看是否有房子出租。)

I'm going to rent a car to travel around the island.

(我要租車環島旅遊。)

1085. **repair** [rɪˋpɛr] vt. & n. 修理

例: Mary's car is in the shop for repairs.

(瑪麗的車在車廠修理中。)

Her car is being repaired.

(她的車正在修理中。)

1086. repeat [rɪ'pit] vt. 重複

例: Could you please repeat the question?
(請你再把問題重複一遍好嗎?)

1087. reply [rɪ'plaɪ] vi. & n. 回答, 回應 (與 to 並用)

reply to a question　　回答問題
= answer a question

例: The teacher waited for the students to reply to her question.
(老師等候學生回答她的問題。)

1088. report [rɪ'pɔrt] n. & vi. 報告; 報到

reporter [rɪ'pɔrtɚ] n. 記者
do a report on...　　做一篇有關……的報導

例: Peter did a report on butterflies.
(彼得做了一篇有關蝴蝶的報導。)

Report to me after class.
(下課後向我報到。)

1089. require [rɪ'kwaɪr] vt. 要求; 需要

requirement [rɪ'kwaɪrmənt] n. 要求
meet one's requirements　　滿足/達到某人的要求

例: I require you to come here after school.
(我要你放學後到這裡來。)

1090. respect [rɪ'spɛkt] n. & vt. 尊敬

have/show respect for...　　向……表示尊敬

例: The little boy has no respect for his parents.
(這小子對父母不尊敬。)

1091. responsible [rɪ'spɑnsəbl] a. 負責的

be responsible for...　　對……負責

例: You should be responsible for what you've done.
(你應對你的所作所為負責。)

1092. **rest** [rɛst] n. & vi. 休息 & n. 剩餘者 (與 the 並用)　　ｒ

take a rest　　休息一下

例: Let's rest for a while before we continue our hike.
= 　Let's take a short rest before we continue our hike.
(咱們暫時休息一下再繼續健行吧。)

Only two students passed the test; the rest failed.
(只有兩個學生考及格，其他人全沒考過。)

1093. **restaurant** [ˈrɛstərənt] n. 餐廳　　ｒ

例: This restaurant serves the best steak.
(這家餐廳供應最棒的牛排。)

1094. **result** [rɪˈzʌlt] n. 結果 & vi. 起因於/導致……　　ｒ

result from...　　起因於……
result in...　　導致……
as a result of...　　由於……
= because of...

例: He failed as a result of laziness.
(由於懶惰，他失敗了。)

Laziness resulted in his failure.
(懶惰導致他的失敗。)

His failure resulted from laziness.
(他的失敗起因於懶惰。)

1095. **return** [rɪˈtɝn] vi. 回來 & vt. 還 & n. 歸還; 回報　　ｒ

in return for...　　以回報……

例: When did you return home?
(你什麼時候回家的？)

You should return the book to the library by Friday.
(你要在星期五以前把這本書還給圖書館。)

I gave him a watch in return for his help.
(我給他一只錶以回報他的幫忙。)

1096. review [rɪ'vju] n. & vt. 複習; 評論

例: You should review all the lessons before the test.
(考前你應複習所有的課文。)

What do you think of the movie review?
(你對此影評有什麼看法？)

1097. rice [raɪs] n. 米; 米飯

例: Fried rice is easy to make.
(炒飯做起來不難。)

1098. rich [rɪtʃ] a. 富有的; 豐富的

be rich in...　　含有豐富的……

例: Strawberries are rich in vitamin C.
(草莓含有豐富的維他命 C。)

＊strawberry ['strɔˌbɛrɪ] n. 草莓
vitamin ['vaɪtəmɪn] n. 維他命

1099. rid [rɪd] vt. 使擺脫 (三態同形, 常用於下列句型)

rid A of B　　使 A 擺脫 B
get rid of...　　擺脫/戒除……

例: Cats help rid our house of mice.
(貓有助於清除屋內的老鼠。)

＊mice [maɪs] n. 老鼠 (本字為複數, 單數為 mouse [maʊs])
You should get rid of the bad habit of smoking.
(你應戒掉抽煙的惡習。)

1100. **ride** [raɪd] n. 乘坐 & vt. 乘坐 (公車); 騎 (馬、自行車)　　**r**

三態為: ride、rode [rod]、ridden [ˈrɪdn̩]。

例: I need a ride to the supermarket.
(我需要搭便車到超市去。)

I ride my bike to and from school every day.
(我每天騎自行車上下學。)

1101. **right** [raɪt] n. 權利 & a. 正確的; 右邊的　　**r**

wrong [rɔŋ] a. 錯誤的

例: You should tell right from wrong.
(你應明辨是非。)

You are too young, so you don't have the right to vote yet.
(你太年輕,因此還沒有投票權。)

1102. **ring** [rɪŋ] n. 戒指; 鈴聲 & vi. (鈴聲) 響起　　**r**

三態為: ring、rang [ræŋ]、rung [rʌŋ]。
a finger ring　　戒指
give sb a ring　　打電話給某人
= give sb a call
= call sb (up)
例: Give me a ring when you have time.
(有空打電話給我。)

The phone has just rung.
(電話剛剛響了。)

1103. **ripe** [raɪp] a. 成熟的　　**r**

例: These apples are ripe and ready to be eaten.
(這些蘋果熟了,可以吃了。)

1104. **rise** [raɪz] n. 上升 & vi. 上升; (價格) 上揚; 起床 (= get up)　　**r**

三態為: rise、rose [roz]、risen [ˈrɪzn̩]。

be on the rise　　上升

例: Prices are on the rise.

= 　Prices are rising.

(物價正在上揚。)

1105. **river** [ˈrɪvɚ] n. 河流

例: We went fishing in the nearby river.

(我們在附近的一條河中釣魚。)

1106. **road** [rod] n. 馬路

roadside [ˈrodsaɪd] n. 路邊

例: I see many cars on the road.

(我看見馬路上有許多車子。)

1107. **rob** [rɑb] vt. 搶奪

robber [ˈrɑbɚ] n. 搶匪

robbery [ˈrɑbərɪ] n. 搶劫

＊使用 rob 時, 始終以人或銀行等被搶奪的對象作受詞。

例: He robbed all my money. (✗)

→ He robbed me of all my money. (○)

(他搶了我所有的錢。)

All my money was robbed. (✗)

→ I was robbed of all my money. (○)

(我所有的錢都被搶了。)

1108. **rock** [rɑk] n. 岩石 & vt. 搖動

rock 'n' roll　　搖滾樂 (= rock music)

rock the boat　　破壞大局

例: When things are going well, do not rock the boat.

(事情進展順利時,不要興風作浪破壞大局。)

1109. role [rol] n. 角色

play a/an...role/part in...　　在……方面扮演……的角色

例: Teamwork plays an important role in achieving success.
(團結合作在獲致成功方面扮演了重要的角色。)
＊teamwork [ˈtimˌwɝk] n. 團結合作

1110. roll [rol] vt. & vi. & n. 滾動

例: Paul rolled the ball to his little sister.
(保羅把球滾到小妹那邊。)
Roll up the window; it's cold in the car.
(把車窗搖起來；車子裡面好冷。)

1111. roof [ruf] n. 屋頂

例: The roof is leaky.
(屋頂會漏水。)
＊leaky [ˈlikɪ] a. 漏的

1112. room [rum] n. 房間 (可數); 空間 (不可數)

make room for...　　騰出空間容納……

例: There are six rooms in the house.
(這房子有六個房間。)
There isn't enough room in the car for five people.
(車裏空間不夠容納五個人。)
Can we make room for one more table?
(我們可以騰出空間再放一張桌子嗎？)

1113. root [rut] n. 樹根; 根源

例: The love of money is the root of all evil.
(金錢是萬惡的根源。──諺語)
＊evil [ˈivl̩] n. 邪惡

1114. rope [rop] n. 繩子

jump rope　　跳繩

be at the end of one's rope　　江郎才盡

例: The children were jumping rope in the park.

（這些孩子在公園裏跳繩。）

1115. rough [rʌf] a. 粗糙的; 大概的

smooth [smuð] a. 平滑的

have a rough idea about...　　約略知道⋯⋯

例: Her skin is rough.

（她的皮膚很粗。）

Do you have a rough idea about what will be on the test?

（你知道考試大概要考什麼嗎？）

1116. round [raʊnd] n. 圓 & 圓的

all year round　　一年到頭

例: He seems to be busy all year round.

（他似乎一年到頭都很忙。）

1117. row [ro] vt. 划 (船)

例: Mary rowed the boat to the shore.

（瑪麗把船划到岸邊。）

＊shore [ʃor] n. 岸邊

1118. rude [rud] a. 粗魯的, 無禮的

例: The boy was rude to his teacher and he got in trouble.

（這男孩對老師無禮，要倒霉了。）

＊get in trouble　　陷入麻煩

1119. rule [rul] n. & vt. 規定; 統治

ruler [rulɚ] n. 統治者; 尺

make it a rule to V　　有……的習慣

as a rule　　按慣例, 通常

例: He makes it a rule to get up early.

(他有早起的習慣。)

　　As a rule, I get up at eight in the morning.

(通常我都是早上八點起床。)

　　The king rules his kingdom.

(國王統治他的王國。)

　　＊kingdom [ˈkɪŋdəm] n. 王國

1120. **run** [rʌn] vi. 跑步 & vt. 經營

run into...　　與……不期而遇

=bump into...

=come across...

run out of...　　用盡……

例: I ran into Mary on my way home.

(我回家途中與瑪麗不期而遇。)

　　Our car almost ran out of gas.

(我們的車子快沒汽油了。)

1121. **rush** [rʌʃ] vi. 猛衝; 火速載運 (某人) & n. 匆忙

be in a rush/hurry　　匆忙

例: He rushed back when he heard the bad news.

(聽到這壞消息時, 他便匆匆趕回家去。)

　　They rushed the patient to the hospital.

(他們把病人火速送到醫院。)

　　Why are you in such a rush?

(你為何那麼匆忙?)

1122. **sad** [sæd] a. 悲傷的　　　　　　　　　　　　Ⓢ

sadness ['sædnɪs] n. 悲傷

例: Mary was very sad after her dog died.

（瑪麗的狗狗死後，她悲傷不已。）

1123. **safe** [sef] a. 安全的 & n. 保險櫃　　　　　Ⓢ

dangerous ['dendʒərəs] a. 危險的

safety ['seftɪ] n. 安全

safe and sound　　安全無恙的

例: I felt happy to learn that John had come back safe and sound.

（知道約翰安全無恙的回來時，我感到高興。）

1124. **sail** [sel] n. 帆; 航行 & vi. 航行　　　　　Ⓢ

sail for...　　　航往……

sailboat ['sel,bot] n. 帆船

sailor ['selɚ] n. 水手

例: The boat sailed to Okinawa. (✗)

→ The boat sailed for Okinawa.

（這艘船航往琉球。）

1125. **salad** ['sæləd] n. 生菜沙拉　　　　　　　　Ⓢ

例: We ate salad and noodles for dinner last night.

（昨晚我們晚餐吃生菜沙拉及麵條。）

1126. **sale** [sel] n. 販售　　　　　　　　　　　　Ⓢ

on sale　　減價出售

for sale　　出售

salesman ['selzmən] n. 售貨員; 業務員

例: The shirt is on sale for NT$500.

（這件襯衫減價出售只賣台幣五百元。）

I'm sorry, but this watch is not for sale.

（很抱歉，這只錶是非賣品。）

1127. salt [sɔlt] n. 鹽

salty [sɔlty] a. 鹹的

sweet [swit] a. 甜的

take...with a grain of salt

(對某人的話) 打折扣, 不要完全信某人的話 (grain [gren] n. 粒)

例: You should take everything he says with a grain of salt.

(他所說的每句話你不要全信。)

1128. same [sem] a. 相同的 (之前恆置 the)

the same...as...　　和⋯⋯相同的⋯⋯

different [ˈdɪfərənt] a. 不同的

be different from...　　與⋯⋯不同

例: I have the same watch as yours.

(我的錶跟你的相同。)

1129. sand [sænd] n. 沙粒

stick one's head in the sand　　持鴕鳥心態

*stick [stɪk] vt. 伸 (stick...into...　　將⋯⋯伸入⋯⋯)

例: Mary and Tom played in the sand at the beach.

(瑪麗與湯姆在海邊玩沙。)

Don't stick your head in the sand whenever there's a problem.

(不要每次有問題時就持鴕鳥心態。)

1130. sandwich [ˈsæn(d)wɪtʃ] n. 三明治 & vt. 將⋯⋯夾在中間

例: Ham and cheese sandwiches are my favorite.

(火腿起士三明治是我的最愛。)

I was sandwiched between my brother and sister in the car.

(我在車裡夾在哥哥跟姊姊的中間。)

1131. satisfy [ˈsætɪsfaɪ] vt. 使滿意; 達到 (某人的需要)

satisfy/meet one's requirements　　達到/符合某人的要求

satisfied [ˈsætɪsfaɪd] a. 感到滿意的

be satisfied with...　　對……感到滿意

例: It's hard to satisfy his requirements.

(他的要求很難達到。)

I'm satisfied with his answer.

(我很滿意他的回答。)

1132. **sauce** [sɔs] n. 醬汁, 滷汁

saucer [ˈsɔsɚ] n. 小碟子

例: Please add some sauce to my rice.

(請在飯上添加一點滷汁。)

1133. **sausage** [ˈsɔsɪdʒ] n. 香腸

例: These sausages are made from pork and beef.

(這些香腸是用豬肉及牛肉做的。)

＊pork [pork] n. 豬肉

beef [bif] n. 牛肉

1134. **save** [sev] vt. 拯救; 節省; 存 (款)

例: You should save money for a rainy day.

(你應存錢以備不時之需。)

The boy saved a drowning man and became a hero.

(這男孩救了一位即將溺斃的人，成了英雄。)

1135. **say** [se] vt. 說 (三態為: say、said [sɛd]、said)

注意第三人稱單數 says 發音為 [sɛz], 而非 [sez]

例: He said, "I'll love you forever and a day."

(他說，『我會愛妳到永遠，甚至比永遠還多一天。』)

1136. **scare** [skɛr] vt. 嚇

例: Don't scare me. I'm a coward.

(別嚇我。我是膽小鬼。)

1137. **scene** [sin] n. 景色 (可數)

scenery [ˈsinərɪ] n. 風景 (不可數)

例: That's really a good scene to see.
　　(那真是個可以看的美景。)

　　　We have a lot of sceneries in Taiwan. (╳)

→ We have a lot of secnery in Taiwan. (○)
　　(台灣有很多風景。)

1138. **schedule** [ˈskɛdʒʊl] n. 時間表

on schedule 　按預定時間

例: Everything was finished on schedule.
　　(一切均按預定時間完成。)

1139. **school** [skʊl] n. 學校

例: John goes to school on time every day.
　　(約翰每天準時上學。)

1140. **science** [ˈsaɪəns] n. 科學; 理化 (科目)

scientist [ˈsaɪəntɪst] n. 科學家

例: Science is my least favorite subject in school.
　　(理化是我在學校最不喜歡的一科。)

1141. **score** [skɔr] n. 分數; 成績 (多用複數) & vi. 得分

例: John scored high on the test.
　　(約翰考試分數很高。)

　　　Peter had poor scores while in high school.
　　(彼得唸高中時,成績很差。)

1142. **sea** [si] n. 海

seafood [ˈsiˌfud] n. 海鮮

例: Mary sat by the sea to watch the sunset.
（瑪麗坐在海邊觀賞日落。）

1143. **search** [sɝtʃ] n. & vi. 尋找 **S**

search for...　　尋找……
例: We're searching for a good way to handle the problem.
（我們正在尋找處理這個問題的好方法。）

1144. **season** [ˈsizn̩] n. 季節 **S**

be in season　　正值盛產季
be out of season　　不在盛產季
例: There are four seasons in a year: spring, summer, autumn and
　　winter.
（一年有春、夏、秋、季四季。）
　　Apples are now in season.
（蘋果是當令水果。）

1145. **seat** [sit] n. 座位 & vt. 使就座 **S**

take/have a seat　　請坐
例: I'm sorry, but this seat is taken.
（很抱歉，這個位子有人佔了。）
　　I was seated by the window.
（我被安排坐在窗邊。）
　　比較:
　　I was sitting by the window.
（我坐在窗邊。）

1146. **second** [ˈsɛkənd] a. 第二的 **S**

be second to none　　是最棒的, 不輸任何人
second-hand [ˌsɛkəndˈhænd] a. 二手的
a second-hand car　　二手車

second-hand smoke　　二手煙

例: When it comes to singing, Peter is second to none.

（說到唱歌，彼得是最棒的。）

1147. secret ['sikrɪt] n. 秘密; 秘訣 (與介詞 to 並用) & a. 秘密的 Ⓢ

keep sth (a) secret　　將某事守秘

例: The secret to his success is hard work.

（他成功的秘訣就是努力。）

　Keep everything I said (a) secret.

（將我所說的每一句話守秘。）

1148. see [si] vt. & vi. 看; 明白 (三態為: see、saw、seen) Ⓢ

例: Did you see Mary talking to that handsome boy?

（你有沒有看到瑪麗跟那位帥哥談話？）

1149. seem [sim] vi. 似乎 Ⓢ

seem (to be) + n./adj.　　似乎是……

It seems that...　　似乎……

例: He seems (to be) a nice guy.

= It seems that he's a nice guy.

（他似乎是個好人。）

1150. seldom ['sɛldəm] adv. 很少 (= rarely ['rɛrlɪ]) Ⓢ

例: We seldom see each other, but we still keep in contact.

（我們很少見面，但彼此仍保持連絡。）

1151. select [sə'lɛkt] vt. 選擇 (= choose) Ⓢ

selection [sə'lɛkʃən] n. 選擇

例: Select the best book for me.

（幫我選最好的書。）

1152. selfish [ˈsɛlfɪʃ] a. 自私的　　Ｓ

selfishness [ˈsɛlfɪʃnɪs] n. 自私

例: A selfish guy is hard to get along with.
（自私的傢伙很難相處。）

1153. sell [sɛl] vt. & vi. 出售 (三態為: sell、sold、sold)　　Ｓ

sell out...　　出賣……

be sold out of...　　賣完……

例: Father will sell his old car before he buys a new one.
（爸爸會把舊車賣掉再買一部新的。）

Never sell out your friends.
（千萬不要出賣朋友。）

Sorry, we're sold out of this book.
= Sorry, we've sold out this book.
（抱歉，這本書我們賣完了。）

1154. send [sɛnd] vt. 寄送 (三態為: send、sent、sent)　　Ｓ

例: Send this letter to Mary, please.
（請把這封信寄給瑪麗。）

1155. senior [ˈsinɪɚ] a. 年紀較長的; 地位較高的 & n. 年長者, 地位較高者　Ｓ

be senior to sb　　比某人年長/地位高

be junior to sb　　比某人幼/地位低

例: He is senior to me in the company.
（他在公司內的地位比我高。）

He is five years my senior.
（他比我大五歲。）

1156. sense [sɛns] n. 感覺; 意義　　Ｓ

make sense　　有意義

a sense of humor/responsibility　　幽默感/責任感

例: What he said doesn't make sense.
(他剛才的話沒有意義。)

1157. **sentence** ['sɛntn̩s] n. 句子 & vt. 判刑

be sentenced to + 刑期　　被判……刑期

例: He was sentenced to five years in prison.
(他被判五年有期徒刑。)
prison ['prɪzn̩] n. 監牢

1158. **serious** ['sɪrɪəs] n. 嚴肅的; 認真的; 嚴重的

例: I'm serious; I'm not joking.
(我是認真的，我可不是在開玩笑。)
Father is a serious person, and I'm a little afraid of him.
(爸爸是個嚴肅的人，我有點兒怕他。)

1159. **serve** [sɝv] vt. 服務; 供應 (餐點)

servant ['sɝvənt] n. 僕人
service ['sɝvəs] n. 服務
be at one's service　　為某人服務
例: I'm glad to be at your service.
(我很樂意為你效勞。)
Breakfast is served at 7 a.m.
(上午七點供應早餐。)

1160. **set** [sɛt] n. 一組, 一套 & vt. 放置 (三態同形) & a. 準備好的 (= ready)

be all set to V　　準備好要……
= be ready to V
set up...　　建立……
例: We are all set to leave.
(我們準備妥當要出發了。)
Set the table for dinner.
(擺碗筷準備吃飯。)

We set up a monument in memory of the hero.
(我們建立一座紀念碑紀念這位英雄。)

We bought a set of coffee cups.
(我們買了一組咖啡杯。)

1161. **several** [ˈsɛvərəl] a. 幾個

例: Several people missed the bus this morning.
(今天早上有幾個人沒趕上公車。)

1162. **shade** [ʃed] n. 樹蔭

例: It's too hot here. Let's sit in the shade of that tree.
(這裡太熱了。咱們待在那個樹蔭下吧。)

1163. **shadow** [ˈʃædo] n. 影子

例: I see my shadow on the wall.
(我看到牆上有自己的影子。)

1164. **shake** [ʃek] vt. & vi. 搖動

(三態為: shake、shook [ʃuk]、shaken [ˈʃekən])
shake hands with...　　與⋯⋯握手
例: Shake the juice before drinking it.
(把果汁搖一搖再飲用。)

1165. **shallow** [ˈʃælo] a. 淺的; 膚淺的

deep [dip] a. 深的
例: The swimming pool is shallow at one end and deep at the
other.
(游泳池一端很淺，另一端則很深。)

1166. **shape** [ʃep] n. 形狀

be in good/poor shape　　身體很好/很差

例: Richard is in good shape for a man of sixty.
(以六十歲的人而言，理查身體算是不錯的了。)

1167. share [ʃɛr] vt. 分享

例: The little girl doesn't like to share her toys with her sister.
(小女孩不願與她妹妹分享玩具。)

1168. sharp [ʃɑrp] a. 銳利的 & adv. 準時地

dull [dʌl] a. 不利的, 鈍的
two o'clock sharp　　兩點整
例: Be careful with that knife because it's very sharp.
(小心那把刀，因為它很利。)
　Meet me at the corner at three o'clock sharp.
(三點整在轉角處等我。)

1169. sheep [ʃip] n. 綿羊

(單複數同形: one sheep、two sheep...)
goat [got] n. 山羊 (one goat、two goats...)
be the black sheep　　是害群之馬
例: He is the black sheep of his family.
(他是他家的害群之馬。)

1170. sheet [ʃit] n. 一張 (紙)

例: Give me a sheet of paper.
=　Give me a piece of paper.
(給我一張紙。)

1171. shelf [ʃɛlf] n. 架子

例: Can you get me the book from that shelf?
(請你把架上的那本書拿給我好嗎？)

1172. shell [ʃɛl] n. 貝殼　　　　　　　　　　　S

例: We collected shells at the beach.
(我們在海邊撿貝殼。)

1173. shine [ʃaɪn] vi. 發亮 (三態為: shine、shone [ʃon]、shone)　S

& vt. 擦亮 (三態為: shine、shined、shined)

例: The sun shone in the sky.
(太陽當空照耀。)

He shined my shoes.
(他替我擦鞋。)

1174. ship [ʃɪp] n. 船 & vt. (以船) 運送　　　　S

例: That ship carries goods from Asia to Europe.
(那艘船從亞洲載貨運往歐洲。)

1175. shirt [ʃɝt] n. 襯衫　　　　　　　　　　S

例: The blue shirt looks much better on you than the red one.
(那件藍襯衫穿在你身上要比紅色的那一件好看。)

1176. shock [ʃɑk] vt. & n. 震驚　　　　　　　S

例: Everyone was shocked to hear the bad news.
(每個人聽到壞消息時都感到震驚。)

1177. shoe [ʃu] n. 鞋子　　　　　　　　　　S

be in one's shoes　　處於某人的立場

例: If you were in my shoes, what would you do?
(你要是處在我的立場，會怎麼做？)

1178. shoot [ʃut] vt. & vi. 射擊　　　　　　S

三態為: shoot、shot [ʃɑt]、shot

例: "Don't move or I'll shoot," said the policeman.
（『別動，否則我就要開槍了。』警察說。）

1179. **shop** [ʃɑp] n. 商店 & vi. 購物 Ⓢ

shop for...　　購買……
＝buy...
go shopping　　購物
go window-shopping　　逛街
例: Let's go shopping at the night market tonight.
（今晚咱們逛夜市去。）

1180. **short** [ʃɔrt] a. 短的; 矮的; 短缺的 Ⓢ

be running short of...　　短缺……
To make a long story short, ...　　長話短說,……
例: I'm running short of money this month.
（我這個月錢不夠用了。）
　　To make a long story short, Ted failed the test.
（長話短說，泰德沒考及格。）

1181. **shortly** [ʃɔrtlɪ] adv. 立刻地, 不久 Ⓢ

例: Shortly after he left, it began to rain.
（他一離開沒多久便開始下雨了。）

1182. **shoulder** [ʃoldɚ] n. 肩膀 vt. 肩負 (責任) Ⓢ

shoulder the burden of...　　負起……的責任
give sb the cold shoulder　　冷淡待某人
例: That girl gave me the cold shoulder when I asked her out.
（我約那女孩子時，她給我吃閉門羹。）

1183. **shout** [ʃaut] vi. 大叫 Ⓢ

例: Don't shout at me! I'm not wrong.
（不要對我大罵！我又沒錯。）

1184. show [ʃo] n. 節目; 秀 & vt. 展示, 展現　　　**S**

三態為: show、showed、shown [ʃon]

本字亦可作不及物動詞, 有下列重要片語:

show up　　　出現

show off　　　炫耀

例: He showed up on time.

(他準時出現。)

I don't like people who show off.

(我不喜歡愛現的人。)

The show on TV was really good.

(那個電視節目真棒。)

1185. shut [ʃʌt] vt. & vi. 關閉 (三態同形)　　　**S**

例: Shut up!

(閉嘴。)

Shut the door, please.

= Close the door, please.

(請關門。)

1186. shy [ʃaɪ] a. 害羞的　　　**S**

例: Don't be shy. I won't bite.

(別害羞。我又不會咬人。)

1187. sick [sɪk] a. 生病的; 有病態心理的; 討厭的　　　**S**

sickness ['sɪknɪs] n. 病

be sick of...　　　厭惡……

be air-sick　　　暈機

be sea-sick　　　暈船

be car-sick　　　暈車

例: I'm sick. I need to take a rest.

(我生病了，需要休息。)

I'm sick of people who lie.
(我厭惡說謊的人。)

1188. side [saɪd] n. 旁邊　　　Ⓢ

be on one's side　　支持某人

例: No matter what happens, I'll always be on your side.

= No matter what happens, I'll always support you.
(不管發生什麼事，我都支持你。)

1189. sight [saɪt] n. 視力 (= eyesight); 景色; 影像　　Ⓢ

at first sight　　第一眼

sightseeing [ˈsaɪtˌsiɪŋ] n. 觀光

例: Mary fell in love with Tom at first sight.
(瑪麗與湯姆一見鍾情。)

We went sightseeing in Japan last month.
(我們上個月在日本觀光。)

1190. sign [saɪn] n. 標示, 標記 & vt. & vi. 簽署; 簽名　　Ⓢ

例: That sign tells you where the school is.
(這個標示告訴你學校的位置。)

Sign your name on the paper.
(把名字簽在這份文件上。)

1191. signal [ˈsɪgnḷ] n. 手勢, 提示　　Ⓢ

traffic signal　　交通號誌, 紅綠燈

例: The traffic signal turned green.
(號誌燈變綠燈了。)

1192. silent [ˈsaɪlənt] a. 安靜的; 沈默的　　Ⓢ

silence [ˈsaɪləns] n. 安靜; 沈默

例: Be silent or someone will hear you.
（安靜，否則別人會聽到你說的話。）
Silence is golden.
（沈默是金。——諺語）

1193. **silly** ['sɪlɪ] a. 愚蠢的　ⓢ

例: The silly father has a clever son.
（蠢爸爸有個聰明的兒子。）

1194. **simple** ['sɪmpl] a. 單純的; 簡單的　ⓢ

例: "The answer to the question is very simple," said Mary.
（瑪麗說，『這個問題的答案很簡單。』）

1195. **since** [sɪns] conj. & prep. 自從 & conj. 由於　ⓢ

since 作連接詞或介詞，表『自從』時，所引導的子句或片語，一定與完成式或完成進行式並用 (have + p.p./have been + Ving)。

例: Ever since I graduated from high school, I've been working for my father.
（自我高中畢業後，就一直為爸爸效力。）

1196. **sing** [sɪŋ] vt. & vi. 唱; 唱歌　ⓢ

三態為: sing、sang [sæŋ]、sung [sʌŋ]

例: Sara sang a beautiful song at the concert.
（莎拉在演唱會唱了一首很美的歌曲。）

1197. **single** ['sɪŋɡl] a. 單一的; 單身的　ⓢ

例: My sister is single, but my brother is married.
（我姊姊未嫁，不過我哥哥已婚。）

1198. **sink** [sɪŋk] n. 洗碗槽 & vt. & vi. (使) 沈沒　ⓢ

三態為: sink、sank [sæŋk]、sunk [sʌŋk]。
sunken ['sʌŋkən] a. 沈沒的 (置於名詞前)

例: Put the dirty dishes in the sink.
(把髒碗盤放在洗碗槽裏。)

Did they find the sunk boat? (✗)

→ Did they find the sunken boat? (○)
(他們找到沈船了嗎?)

The enemy has sunken two of our ships. (✗)

→ The enemy has sunk two of our ships. (○)
(敵人擊沈了我們兩艘船。)

1199. **sister** ['sɪstɚ] n. 妹妹 (= younger sister); 姊姊 (= older sister) Ⓢ

brother ['brʌðɚ] n. 弟弟; 哥哥 (= older brother)

例: I have one sister and two brothers.
(我有一個妹妹兩個哥哥。)

1200. **sit** [sɪt] vi. 坐 (三態為: sit、sat [sæt]、sat) Ⓢ

sit down　　坐下

sit up　　敖夜, 不睡覺; 坐起來

例: Sit down, please.
(請坐。)

I sat up watching TV all night.
(我整晚看電視到通霄。)

1201. **size** [saɪz] n. 尺寸; 大小; 規模 Ⓢ

例: This shirt comes in three sizes: small, medium and large.
(這件襯衫有三個尺寸:小、中、大。)

1202. **skate** [sket] vi. 溜冰 Ⓢ

go skating　　溜冰去

例: Let's go skating tomorrow.
(咱們明天溜冰去。)

1203. ski [ski] vi. 滑雪

go skiing　　滑雪去

例: We went skiing in Canada last year.
（我們去年到加拿大滑雪。）

1204. skin [skɪn] n. 皮膚

by the skin of one's teeth　　僅以牙齒表皮的差距 (喻有驚無險)

例: Beauty is only skin-deep.
（美貌是膚淺的——諺語，喻外在美不重要，重要的是內在美。）

Tom passed the test by the skin of his teeth.
（湯姆勉強考及格了。）

1205. skirt [skɝt] n. 裙子

例: Mary doesn't like to wear skirts because she has hairy legs.
（瑪麗不喜歡穿裙子因為她有腿毛。）

1206. sky [skaɪ] n. 天空

例: I see a bird flying high in the sky.
（我看到一隻鳥在空中翱翔。）

1207. sleep [slip] n. 睡眠 & vi. 睡覺

三態為: sleep、slept [slɛpt]、slept

go to sleep　　入睡

sleepy [ˈslipɪ] a. 想睡的

asleep [əˈslip] a. 睡著的

fall asleep　　睡著了

have a good night's sleep　　睡得好

例: Did you have a good night's sleep last night?
（你昨晚睡得好嗎？）

I fell asleep in the middle of the meeting.
（會開到一半我就睡著了。）

1208. slow [slo] a. 慢的 & vi. 慢下來 (與 down 並用) ⑤

slowly [ˈsloɪɪ] a. 慢慢地

例: Slow down or you'll get a ticket.
(放慢速度,否則你會吃罰單。)

I don't like slow workers.
(我不喜歡做事慢吞吞的人。)

1209. small [smɔl] a. 小的; 個子小的 ⑤

例: This shirt is too small for me to wear anymore.
(這件襯衫太小我穿不下了。)

1210. smart [smɑrt] a. 聰明的 ⑤

例: Tom is smart and good-looking.
(湯姆聰明又瀟灑。)

1211. smell [smɛl] n. 氣味 & vi. 聞起來; 有異味 ⑤

三態為: smell、smelt [smɛlt]、smelt

例: I don't like the smell of that coffee.
(我不喜歡那個咖啡的氣味。)

Those flowers smell wonderful.
(那些花很香。)

You smell. Stay away from me.
(你好臭。離我遠一點。)

1212. smile [smaɪl] n. & vi. 微笑 ⑤

smile at...   對……微笑

例: Look! That girl is smiling at you.
(瞧!那個女孩子正對著你微笑。)

1213. smoke [smok] n. 煙 & vi. 抽煙

例: You're not allowed to smoke in here.
(這裏面禁煙。)

1214. smooth [smuð] a. 平滑的; 順暢的

smoothly [ˈsmuðlɪ] adv. 平滑地; 順暢地

例: Sue has smooth and shiny hair.
(蘇有一頭光滑亮麗的秀髮。)

The test went smoothly this morning.
(今天早上的測驗進行得滿順利。)

1215. snack [snæk] n. (正餐之外的) 便餐; 點心

例: After class we had a snack.
(下課後我們吃了點東西。)

1216. snake [snek] n. 蛇

例: Be careful. This snake is poisonous.
(小心。這條蛇有毒。)

＊poisonous [ˈpɔɪzənəs] a. 有毒的

1217. snow [sno] n. 雪 & vi. 下雪

例: The weatherman says it will snow tomorrow.
(氣象播報員說明天會下雪。)

The snow caused many car accidents.
(大雪造成多起車禍。)

1218. so [so] conj. 因此 & adv. 如此地

so..that... 如此……以致……

例: Tom was sick, so he couldn't go to school.
(湯姆生病了，因此他無法上學。)

I'm so tired that I need to take a rest.
(我太累，因此需要休息一下。)

1219. **soap** [sop] n. 肥皂 (不可數) Ⓢ

a cake of soap　　一塊肥皂

例: I bought two soaps. (✗)

→ I bought two cakes of soap. (○)
(我買了兩塊肥皂。)

1220. **soccer** ['sɑkɚ] n. 足球 Ⓢ

例: Can you play soccer?
(你會踢足球嗎?)

1221. **soft** [sɔft] a. 軟的 Ⓢ

例: This bread is soft and delicious.
(這麵包鬆軟好吃。)

1222. **software** ['sɔftwɛr] n. 軟體 (不可數) Ⓢ

hardware ['hɑrdwɛr] n. 硬體 (不可數)

例: Some software can be much more expensive than hardware.
(有些軟體要比硬體更貴。)

1223. **soldier** ['soldʒɚ] n. 軍人; 士兵 Ⓢ

例: The brave soldier fought in three battles.
(這個勇敢的軍人曾參加過三次戰役。)

1224. **solve** [sɑlv] vt. 解決 (問題) Ⓢ

solution [sə'luʃən] n. 解決; 解決之道 (與介詞 to 並用)

例: Help me solve this problem.
(幫我解決這個問題。)

I have a good solution to that problem.
(那個問題我有一個不錯的解決之道。)

1225. somebody [ˈsʌmˌbɑdɪ] n. 某人　　Ⓢ

= someone [ˈsʌmwʌn] n.

nobody [ˈnoˌbɑdɪ] n. 無人

= no one [ˈnowʌn]

anybody [ˈɛnɪˌbɑdɪ] n. 任何人

= anyone [ˈɛnɪwʌn]

everybody [ˈɛvrɪˌbɑdɪ] n. 每個人

= everyone [ˈɛvrɪwʌn]

例: I need somebody to help me with the work.

(我需要找個人來幫我做這工作。)

1226. something [ˈsʌmθɪŋ] n. 某件事; 某個東西　　Ⓢ

nothing [ˈnʌθɪŋ] n. 無事; 無物

anything [ˈɛnɪˌθɪŋ] n. 任何事; 任何東西

everything [ˈɛvrɪˌθɪŋ] n. 每件事; 每個東西

例: I have something to tell you.

(我有事要告訴你。)

There is nothing he can't do.

(他什麼事都會做。)

1227. somewhere [ˈsʌmˌwɛr] adv. 某處　　Ⓢ

nowhere [ˈnoˌwɛr] adv. 無處

anywhere [ˈɛnɪˌwɛr] adv. 任何地方

everywhere [ˈɛvrɪhˌwɛr] adv. 每個地方

例: I believe somewhere in the world there's a boy for me.

(我知道世界某處我的意中人在等我。)

1228. sometimes [ˈsʌmtaɪmz] adv. 有時候　　Ⓢ

例: Sometimes I just like to stay at home and relax.

(有時候我只想待在家裏輕鬆一下。)

1229. **son** [sʌn] n. 兒子

daughter [ˈdɔtɚ] n. 女兒

例: I have two sons and five daughters.
(我有兩個兒子五個女兒。)

1230. **song** [sɔŋ] n. 歌曲

例: That song playing on the radio is my favorite.
(正在收音機播放的那首歌是我的最愛。)

1231. **soon** [sun] adv. 很快地

as soon as...　一……就……

例: Paul will be here very soon.
(保羅很快就要來了。)

As soon as I saw my teacher, I ran away.
(我一看到老師拔腿就跑。)

1232. **sore** [sɔr] a. 酸痛的

例: After such a long walk, my legs are sore.
(走了那麼一大段路，我的腿酸死了。)

1233. **sorry** [ˈsɔrɪ] a. 抱歉的

例: I'm sorry, but I must be leaving.
(很抱歉，我得離開了。)

1234. **sound** [saʊnd] n. 聲音 & a. 健全的; 不錯的 & vi. 聽起來

例: I love the sound of music.
(我喜歡音樂的聲音。)

Thank you for your sound idea.
(謝謝你的好點子。)

That idea sounds good.
(那個點子聽起來不錯。)

1235. **soup** [sup] n. 湯 (不可數)

a soup (✗)
→ a bowl of soup (○)　　一碗湯
drink soup (✗)
→ eat soup (○)　　喝湯
例: Eat the soup while it's hot.
(趁熱把湯喝了吧。)

1236. **sour** [saʊr] a. (味道) 酸的

例: This milk has turned sour.
(牛奶變酸了。)

1237. **space** [spes] n. 太空; 空間

spaceman [ˈspesmən] n. 太空人
例: Do you believe there is life in space?
(你相信太空有生物嗎?)

1238. **speak** [spik] vi. 說 (語言)

三態為: speak、spoke [spok]、spoken [ˈspokən]
speech [spitʃ] n. 演講
give a speech　　演講
例: How many languages do you speak?
(你會說多少種語言?)
He gave a wonderful speech to us yesterday.
(他昨天對我們做了一篇精湛的演講。)

1239. **special** [ˈspɛʃəl] a. 特別的

例: What's so special about this car?
(這輛車有什麼特別之處?)

1240. speed [spid] n. 速度 & vi. 超速; 加速 Ⓢ

三態為: speed、sped [spɛd]/speeded ['spidɪd]、sped/speeded

例: Our car was traveling at a high speed.
(我們車子正高速行駛。)

Speed up, or we'll be late.
(快一點,否則我們會遲到了。)

1241. spell [spɛl] vt. 拼 (字) Ⓢ

例: How do you spell that word?
(那個字是怎麼拼的?)

1242. spend [spɛnd] vt. 花費 (時間、金錢) Ⓢ

三態為: spend、spent、spent。

spend time + Ving　　花時間從事……

spend money on + N　　把錢花在……之上

例: I spent almost five hours to write that letter. (✗)

→ I spent almost five hours writing that letter. (○)
(我花了幾近五個鐘頭寫那封信。)

Tom spent a lot of money on comic books.
(湯姆把大筆錢都花在漫畫書上。)

1243. spoil [spɔɪl] vi. (食物) 變壞 & vt. 寵壞 Ⓢ

例: The food has spoiled; it can't be eaten anymore.

= The food has gone bad; it can't be eaten anymore.
(這個食物已餿了,不能再吃了。)

Don't spoil your child.
(別把孩子寵壞了。)

1244. spoon [spun] n. 湯匙 Ⓢ

例: Put the spoon next to the fork.
(把湯匙放在叉子旁邊。)

1245. sport [spɔrt] n. 運動　Ⓢ

例: Basketball is a popular sport in the United States.
（在美國籃球是很受歡迎的運動。）

1246. spread [sprɛd] vi. & vt. 蔓延, 傳播 & vt. 塗抹 (三態同形)　Ⓢ

例: The rumor about Mary spread like wild fire.
（有關瑪麗的謠言像野火般傳開。）

Spread butter on the bread.
（把奶油塗在麵包上。）

1247. spring [sprɪŋ] n. 春天; 泉水; 彈簧　Ⓢ

hot spring　　溫泉

例: This spring I'll go to Japan.
（今年春天我會到日本去。）

1248. stage [stedʒ] n. 舞台　Ⓢ

例: I feel nervous whenever I stand on the stage.
（每次我站在舞台上就感到緊張。）

1249. stand [stænd] vi. 站立 & vt. 容忍　Ⓢ

三態為: stand、stood [stʊd]、stood

例: Don't stand on that chair. It might break.
（別站在椅子上。它可能會斷裂。）

I just can't stand his selfishness.
= I just can't put up with his selfishness.
（我受不了他的自私。）

1250. star [stɑr] n. 星星; 恆星　Ⓢ

例: Every night, I wish upon a star.
（每晚我會對一顆星星許願。）

1251. start [stɑrt] n. & vt. & vi. 開始; 起動

=begin [brɪ'gɪn] vt. & n. 開始; 起動

例: When does the show start?

(這個節目什麼時候開始？)

1252. station ['steʃən] n. 車站

例: The bus station is two blocks away.

(公車站過兩條街就到了。)

1253. stay [ste] n. 逗留 & vi. 逗留; 保持 (= remain)

stay up 開夜車

stay away from... 遠離……

stay young 保持青春

例: Last night I stayed up until one.

(我昨晚開夜車到一點。)

Stay away from him. He's a bad guy.

(遠離他。他不是善類。)

1254. steak [stek] n. 牛排

例: I'd like my steak well done.

(我的牛排要全熟。)

1255. steal [stil] vt. & vi. 偷竊

三態為: steal、stole [stol]、stolen ['stolən]

例: Who has stolen my money?

(誰偷了我的錢？)

1256. steel [stil] n. 鋼

例: That knife is made from steel.

(那把刀是鋼製的。)

1257. step [stɛp] n. 一步 vi. 踏步, 走 (= walk) Ⓢ

例: Watch your step. The floor is wet.
(小心慢行。地板是溼的。)
He stepped up to the blackboard and wrote his name on it.
(他走向黑板,把名字寫在上面。)

1258. stick [stɪk] n. 棍子; 拐杖 & vi. 黏, 堅守 Ⓢ

三態為: stick、stuck [stʌk]、stuck
stick to...　　堅守……
例: The old man uses a stick to walk with.
(這位老先生用拐杖走路。)
Stick to your principles, son.
(兒子,你要堅守原則。)

1259. still [stɪl] adv. 仍然 & a. 靜止的 Ⓢ

例: Tom is poor, but I still love him.
(湯姆很窮,不過我仍然愛他。)
Still waters run deep.
(靜水流深,大智若愚。──諺語)

1260. stomach [ˈstʌmək] n. 胃; 肚子 Ⓢ

stomachache [ˈstʌməkˌek] n. 胃痛
例: He was lying on his stomach/on his back.
(他俯臥著／仰臥著。)
I had a stomachache yesterday.
(我昨天肚子痛。)

1261. stone [ston] n. 石頭 Ⓢ

within a stone's throw　　在步行範圍之內
例: My school is within a stone's throw from here.
(我的學校離這兒走幾步路就到了。)

1262. **stop** [stɑp] n. 停止 & vt. & vi. 停止; 阻止　　　　Ⓢ

a bus stop　　　公車站牌
stop Ving　　　停止做某事
stop to V　　　停下原有工作開始從事……

例: He stopped to talk to me when he saw me.
（他看到我時，便停下來跟我說話。）
　　He stopped talking to me when he saw Mary.
（他看到瑪麗時便不再與我說話。）

1263. **store** [stɔr] n. 商店 & vt. 儲存　　　　　　Ⓢ

例: I went to the store to buy some milk.
（我到商店去買些牛奶。）
　　This disk stores a lot of information.
（這張磁碟片可儲存許多資料。）

1264. **storm** [stɔrm] n. 暴風雨　　　　　　　　Ⓢ

例: The storm caused a lot of damage.
（這場暴風雨造成許多損害。）

1265. **story** [ˋstɔrɪ] n. 故事; 樓層　　　　　　　Ⓢ

例: Every night Jim tells his son a story.
（吉姆每晚都跟兒子說故事。）
　　That building is ten stories high.
（那幢大樓有十層樓高。）

1266. **stove** [stov] n. 爐子　　　　　　　　　Ⓢ

例: That stove uses gas.
（那個爐子用的是瓦斯。）

1267. straight [stret] a. 直的 & adv. 一直　Ⓢ

例: My hair is curly, but my sister's hair is straight.
(我的頭髮是捲的,不過我妹妹的頭髮則是直的。)

To get to the store, go straight and then turn right at the corner.
(要去商店就直走,到轉角右轉就行了。)

1268. strange [strendʒ] a. 陌生的; 奇怪的　Ⓢ

stranger [ˈstrendʒɚ] n. 陌生人

例: Why is Bill acting so strange?
(比爾的舉止為何那麼怪異?)

1269. street [strit] n. 街; 街道　Ⓢ

例: What street do you live on?
(你住在哪條街?)

1270. strict [strɪkt] a. 嚴格的　Ⓢ

be strict with...　　對⋯⋯很嚴格

例: Bill's parents were very strict with him.
(比爾的父母對他很嚴格。)

1271. strike [straɪk] n. 罷工 & vt. 打擊　Ⓢ

三態為: strike、struck [strʌk]、struck

go on strike　　罷工

例: The workers have been on strike for a month.
(工人罷工已一個月了。)

Tom was struck in the face with a ball.
(湯姆的臉被球打到。)

1272. strong [strɔŋ] a. 強的; 強壯的　Ⓢ

weak [wik] a 柔弱的; 無力的

例: That man is strong because he exercises every day.
(那名男子因為天天運動，所以身體很壯。)

1273. **student** [ˈstjudənt] n. 學生　S

　　例: Several students were late for the exam.
　　(有幾個學生考試遲到了。)

1274. **study** [ˈstʌdɪ] n. 讀書; 研究; 書房 & vt. 研究 & vi. 讀書, 研讀　S

　　studies [ˈstʌdɪz] n. 學業 (恆用複數)
　　例: Studying English takes a lot of effort.
　　(學英文很費工夫。)
　　　My sister is studying law.
　　(我妹妹正在攻讀法律。)
　　　John is doing his homework in his study.
　　(約翰正在書房做功課。)
　　　Peter did well in his studies.
　　(彼得的功課很好。)

1275. **stupid** [ˈstjupɪd] a. 愚蠢的　S

　　例: That was a stupid question.
　　(那真是個蠢問題。)

1276. **style** [staɪl] n. 風格; 流行　S

　　be in style　　流行
　=be in fashion
　　be out of style　　不流行
　=be out of fashion
　　例: Miniskirts are no longer in style.
　　(迷你裙不再流行了。)

1277. subject ['sʌbdʒɪkt] n. 學科; 主題　　S

例: That subject is easy to learn.
(那門課很容易學。)

The subject of the speech this morning was smoking.
(今天早上演講的主題是抽煙。)

1278. submarine ['sʌbməˏrin] n. 潛水艇　　S

例: The submarine sank the boat.
(潛水艇把船擊沉了。)

1279. subway ['sʌbwe] n. 地鐵　　S

例: The subway was closed for two weeks after the typhoon.
(颱風之後地鐵關閉了兩個星期。)

1280. succeed [sək'sid] vi. 成功 & vt. 繼承　　S

例: Mom often says that I will succeed at anything if I try hard enough.
(媽媽常說我只要努力的話,做什麼都會成功。)

The boy succeeded his father as king.
(這男孩繼承他的父親,當上了國王。)

1281. success [sək'sɛs] n. 成功 (不可數); 成功者/成功的事 (可數)　　S

successful [sək'sɛsfḷ] a. 成功的

例: Failure is the mother of success.
(失敗為成功之母。——諺語)

The party last night was quite a success.

= The party last night was quite successful.
(昨晚的派對很成功。)

1282. such [sʌtʃ] a. 這樣的　　S

such...as...　　像……這樣的……

例: I've never seen such a beautiful girl as Mary.
(我從沒見過像瑪麗這樣的美女。)

He has many hobbies, such as singing, swimming and skating.
(他有很多嗜好，諸如唱歌、游泳及溜冰。)

1283. **sudden** [ˈsʌdn̩] a. 突然的　Ⓢ

all of a sudden　　突然間

= suddenly

例: It began to rain all of a sudden.

= It began to rain suddenly.
(突然下起雨來了。)

1284. **suffer** [ˈsʌfɚ] vt. 遭受 (打擊、損失等) & vi. 受苦　Ⓢ

suffer from + 疾病　　飽受某疾病之苦

例: John suffers from AIDS.
(約翰飽受愛滋病的折磨。)

The company suffered a big loss because of the wrong direction.
(因為方向錯誤，公司蒙受很大的損失。)

1285. **sugar** [ˈʃʊgɚ] n. 糖　Ⓢ

例: Sugar is fattening.
(糖會令人發胖。)

＊fattening [ˈfætn̩ɪŋ] a. 令人發胖的

1286. **suggest** [səgˈdʒɛst] vt. 建議; 暗示　Ⓢ

suggest that + 主詞 + (should) + 原形動詞　　建議……

例: I suggest that he study English before he goes to Canada.
(我建議他去加拿大之前先唸英文。)

His words suggest that he is angry.
(他的話意味著他生氣了。)

1287. suit [sut] n. 西裝 & vt. 適合　　S

例: That suit looks great on you.
(你穿上那套西裝有夠帥。)

That job doesn't suit you.
(那份工作不適合你。)

1288. summer ['sʌmɚ] n. 夏天　　S

例: Summer is around the corner.
= Summer is coming soon.
(夏天就要到了。)

1289. sun [sʌn] n. 太陽　　S

sunburn ['sʌn,bɝn] n. 曬傷

例: Tom got a sunburn because he didn't wear a hat.
(湯姆因為沒戴帽子被曬傷了。)

1290. supermarket ['supɚ,markɪt] n. 超市　　S

例: Supermarkets make life easy.
(超市使生活方便多了。)

1291. supper ['sʌpɚ] n. 晚餐　　S

例: Mother usually makes supper at seven.
(媽媽通常在七點弄晚飯。)

1292. supply [sə'plaɪ] vt. 供應　　S

supply sb with sth　　供應某人某物
= provide sb with sth
supplies [sə'plaɪz] n. 供應品 (恆用複數)

例: We supplied the orphans with food.
(我們供應食物給那些孤兒。)

＊orphan ['ɔrfən] n. 孤兒

1293. suppose [sə'poz] vt. 推定, 料想 **S**

be supposed to V 　　理應……; 應當……

例: He is supposed to arrive at ten.
(他理應在十點到。)

What makes you suppose that he will leave the company?
(是什麼讓你推論他會離開公司？)

1294. sure [ʃur] a. 肯定的, 確定的 **S**

be sure (that)... 　　確定

be sure of + N 　　確定……

例: Are you sure that he'll come?
(你確定他會來嗎？)

Are you sure of this answer?
(你確定這個答案嗎？)

1295. surely ['ʃurlɪ] adv. 確定地 **S**

= certainly ['sɝtn̩lɪ]

例: We will surely get there on time if we leave now.
(我們若現在動身一定會準時到達那裏。)

1296. surprise [sə'praɪz] n. 驚訝 & vt. 使吃驚 **S**

be surprised at... 　　對……感到驚訝

例: Everyone was surprised to see Tom Cruise at the night
market.
(大家在夜市見到阿湯哥時都大感驚訝。)

I was surprised at his good English.
(他的英文很好，令我驚訝。)

1297. sweat [swɛt] n. 汗 & vi. 出汗 **S**

例: I see sweat on your face.
(我看到你臉上有汗水。)

I sweat a lot when it's hot.
(天熱時我汗流得很多。)

1298. **swear** [swɛr] vt. 發誓 & vi. 咒罵 (與 at 並用)　**S**

三態為: swear、swore [swɔr]、sworn [swɔrn]。

例: I swear I didn't steal the money.
(我發誓我沒偷那筆錢。)

Don't swear at me!
(別咒罵我！)

1299. **sweep** [swip] vt. 清掃　**S**

三態為: sweep、swept [swɛpt]、swept

例: The cleaner sweeps the floors every night.
(清潔工每晚清掃地板。)

1300. **sweet** [swit] a. 甜的; 甜美的　**S**

例: This coffee is too sweet.
(這咖啡太甜了。)

Mary is a sweet girl.
(瑪麗是個甜姐兒。)

1301. **sweets** [swits] n. 甜食 (恆用複數)　**S**

例: John enjoys sweets.
= John has a sweet tooth. (此處 tooth 恆為單數)
(約翰喜歡甜食。)

1302. **swim** [swɪm] vi. 游泳　**S**

三態為: swim、swam [swæm]、swum [swʌm]

例: Peter swims like a fish.
= Peter is good at swimming.
(彼得很會游泳。)

1303. **system** [ˈsɪstəm] n. 系統　　　　　**S**

systematic [ˌsɪstəˈmætɪk] a. 有系統的

例: The computer system was out of order.

(這個電腦系統故障了。)

1304. table ['tebḷ] n. 餐桌

例: "Set the table for dinner!" Mom said.
(媽媽說:『擺碗筷準備吃晚飯!』)

1305. tail [tel] n. 尾巴

tale [tel] n. 故事 (= story)

例: The dog was chasing its own tail.
(那隻狗正在追逐自己的尾巴。)

He told us a very interesting tale.
(他為我們說了一個有趣的故事。)

1306. take [tek] vt. 拿取; 帶走 (從近處帶到遠處)

三態為: take、took [tʊk]、taken ['tekən]
bring [brɪŋ] vt. 帶來 (從遠處帶到近處)

例: Take this book to Mary but bring it back two days from now.
(把這本書帶給瑪麗,不過兩天後再帶回來。)

1307. talk [tɔk] n. & vi. 談話

例: I'd like to have a talk with you about your son.
= I'd like to talk with you about your son.
(我想跟你談談有關令郎的事。)

1308. talent ['tælənt] n. 才華, 天份

talented ['tæləntɪd] a. 有天份的
have a talent for... 在……有天份
= be talented in...

例: Mary has a talent for music.
= Mary is talented in music.
(瑪麗有音樂方面的天賦。)

1309. tall [tɔl] a. 高的, 高個子的

例: The man is short while his wife is tall.
(這男子很矮，而他太太卻很高。)

1310. tame [tem] a. 馴良的 & vt. 馴服

例: The dog is tame; it won't bite.
(這狗很溫馴，不會咬人。)

Mary tried to tame the wild dog.
(瑪麗設法要馴服那隻野狗。)

1311. tank [tæŋk] n. 油箱; 坦克車

tanker [ˈtæŋkɚ] n. 油輪

例: Fill the tank with gas.
(把油箱加滿汽油。)

1312. tap [tæp] n. (自來水) 水龍頭 & vi. 輕敲

tap water   自來水

例: Paul tapped on my shoulder to ask me a question.
(保羅輕敲我的肩膀要問我問題。)

1313. tape [tep] n. 膠帶; 錄音帶 & vt. 用膠帶貼; 錄音

例: Tape up the box and mail it out.
(把箱子用膠帶封好再寄出去。)

Will you tape that song for me?
(請你替我把那首歌錄下來好嗎？)

1314. taxi [ˈtæksɪ] n. 計程車 & vi. (飛機) 滑行

hail a taxi   用手招計程車

例: Mary hailed a taxi in front of the store.
(瑪麗在商店前招了一部計程車。)

The airplane taxied down the runway.
(飛機沿著跑道滑行。)

1315. **taste** [test] n. 味道; 品嚐; 品味 & vt. 品嚐 & vi. 嚐起來 **t**

have good/bad taste　　有品味/沒品味

例: May I have a taste of your cake?
(我可不可以嚐一口你的蛋糕?)

This food tastes delicious.
(這道食物嚐起來真好吃。)

Tom has good taste in clothing.
(湯姆對衣服有品味。)

1316. **tea** [ti] n. 茶 **t**

例: Green tea is good for your health.
(綠茶對你健康有益。)

1317. **teach** [titʃ] vt. & vi. 教 (書); 教導 **t**

三態為: teach、taught [tɔt]、taught
teacher [ˈtitʃɚ] n. 教師

例: Mr. Wang has been teaching English for ten years.
(王老師教英文已有十年了。)

1318. **team** [tim] n. (球) 隊 & vi. 團結 (與 up 並用) **t**

team up　　團結合作; 發揮團隊精神

例: Let's team up and get the job done.
(咱們團結合作把工作做完。)

Our team lost the game last night.
(我隊昨晚輸了這場比賽。)

1319. **tear** [tɪr] n. 眼淚 & [tɛr] vt. 撕/拆開 **t**

三態為: tear、tore [tor]、torn [torn]
burst into tears　　突然大哭

= burst out crying

tear up... 　　將……撕爛

tear down... 　　將……拆毀

例: He burst into tears when he heard the bad news.

(他聽到這消息時，大哭失聲。)

He tore up the letter.

(他把信撕爛了。)

They tore down the house.

(他們把房子拆毀。)

1320. **telephone** [ˈtɛləfon] n. 電話 (常縮寫成 phone [fon]) & vt. 打電話

例: Telephone me at six tonight.

= 　Call me at six tonight.

= 　Phone me at six tonight.

(今晚六點打電話給我。)

The telephone was off the hook all day.

(電話整天沒掛好。)

＊be off the hook 　　脫離鉤子

hook [hʊk] n. 鉤子

1321. **television** [ˈtɛləˌvɪʒən] n. 電視 (常縮寫成 TV)

例: Watching television is how I relax in the evening.

(看電視就是我每晚放鬆的方式。)

1322. **tell** [tɛl] vt. 說 (故事/謊言); 告訴; 分辨; 預測

tell a story/a lie 　　說故事/說謊

tell A from B 　　分辨 A 與 B 的不同

例: We should learn to tell right from wrong.

(我們應學習明辨是非。)

I can tell that he is going to succeed.

(我可以預測他會成功。)

Tell me the truth.
(把真相告訴我。)

1323. temper [ˈtɛmpɚ] n. 脾氣

lose one's temper　　發脾氣
have a bad temper　　脾氣壞
例: He lost his temper and hit his wife.
(他發脾氣便打了他太太。)

1324. temperature [ˈtɛmprətʃɚ] n. 溫度; 體溫

run a temperature　　發燒
take one's temperature　　量某人體溫
例: The nurse took my temperature.
(護士量我體溫。)
　　The baby is running a temperature.
(小寶寶發燒了。)

1325. temple [ˈtɛmpḷ] n. 廟宇

例: At the temple my mother prayed for my grandfather to get better.
(在寺廟的時候，我媽媽祈求讓我爺爺身體復元。)

1326. tennis [ˈtɛnɪs] n. 網球

例: That tennis player is very famous.
(那位網球選手很有名。)

1327. tent [tɛnt] n. 帳蓬

pitch a tent　　架設帳蓬
例: Let's pitch our tent over there.
(咱們帳蓬架在那邊吧。)

1328. term [tɝm] n. 關係 (恆用複數); 學期; 任期

be on good terms with... 　與……關係融洽

in terms of... 　就……而言

例: Paul is on good terms with his teachers.

(保羅與他老師間的關係融洽。)

　In terms of music, I like jazz best.

(就音樂而言，我最喜歡爵士樂。)

1329. terrible [ˈtɛrəbl] a. 可怕的; 糟糕的

terror [ˈtɛrə] n. 恐怖

例: His English is terrible.

(他的英文爛透了。)

1330. test [tɛst] n. 測驗 & vt. 測試

例: The test was a piece of cake.

(這次的測驗簡單極了。)

　＊be a piece of cake 　很容易

　= be quite easy

1331. than [ðæn] conj. 比 (與 more 或 less 等比較級並用)

more/less...than... 　比……更加/更不……

would rather V than V 　寧願……也不願……

例: She is far more beautiful than Mary.

(她比瑪麗漂亮多了。)

　I would rather stay at home than go out.

(我寧願待在家裏，也不願外出。)

1332. thank [θæŋk] n. & vt. 感謝

thankful [ˈθæŋkfl] a. 感謝的

be thankful to sb for sth 　因某事感謝某人

thanks to... 　由於/幸虧……

例: Thank you for all of your help.
(謝謝你給我的全力幫助。)

I should be thankful to you for your support.
(我應感謝你的支持。)

Thanks to your help, I was able to finish the work on time.
(幸虧你的幫助,我終於能準時完成工作。)

1333. **theater** [ˈθɪətɚ] n. 戲院; 電影院

例: The theater was full of movie-goers.
(戲院擠滿了看電影的人。)

1334. **thick** [θɪk] a. 厚的

例: The thick book was hard to read.
(這本厚的書很難讀。)

1335. **thin** [θɪn] a. 薄的; 瘦的

例: Jane is thin, but Mary is fat.
(阿珍很瘦,瑪麗卻很胖。)

1336. **thing** [θɪŋ] n. 東西; 事情

例: I have several things to deal with.
(我有幾件事要處理。)

1337. **think** [θɪŋk] vt. 認為 (以 that 子句作受詞) & vi. 想

三態為: think、thought [θɔt]、thought)
thought [θɔt] n. 思想; 念頭
think of/about...　　想⋯⋯
think of A as B　　將 A 視作 B
at the thought of...　　一想到⋯⋯

例: We all think of John as a hero.
(我們大家都把約翰視為英雄。)

I cried at the thought of Mary.
（一想到瑪麗，我就哭了。）

1338. thoughtful [ˈθɔtfl] a. 體諒的

例: John is a thoughtful young man.
（約翰是個很體諒人的年輕人。）

1339. though [ðo] conj. 雖然

= although [ɔlˈðo]

例: Though he is handsome, he's not smart.
（雖然他是個帥哥，卻不夠聰明。）

1340. through [θru] prep. 經過 & a. 做完的

be through with...　　做完……

= be finished with...

= finish...

例: Through his help, I finished my work.
（透過他的幫助，我把工作做完了。）

I'm through with my work.

= I've finished my work.
（我工作做完了。）

1341. throw [θro] vt. 扔, 擲

三態為: throw、threw [θru]、thrown [θron]

本字亦可作不及物動詞，有下列重要片語：

throw up　　嘔吐

例: I threw up when I smelt that smell.
（我聞到那個東西時就吐了。）

He threw a stone at me.
（他向我扔石頭。）

1342. thunder [ˈθʌndɚ] n. 雷聲 & vi. 打雷

例: The thunder scared the dog.
(雷聲把狗嚇了一跳。)

1343. ticket [ˈtɪkɪt] n. 票; 罰單

例: I bought two tickets to the movies.
(我買了兩張電影票。)

1344. tie [taɪ] n. 領帶 & vt. 綁

tie A to B　　把 A 綁在 B 上
tie the knot with sb　　與某人結婚/結為連理
例: Can you help me tie this rope?
(請你幫我綁這繩子好嗎?)

1345. tiger [ˈtaɪgɚ] n. 老虎

例: My sister was born in the Year of the Tiger.
(我妹妹是虎年生的。)

1346. tight [taɪt] a. 緊的

tightly [ˈtaɪtlɪ] adv. 緊緊地
tighten [ˈtaɪtn̩] vt. 使緊
例: The shoes are too tight to wear.
(鞋子太緊穿不下。)

1347. till [tɪl] conj. & prep. 直到

= until [ʌnˈtɪl] conj.
例: We can't leave till the work is done.
(我們要到工作做完才能離開。)

1348. **time** [taɪm] n. 時間

例: Time is money.
(時間就是金錢。──諺語)
Do you have time?
(你有空嗎？)
Do you have the time?
(你的錶現在幾點了？)

1349. **tiny** ['taɪnɪ] a. 小的; 極小的

例: The tiny baby cried for milk.
(小寶寶哭著要喝奶。)

1350. **tired** [taɪrd] a. 累的

tiring ['taɪrɪŋ] a. 累人的
be sick and tired of...   厭倦……
例: I'm sick and tired of this job.
(這個工作我做煩了。)
The baby is tiring; he keeps crying.
(這小寶寶真磨人；他哭個不停。)

1351. **title** ['taɪtl] n. 頭銜, 名號

例: The title of the book is on the cover.
(這本書的書名在封面上。)

1352. **tip** [tɪp] n. 小費 & vt. 付 (某人) 小費

例: He gave me a tip of NT$100 for the service.
= He tipped me NT$100 for the service.
(他給我台幣一百元小費，謝謝我的服務。)

1353. toast [tost] n. 土司 & vt. 向……敬酒

例: I had a piece of toast and a boiled egg for breakfast.
(我早餐吃了一片土司和一枚水煮蛋。)
＊boiled [bɔɪld] a. 被水煮過的

1354. today [tə'de] n. & adv. 今天

yesterday ['jɛstɚˌde] n. & adv. 昨天
tomorrow [tə'mɑro] n. & adv. 明天
the day before yesterday　　前天
the day after tomorrow　　後天
a year from today　　一年後的今天
例: Today is my birthday.
(今天是我的生日。)

1355. tomorrow [tə'mɑro] n. & adv. 明天

例: I won't be here tomorrow.
(我明天不會在這裏。)

1356. together [tə'gɛðɚ] adv. 一起

例: Let's go to the movies together.
(咱們一起看電影去。)
Birds of a feather flock together.
(物以類聚。——諺語)
＊feather ['fɛðɚ] n. 羽毛
flock [flɑk] vi. 聚集

1357. toilet ['tɔɪlɪt] n. 廁所; 馬桶

例: Excuse me, but where's the toilet?
(對不起，廁所在哪裏？)

1358. **tongue** [tʌŋ] n. 舌頭

mother tongue　　母語

= mother language

例: My mother tongue is Mandarin Chinese.
(我的母語是中文。)

1359. **tool** [tul] n. 工具

例: The only tool you need is a hammer.
(你需要的唯一工具就是榔頭。)
＊hammer [ˈhæmɚ] n. 榔頭

1360. **tooth** [tuθ] n. 牙齒 (複數形為 teeth [tiθ])

toothache [ˈtuθ͵ek] n. 牙疼

have a sweet tooth　　喜歡吃甜食

例: Mary has gained weight because she has a sweet tooth.
(瑪麗發胖了，因為她愛吃甜食。)

1361. **top** [tɑp] n. 頂端 & a. 頂端的

例: Tom lives on the top floor.
(湯姆住在頂樓。)

Bill is at the top of his class.
(比爾在班上名列前茅。)

1362. **touch** [tʌtʃ] n. & vt. 接觸

keep/stay in touch with...　　與……保持連絡

get in touch with...　　與……連絡

例: Please get in touch with me as soon as possible.
(請儘快跟我連絡。)

Don't touch the paint! It's still wet.
(不要觸碰那油漆！還沒乾。)

1363. toward [tɔrd] prep. 朝向

= towards [tɔrdz]

例: Paul walked toward Mary and gave her a warm kiss.
(保羅走向瑪麗給她一個熱吻。)

1364. tow [to] vt. 拖吊

例: Mary had to have her car towed after it broke down.
(瑪麗的車拋錨，只好叫人把車拖走。)
＊break down　(汽車) 拋錨

1365. towel [ˈtauəl] n. 毛巾

例: After you go swimming, dry off with a towel.
(游完泳後，用毛巾把身體擦乾。)

1366. tower [ˈtauɚ] n. 塔

例: The tower is about 100 meters high.
(這座塔約有一百公尺高。)

1367. town [taun] n. 城

in town　在城內
out of town　不在城內
例: Mom will be out of town until the end of next week.
(下個週末媽媽才會在城內。)

1368. toy [tɔɪ] n. 玩具

例: The little boy is playing with his toys.
(小男孩在把玩他的玩具。)

1369. track [træk] n. 蹤跡; 軌道

keep track of...　掌握……的行蹤

例: Keep track of everything he does.
（追蹤他所做的每件事。）

1370. **trade** [tred] n. 貿易 & vt. 交換

trade A for B　　以 A 換取 B

trade in...　　換購

例: Can I trade my car for your daughter, sir?
（先生，我可以用我的車來換取您的女兒嗎？）

I just traded in my used car for a new one.
（我才把舊車賣掉換了一部新車。）

1371. **traffic** [ˈtræfɪk] n. 交通

a traffic accident　　車禍

a traffic jam　　交通阻塞

例: Traffic is really heavy during rush hour.
（尖峰時間交通真的很擁塞。）

＊rush hour　　上下班尖峰時間

1372. **train** [tren] n. 火車 & vt. 訓練 & vi. 接受訓練

例: By the time I got to the station, the train had left.
（我趕到車站時，火車已經離開了。）

Mary was trained to be a nurse.
（瑪麗接受護士養成訓練。）

1373. **trap** [træp] n. 陷阱 & vt. 使落入陷阱

例: The fox got caught in the trap.
（這隻狐狸落入陷阱。）

1374. **travel** [ˈtrævḷ] vi. & n. 旅行

例: My sister is traveling in Europe right now.
（我妹妹目前正在歐洲旅行。）

1375. tray [tre] n. 自助餐餐盤

例: The waitress carried the food on a tray.
(女服務生用餐盤盛食物。)

1376. treasure [ˈtrɛʒɚ] n. 財寶 & vt. 珍惜

例: My cute granddaughter is my treasure.
(我那可愛的孫女就是我的寶貝。)

I treasure your love, honey.
(親愛的，我很珍惜妳的愛。)

1377. treat [trit] vt. 對待; 請 (某人) 客 & n. 樂事; 請客

treat sb to sth　　請某人某物

例: Can I treat you to dinner?
(我可以請妳吃晚飯嗎？)

It's my treat today.
(今天我請客。)

It's a treat going out for ice cream.
(外出吃冰淇淋是件樂事。)

1378. triangle [ˈtraɪˌæŋgl̩] n. 三角形

例: The button is shaped like a triangle.
(這個鈕扣呈三角形。)

1379. trip [trɪp] n. 旅程; 旅行

take a trip to + 地方　　到某地旅行
= go on a trip to + 地方

例: My family and I took a trip to Japan last year.
(我和家人去年到日本走了一趟。)

1380. trouble ['trʌbḷ] n. 麻煩 & vt. 困擾

get in/into trouble　　陷入麻煩, 倒霉

例: If you don't stop talking in class, you'll get in trouble.
（你上課繼續講話的話，就會倒霉了。）

1381. trousers ['trauzɚz] n. 長褲 (英式用法, = pants)

a pair of trousers　　一條褲子

例: Those trousers are too tight on you.
（這條褲子穿在你身上太緊了。）

1382. true [tru] a. 真實的; 忠實的

truly ['trulɪ] adv. 真正地
come true　　成真, 實現
be true to sb　　對某人忠實

例: Because of hard work, his dreams finally came true.
（由於努力，他的夢想實現了。）
　　You should be true to your wife.
（你應對太太忠實。）

1383. trunk [trʌŋk] n. (汽車) 後車廂; 樹幹; 象鼻

例: Bill put the bags in the trunk of the car.
（比爾把袋子全都放在後車廂內。）

1384. truth [truθ] n. 真理; 真相

To tell (you) the truth, ...　　老實說,……

例: To tell the truth, I don't like him.
（老實說，我不喜歡他。）

1385. try [traɪ] vt. 嚐試; 設法 & n. 嚐試

try + N/Ving　　嚐試……
try to + V　　設法……

give it a try　　試試看

例: I tried his way, but it didn't work.
(我試過他的方法，但沒有效。)

　I'll try to be there by 10.
(我會設法十點以前趕到那兒。)

1386. **tunnel** [ˈtʌnḷ] n. 隧道

例: The tunnel is so dark that I can't see anything in here.
(隧道好黑，這裡面我什麼都看不見。)

1387. **turkey** [ˈtɜkɪ] n. 火雞

cold turkey　　一勞永逸地 (俚語)
= once and for all

例: You should quit smoking cold turkey.
(你應一次把煙戒掉。)

1388. **turn** [tɜn] vt. & vi. 轉動 & n. 轉動; 輪流

turn around　　向後轉
turn up　　出現
turn down...　　拒絕……
turn into...　　轉變成……
take turns　　輪流

例: They took turns doing the dishes.
(他們輪流洗盤子。)

1389. **turtle** [ˈtɜtḷ] n. 烏龜

例: The turtle beat the rabbit in the race.
(此次賽跑烏龜贏了兔子。)

1390. **twice** [twaɪs] adv. 兩倍; 兩次

例: I go out for dinner twice a month.
(我一個月吃兩次館子。)

1391. twin [twɪn] n. 雙胞胎

例: Tom has a twin brother named Peter.
(湯姆有個雙胞胎弟弟，名叫彼得。)

1392. twinkle [ʼtwɪŋkl̩] vi. (星光) 閃爍

例: The stars twinkle at night.
(星星在夜中閃爍。)

1393. type [taɪp] n. 型式, 類型 (= kind) & vt. 打 (字)

例: Type the report before you turn it in.
(把報告打好再繳出來。)
What type of music do you like?
(你喜歡哪一類的音樂？)

1394. typhoon [taɪʼfun] n. 颱風

例: A typhoon is coming soon.
(颱風就要來了。)

1395. ugly [ˈʌglɪ] a. 醜陋的　　u

例: Even though he's ugly, he's very smart and kind.
(雖然他醜，卻很聰明，心腸也好。)

1396. umbrella [ʌmˈbrɛlə] n. 雨傘　　u

例: It looks like it's going to rain. You'd better carry an umbrella.
(看起來要下雨的樣子。你最好帶把傘。)

1397. uncle [ˈʌŋk!] n. 叔叔; 伯父　　u

　aunt [ænt/ɑnt] n. 阿姨; 伯母; 嬸嬸
例: My uncle has three children and a cat.
(我叔叔有三個孩子外加一隻貓。)

1398. under [ˈʌndɚ] prep. 在⋯⋯的下方　　u

例: The dog hid under the table.
(狗躲在桌下。)

1399. underground [ˈʌndɚˌgraʊnd] a. 地下的 & adv. 在地下　　u

例: The subway goes underground in many areas.
(在許多地區地鐵都是在地下行駛。)

1400. understand [ˌʌndɚˈstænd] vt. 了解　　u

understanding [ˌʌndɚˈstændɪŋ] n. 了解 & a. 體諒的 (= thoughtful)
例: I was unable to understand what he was saying.
(我無法了解他在說什麼。)
　He has a good understanding of music.
(他很懂音樂。)
　I like him because he's understanding.
(他很體貼，所以我喜歡他。)

1401. university [ˌjunəˈvɜˌsətɪ] n. 大學　　　**u**

例: That university is the best in the country.
(那所大學是該國最好的一所。)

1402. uniform [ˈjunəˌfɔrm] n. 制服　　　**u**

例: Everyone must wear a uniform at my school.
(我們學校每個人都須穿制服。)

1403. unless [ʌnˈlɛs] conj. 除非　　　**u**

例: I won't marry you unless you promise to be nice to me.
(除非你承諾對我好，否則我不會嫁給你。)

1404. until [ʌnˈtɪl] conj. & prep. 直到 (= till [tɪl])　　　**u**

例: I'll stay here until you come back.
(我會在這兒待到你回來為止。)

1405. unusual [ʌnˈjuʒuəl] a. 不尋常的　　　**u**

例: Even today, it's still unusual for girls to chase boys.
(即使時到今日，女追男仍然是少有的事。)
　　chase [tʃes] vt. 追求

1406. up [ʌp] adv. 向上地　　　**u**

grow up　　　長大
bring up...　　將……撫養長大
例: Peter grew up in the country.
= 　Peter was brought up in the country.
(彼得是在鄉下長大的。)

1407. upset [ʌpˈsɛt] vt. 使不悅 (三態同形) & a. 難過的, 心情不好的　　　**u**

例: Bill was upset because he failed the test.
(比爾沒考及格所以心情不好。)

1408. upstairs [ˌʌpˈstɛrz] adv. 在樓上

downstairs [daʊnˈstɛrz] adv. 在樓下

例: A noisy family lives upstairs from me.

（一戶喧鬧的人家就住在我樓上。）

1409. use [jus] n. 利用, 使用 & [juz] vt. 利用, 使用

used [juzd] a. 習慣的; 用過的; 舊的

useful [ˈjusfḷ] a. 有用的

useless [ˈjuslɪs] a. 無用的

make use of...　　利用

＝ use...

例: You should make use of every chance to learn English.

（你應利用每個機會學英文。）

　That's a used car, not a new one.

（那是中古車而非新車。）

1410. usual [ˈjuʒʊəl] a. 普通的; 通常的

usually [ˈjuʒʊəlɪ] adv. 通常

例: Paul usually stays at home on the weekends.

（週末時保羅通常待在家裏。）

1411. vacation [vəˈkeʃən] n. 假期

go on (a) vacation　　渡假去

be on vacation　　渡假中

例: Mary is on vacation in France.

（瑪麗正在法國渡假。）

1412. valley [ˈvælɪ] n. 山谷

例: Down in the valley there is a small town.

（山谷裏有個小鎮。）

1413. value [ˈvælju] n. 價值 & vt. 珍惜 (= treasure)

be of great value/be of no value　　頗有價值/毫無價值

例: The value of life lies in hard work.

（人生的價值在於努力。）

I value your love.

（我珍惜你的愛。）

1414. vase [ves] n. 花瓶

例: Put the flowers in the vase on the table.

（把花放在桌上的花瓶裏。）

1415. vegetable [ˈvɛdʒtəbl] n. 蔬菜

例: The vegetables were fresh from the garden.

（這些蔬菜是剛從菜園拔起來的。）

1416. vehicle [ˈviɪkl] n. 車輛 (指所有有輪子的交通工具)

例: You'll see all kinds of vehicles on the road.

（你會看到馬路上有各種類型的車輛。）

1417. view [vju] n. 觀點; 景色

In one's view...　　依某人之見，……

例: In my view, John is a nice guy.
（依我之見，約翰是個好人。）

That room has a great view.
（那房間視野很棒。）

1418. village [ˈvɪlɪdʒ] n. 村莊

例: The small village was destroyed in the earthquake.
（小村落在地震中毀了。）

1419. very [ˈvɛrɪ] adv. 很

例: It's very important to learn English.
（學英文很重要。）

1420. visit [ˈvɪzɪt] n. & vt. 拜訪, 探訪

visitor [ˈvɪzɪtɚ] n. 訪客; 遊客
pay a visit to...　　拜訪……
= visit...

例: I'll pay a visit to my uncle this weekend.
（這個週末我會去看我叔叔。）

1421. voice [vɔɪs] n. 聲音

例: Peter has a great singing voice.
（彼得的歌喉很美妙。）

1422. vitamin [ˈvaɪtəmɪn] n. 維他命

例: This fruit is high in vitamin C.
（這種水果含有豐富的維他命 C。）

1423. vote [vot] n. 選擇; 選票 & vi. 選舉

vote for sb　　選某人, 對某人投贊成票
例: Who will you vote for?
（你會選誰呀？）

1424. wait [wet] n. & vi. 等候 **W**

wait for...　　等候

wait on...　　(餐廳中服務生) 招呼 (客人)

例: I've been waiting for him for two hours.

(我等了他有兩個鐘頭了。)

　Are you being waited on, sir?

(先生，有人招呼您嗎？)

1425. waiter [ˈwetɚ] n. 男服務生 **W**

waitress [ˈwetrɪs] n. 女服務生

例: All the waiters and waitresses have been very helpful.

(所有的男女服務生都很有熱忱。)

1426. wake [wek] vi. 醒來 (與 up 並用) **W**

三態為: wake、woke [wok]、woken [ˈwokən]。

awake [əˈwek] a. 醒著的 & vi. 醒來

三態為: awake、awoke、awoken。

wake up　　醒來

= awake

例: I woke up at ten.

= I awoke at ten.

(我十點醒來。)

I stayed awake all night.

(我整晚未眠。)

1427. walk [wɔk] n. 走路; 散步 & vi. 步行 & vt. 遛 (狗); 陪 (某人) 走路 **W**

take a walk　　散步

= go for a walk

walk a dog　　遛狗

例: Let's take a walk after work.

(下班後咱們散個步吧。)

Please walk me home.
(請陪我走路回家。)

1428. wall [wɔl] n. 牆壁　　　　　　　　　**W**

drive sb up the wall　　逼某人走投無路

例: The little girl drew on the wall.
(小女孩在牆上塗鴉。)

1429. wallet [ˈwɑlɪt] n. 皮夾子　　　　　　**W**

例: Paul's wallet was stolen when he was on the train.
(保羅在火車上的時候皮夾子被偷了。)

1430. want [wɑnt] vt. 要; 想要　　　　　　　**W**

例: What do you want to do tonight?
(你今晚要做什麼？)

1431. war [wɔr] n. 戰爭　　　　　　　　　　**W**

be at war with...　　與 (某國) 交戰

例: War takes hundreds of thousands of lives.
(戰爭會奪走成千上萬的生命。)

1432. warm [wɔrm] a. 溫暖的; 熱情的 & vi. 熱身 (與 up 並用)　**W**

warmth [wɔrmθ] n. 溫暖

例: It was warm yesterday, but it is cold today.
(昨天天氣暖和, 今天卻冷了起來。)
Warm up before you exercise.
(你要熱身之後再運動。)

1433. warn [wɔrn] vt. 警告　　　　　　　　**W**

warning [ˈwɔrnɪŋ] n. 警告
warn sb of sth　　警告某人某事
warn sb against Ving　　警告某人不要……

例: Our teacher warns us of the danger of smoking.
（我們老師警告我們抽煙的危險。）

　Our teacher warns us against smoking.
（我們老師警告我們不要抽煙。）

1434. **wash** [wɑʃ] vt. 洗　　　　W

例: Make sure you wash your hands before you eat.
（確實做到洗手後再吃東西。）

1435. **waste** [ʹwest] n. 浪費; 廢棄物 (不可數) vt. 浪費　　W

wasteful [ʹwestfl] a. 浪費的

waste time + Ving　　浪費時間從事……

例: Watching TV all day is a waste of time.
（整天看電視就是浪費時間。）

　Don't waste your time watching TV.
（不要浪費時間看電視。）

1436. **watch** [wɑtʃ] n. 手錶; 看守 & vt. & vi. 注意; 觀看 (電視)　　W

watch out　　　留神; 注意

= look out

例: What time is it by your watch?

= What time does your watch have?
（你的錶幾點了？）

　Watch out! That car almost hit you.
（小心！那輛車差一點撞到你。）

1437. **water** [ʹwɑtɚ] n. 水 & vt. 澆 (花) & vi. 流口水　　W

例: I have to remember to water my plant every day.
（我得記住每天要澆我的盆栽。）

＊ plant [plænt] n. 植物; 盆栽

例: My mouth watered when I saw the food.
（我看到那些食物時，便流口水了。）

1438. wave [wev] n. 波浪 & vi. & vt. 搖擺　**W**

make waves　興風作浪
wave at/to sb　向某人揮手
例: I hate people who like to make waves.
(我痛恨興風作浪的人。)
　　The girl waved at her parents when she saw them.
(女孩子看到父母時便向他們揮手。)

1439. way [we] n. 方法, 方式; 方向　**W**

例: Could you show me the way to the station?
(能否告訴我到車站怎麼走？)
　　I don't like the way he treats people.
(我不喜歡他待人的方式。)

1440. weak [wik] a. 弱的; 柔弱的; 體弱的　**W**

weakness [ˋwiknɪs] n. 虛弱 (不可數); 弱點 (可數)
例: After being sick, I felt very tired and weak.
(生病後，我覺得身體又累又虛弱。)

1441. wealth [wɛlθ] n. 財富　**W**

wealthy [ˋwɛlθɪ] a. 富有的 (= rich)
例: Though he is wealthy, he is stingy.
(他雖然有錢，卻很小器。)
＊ stingy [ˋstɪndʒɪ] a. 小器的

1442. wear [wɛr] vt. 穿戴; 施 (粧); 磨損　**W**

三態為: wear、wore [wɔr]、worn [wɔrn]
be worn out　累壞了
= be tired out
例: She didn't wear any makeup, but she still looked beautiful.
(她沒化粧，但看起來仍然美麗。)

I was worn out after all the work.
(把工作做完後，我累壞了。)

1443. **weather** ['wɛðɚ] n. 天氣

(不可數, 不可說 a weather、two weathers)

例: What's the weather like today?
(今天天氣怎麼樣？)

1444. **wedding** ['wɛdɪŋ] n. 婚禮

例: The wedding is planned for the middle of June.
(婚禮預定在六月中旬舉行。)

1445. **week** [wik] n. 星期

例: Next week I'll be on business in Tainan.
(下星期我會到台南出差。)

1446. **weekend** ['wikɛnd] n. 週末 (與 on 並用)

例: On the weekends, I go out with my friends.
(週末的時候我都會跟友人外出。)

1447. **weigh** [we] vt. 量 (某人) 體重 & vi. 重達

weight [wet] n. 重量
lose weight   瘦下來
gain weight   胖起來
= put on weight

例: How much do you weigh?
=   What's your weight?
(你多重？)

1448. **welcome** ['wɛlkəm] a. 受歡迎的 & vt. 歡迎

三態為: welcome、welcomed、welcomed

例: A: Thank you very much for your help.
　B: You're welcome.
（甲：多謝你的幫助。）
（乙：別客氣。）

1449. **west** [wɛst] n. 西方 (與 the 並用) & adv. 往西方

western [ˈwɛstə-n] a. 西方的

例: The sun rises in the east and sets in the west.
（太陽在東方升起，西方落下。）

1450. **wet** [wɛt] n. 濕的

例: Don't wear those clothes because they're wet.
（那些衣服是濕的，所以不要穿。）

1451. **whale** [wel] n. 鯨魚

have a whale of a time　玩得很愉快
= have a good time

例: The movie was about a boy and a whale.
（那部電影演的是有關某男孩與鯨魚的故事。）

We had a whale of a time at the party.
（我們在派對上玩得很愉快。）

1452. **what** [wɑt] n. 什麼

例: What's the matter with you?
= What's wrong with you?
（你怎麼了？）

1453. **when** [wɛn] conj. 當 & adv. 何時

例: When I heard the bad news, I couldn't help crying.
（我聽到這壞消息時，忍不住哭了。）

When will he come?
（他何時來？）

1454. where [wɛr] adv. 何處 & conj. 在……的地方　W

例: Where do you live?
(你住在何處？)
Where there is a will, there is a way.
(在有意志力的地方，就有一條道路／有志者事竟成。——諺語)

1455. whether ['wɛðɚ] conj. 是否; 不論是否　W

例: Tell me whether he'll come.
(告訴我他是否會來。)
Whether he goes or not, I'll go.
(不論他是否會去，我都會去。)

1456. which [wɪtʃ] pron. 哪一個; 那個　W

例: Which answer is the best one?
(哪一個答案是最好的？)
The book which you bought yesterday is really good.
(你昨天買的那本書真棒。)

1457. while [waɪl] conj. 當; 而　W

例: While you were gone, your mother called.
(你不在的時候，你媽媽打電話過來。)
Mary is clever, while Peter is stupid.
(瑪麗很聰明，而彼得卻很笨。)

1458. white [waɪt] n. & a. 白色 (的)　W

a white lie　善意的謊言 (你明明沒吃過飯,有人問你吃過了沒,出於
客氣,你卻說吃過了,這就是 a white lie。)
例: John told a white lie to his wife.
(約翰對他太太說了一個善意的謊言。)

1459. who [hu] pro. 誰; 那個人

例: Who is that man over there?
(那邊那個人是誰呀？)

I like people who work hard.
(我喜歡勤奮的人。)

1460. whole [hol] a. 整個的, 全球的 & n. 全部

On the whole,...　　一般而言,……
= In general,...

例: Tell me the whole story.
(把故事原原本本地告訴我。)

On the whole, girls are more shy than boys.
(一般而言，女孩子比男孩子害羞。)

1461. why [hwaɪ] adv. 為什麼

例: Why are you angry with me?
(你為什麼生我的氣？)

Tell me the reason why you're angry.
(告訴我你生氣的理由。)

1462. wide [waɪd] a. 寬的; 寬闊的

width [wɪdθ] n. 寬度; 寬闊

例: The river is 200 meters wide.
= The river is 200 meters in width.
(這條河寬兩百公尺。)

1463. widow [ˈwɪdo] n. 寡婦

widower [ˈwɪdoˑ] n. 鰥夫

例: When a woman's husband dies, she becomes a widow.
(女人的丈夫過逝時，她就成了寡婦。)

1464. **wife** [waɪf] n. 妻人 (複數形為 wives [waɪvz])

husband [ˈhʌzbənd] n. 丈夫

例: A man would be in great trouble if he had more than one wife.

(男人的太太不止一個時，代誌就大條了。)

1465. **wild** [waɪld] a. 野生的; 野蠻的; (暴風雨) 猛烈的

be wild about...　　瘋狂喜愛……

= be crazy about...

wilderness [ˈwɪldənɪs] n. 蠻荒

in the wilderness　　在蠻荒地區

例: The wild dog bit the little girl.

(野狗咬了那小女孩。)

Peter is wild about Mary.

(彼得瘋狂愛上瑪麗。)

1466. **will** [wɪl] aux. 將要 & n. 意志力; 遺囑

make a will　　立下遺囑

例: When will you be home?

(你何時會在家？)

Never lose the will to live.

(千萬不要失去求生的意志力。)

1467. **win** [wɪn] vt. & vi. 贏

三態為: win、won [wʌn]、won

例: Our team won the game.

(我隊贏了這場比賽。)

1468. **wind** [wɪnd] n. 風

windy [ˈwɪndɪ] a. 颳風的, 起風的

例: The wind is blowing hard.
(風颳得很厲害。)

1469. window ['wɪndo] n. 窗戶　　　**W**

例: Open the window; it's stuffy in here.
(把窗戶打開,這裏面很悶。)
stuffy ['stʌfɪ] a. 悶的, 不通風的

1470. wing [wɪŋ] n. 翅膀　　　**W**

例: The bird broke its wing.
(這隻鳥的翅膀折斷了。)

1471. winter ['wɪntɚ] n. 冬天　　　**W**

例: I don't like winter because it's too cold.
(我不喜歡冬天,因為太冷了。)

1472. wipe [waɪp] vt. 擦拭　　　**W**

wipe up...　　將……擦拭乾淨
例: Wipe up the water on the floor.
(把地板上的水擦乾淨。)

1473. wire [waɪr] n. 鐵絲; 電線　　　**W**

例: The coat hanger is made of wire.
(這個衣架是鐵絲做的。)

1474. wise [waɪz] a. 有智慧的; 明智的　　　**W**

例: Going to college is a wise decision.
(上大學是個明智的決定。)

1475. wisdom ['wɪzdəm] n. 智慧　　　**W**

例: Wisdom comes from experience.
(智慧來自經驗。)

1476. wish [wɪʃ] n. 願望 & vt. 希望　　**W**

make a wish　　許個願

例: Make a wish on a falling star.
(對流星許個願。)

I wish he were here now.
(我真希望他現在在這裏，但卻不在。)

1477. woman [wʊmən] n. 女人 (複數形為 women [ˈwɪmən])　　**W**

例: That woman over there is my wife.
(那邊那個女人是我太太。)

1478. wonder [ˈwʌndɚ] n. 奇蹟 & vt. 想知道　　**W**

work wonders　　產生奇蹟

例: The medicine worked wonders.
(這個藥真靈。)

I wonder whether he'll come.
(我不知道他是否會來。)

1479. wonderful [ˈwʌndɚfḷ] a. 很棒的 (= great、cool)　　**W**

例: Thank you for your wonderful idea.
(謝謝你這麼棒的點子。)

1480. wood [wʊd] n. 木頭　　**W**

wooden [ˈwʊdṇ] a. 木質的, 木造的

例: That's a wooden table. In other words, it's made of wood.
(那是一張木桌。換言之，那是木造的。)

1481. wool [wʊl] n. 羊毛　　**W**

woolen [ˈwʊlən] a. 羊毛製的

例: It's a woolen shirt. In other words, it's made of wool.
(那是羊毛衫。換言之，那是羊毛製的。)

1482. word [wɝd] n. 文字 (可數); 承諾 (不可數)　

例: Do you know how to say this word?
(你知道這個字怎麼唸嗎？)

He is a man of his word.
(他是個言而有信的人。)

1483. wordy [ˈwɝdɪ] a. 字數太多的, 冗長的　**W**

例: That composition is too wordy. Make it short.
(那篇作文太冗長。把它化簡。)

1484. work [wɝk] n. 工作 (不可數); 作品 (可數) & vi. 工作; 發生功能　**W**

worker [ˈwɝkɚ] n. 工人; 員工

例: His works are on display at the museum.
(他的作品正在博物館展出。)

The machine doesn't work.
(這機器故障了。)

1485. world [wɝld] n. 世界　**W**

例: Tom is my best friend in the world.
(湯姆是我世上最好的朋友。)

1486. worry [ˈwɝɪ] n. 憂慮 & vt. & vi. (使) 擔憂　**W**

worry about...　　擔心……
worry sb sick　　使某人擔心極了

例: I really worry about him. He hasn't eaten for a week.
(我真擔心他。他一個星期沒吃飯了。)

He worries me sick.
(他令我擔心要死。)

1487. worried [ˈwɝɪd] a. 感到憂心的　**W**

be worried about...　　擔心
= worry about...

例: I'm worried about Mary. She has been acting strange since her boyfriend left her.
(我很擔心瑪麗。自她男友離開她之後，他的舉止就怪怪的。)

1488. **worse** [wɝs] a. 更糟的 (是 bad 的比較級) Ｗ

what's worse　　更糟的是
what's better　　更好的是

例: He's stupid. What's worse, he's lazy.
(他很蠢。更糟的是，他很懶。)

1489. **worth** [wɝθ] n. 價值 & prep. 值得 Ｗ

(多用於"be worth + Ving"的句構中)
worthy ['wɝðɪ] a. 值得的 (多用於"be worthy of + N"的句構中)
worthwhile [ˌwɝθ'waɪl] a. 值得的 (多用於"It is worthwhile to V"的句構中)

例: This book is worth reading.
(這本書值得看。)

This question is worthy of our attention.
(這個問題值得我們注意。)

It is worthwhile to learn English.
(學英文是值得的。)

1490. **write** [raɪt] vt. & vi. 寫 (三態為: write、wrote [rot]、written) ['rɪtn̩] Ｗ

例: He wrote me a letter.
(他寫了一封信給我。)

He can't read, nor can he write.
(他不識字，也不會寫字。)

1491. **wrong** [rɔŋ] a. 錯誤的 Ｗ

例: Sorry, you've got the wrong number.
(抱歉，你打錯電話號碼了。)

1492. **X'mas** [ˈkrɪsməs] n. 聖誕節

(是 Christmas 的縮寫)，本字只用於賀卡上。

1493. **yard** [jɑrd] n. 碼; 院子

backyard [ˌbækˈjɑrd] n. 後院

例: Father grows many roses in the backyard.
(爸爸在後院種了許多玫瑰。)

1494. **year** [jɪr] n. 年

例: This year I hope to do better in school.
(今年我希望在學成績有更好的表現。)

1495. **yellow** [ˈjɛlo] n. & n. 黃色 (的)

例: When the light turns yellow, you should slow down.
(變黃燈時你要減速。)

1496. **yesterday** [ˈjɛstəˌde] n. & adv. 昨天

例: Don't fool me. I wasn't born yesterday.
(別騙我。我又不是三歲小孩。──諺語。)

1497. **yet** [jɛt] conj. 但是 (= but) & adv. 尚未 (與 not 並用)

例: He's nice, yet I don't like him.
(他很好，但我不喜歡他。)
He hasn't shown up yet.
(他還未出現。)

1498. **young** [jʌŋ] a. 年輕的

youngster [ˈjʌŋstə] n. 年輕人
youth [juθ] n. 青春 (不可數); 青年 (可數)

例: You look young for your age.
(你看起來比實際年紀年輕。)

1499. **zero** [ˈzɪro] n. 零; 零分　　　**Z**

例: Bill got a zero on the test.
（這次考試比爾得了個鴨蛋。）

1500. **zoo** [zu] n. 動物園　　　**Z**

例: My class went to the zoo yesterday to see the baby penguins.
（我們全班昨天到動物園去看小企鵝。）
　＊penguin [ˈpɛŋgwɪn] n. 企鵝

標 誌 篇

	1. **Two-way Traffic**　　雙行道 traffic ['træfɪk] n. 交通
	2. **One Way**　　單行道
	3. **Do Not Enter**　　請勿進入 enter ['ɛntɚ] vi. 進入
	4. **Lost and Found**　　失物招領 found [faʊnd] vt. 發現 (find 的過去式及過去分詞)
	5. **Gas Station**　　加油站
	6. **Taxi Stand**　　計程車招呼站
	7. **Viewing Area**　　觀景區 area ['ɛrɪə] n. 地區
	8. **Parking**　　停車場
	9. **Elevator**　　電梯
	10. **Telephone**　　公用電話

11. **No Crossing** 禁止跨越

 12. **Hospital** 醫院

 13. **Camping** 露營區

 14. **Restaurant** 餐廳

 15. **Post Office** 郵局

 16. **First Aid** 急診室

 17. **No Smoking** 禁止吸煙

 18. **Information** 詢問處

 19. **No Parking** 禁止停車

 20. **Handicapped Only** 殘障專用

21. **Airport**　　機場

22. **Pedestrian Crossing**　　行人穿越道
pedestrian [pə'dɛstrɪən] n. 行人

23. **Women's Toilet**　　女廁所
toilet ['tɔɪlɪt] n. 廁所
= restroom
= lavatory ['lævətɔrɪ]

24. **Men's Toilet**　　男廁所

25. **No Left Turn**　　禁止左轉

26. **No Right Turn**　　禁止右轉

27. **No U Turn**　　禁止迴轉

28. **Fasten Your Seatbelt**　　請繫好安全帶
fasten ['fæsn̩] vt. 綁

── 動物昆蟲篇 ──

1. **ant** [ænt] n. 螞蟻

2. **bat** [bæt] n. 蝙蝠

3. **bear** [bɛr] n. 熊

4. **butterfly** ['bʌtɚ͵flaɪ] n. 蝴蝶

5. **camel** ['kæml̩] n. 駱駝

6. **chicken** ['tʃɪkɪn] n. 雞

7. **cock** [kak] n. 公雞

8. **cockroach** ['kak͵rotʃ]
   n. 蟑螂

9. **cow** [kau] n. 乳牛

10. **crow** [kro] n. 烏鴉

11. **crab** [kræb] n. 螃蟹

12. **donkey** ['daŋkɪ] n. 驢子

13. **dolphin** ['dalfɪn] n. 海豚

14. **dove** [dʌv] n. 鴿子

15. **duck** [dʌk] n. 鴨子

16. **elephant** ['ɛləfənt] n. 大象

17. **fox** [faks] n. 狐狸

18. **frog** [frag] n. 青蛙

19. **giraffe** [dʒə'ræf] n. 長頸鹿

20. **goose** [gus] n. 鵝

21. **grasshopper**
    ['græs͵hapɚ] n. 蚱蜢

22. **hen** [hɛn] n. 母雞

23. **kangaroo**
    [͵kæŋgə'ru] n. 袋鼠

24. **lamb** [læm] n. 羔羊

25. **lion** ['laɪən] n. 獅子

26. **monkey** ['mʌŋkɪ] n. 猴子

27. **mosquito** [mə'skito] n. 蚊子

28. **mouse** [maus] n. 老鼠 (單數)
    mice [maɪs] n. 老鼠 (複數)

29. **ox** [aks] n. 公牛

30. **panda** ['pændə] n. 熊貓

31. **parrot** ['pærət] n. 鸚鵡

32. **peacock** ['pi͵kak] n. 孔雀

33. **penguin** ['pɛngwɪn] n. 企鵝

34. **puppy** ['pʌpɪ] n. 小狗

35. **seagull** ['si͵gʌl] n. 海鷗

36. **shark** [ʃark] n. 鯊魚

37. **sheep** [ʃip] n. 綿羊 (單複數同形)

38. **shrimp** [ʃrɪmp] n. 蝦子

39. **silkworm** ['sɪlk͵wɝm] n. 蠶

40. **snake** [snek] n. 蛇

41. **spider** ['spaɪdɚ] n. 蜘蛛

42. **squirrel** ['skwɝl] n. 松鼠

43. **tiger** ['taɪgɚ] n. 老虎

44. **turkey** ['tɝkɪ] n. 火雞

45. **turtle** ['tɝtl̩] n. 烏龜

46. **whale** [wel] n. 鯨魚

47. **wolf** [wulf] n. 狼 (單數)
    wolves [wulvz] n. 狼 (複數)

── 運動篇 ──

1. **tennis** [ˈtɛnɪs] n. 網球
2. **running** [ˈrʌnɪŋ] n. 賽跑
3. **volley ball** [ˈvɑlɪ ˌbɔl] n. 排球
4. **baseball** [ˈbesbɔl] n. 棒球
5. **basketball**
   [ˈbæskɪtbɔl] n. 籃球
6. **swimming**
   [ˈswɪmɪŋ] n. 游泳
7. **high jump**
   [ˈhaɪ ˌdʒʌmp] n. 跳高
8. **golf** [gɔlf] n. 高爾夫球
9. **long jump**
   [ˈlɔŋ ˌdʒʌmp] n. 跳遠
10. **jogging** [ˈdʒɑgɪŋ] n. 慢跑
11. **badminton**

   [ˈbædmɪntən] n. 羽毛球
12. **in-line skating**
   [ˈɪnˌlaɪn ˈsketɪŋ] n. 直排溜冰
13. **skiing** [ˈskiɪŋ] n. 滑雪
14. **boxing** [ˈbɑksɪŋ] n. 拳擊
15. **hockey** [ˈhɑkɪ] n. 曲棍球
16. **bowling** [ˈbolɪŋ] n. 保齡球
17. **table tennis**
   [ˈtebḷ ˌtɛnɪs] n. 桌球
18. **billiard** [ˈbɪljəd] n. 撞球
19. **soccer** [ˈsɑkɚ] n. 足球
20. **football** [ˈfʊtbɔl] n. 美式足球
21. **rugby** [ˈrʌgbɪ] n. 英式橄欖球
22. **cycling** [ˈsaɪkḷɪŋ] n. 自由車

── 蔬菜水果篇 ──

1. **banana** [bəˈnænə] n. 香蕉
2. **peach** [pitʃ] n. 水蜜桃
3. **cherry** [ˈtʃɛrɪ] n. 櫻桃
4. **honeydew melon**
   [ˈhʌnɪdju ˌmɛlən] n. 香瓜
5. **orange** [ˈɔrɪndʒ] n. 柳橙
6. **watermelon**
   [ˈwɑtɚˌmɛlən] n. 西瓜

7. **kiwi fruit**
   [ˈkiwɪ ˌfrut] n. 奇異果
8. **pineapple** [ˈpaɪnˌæpḷ] n. 鳳梨
9. **mango** [ˈmæŋgo] n. 芒果
10. **grape** [grep] n. 葡萄
11. **grapefruit**
   [ˈgrepfrut] n. 葡萄柚
12. **papaya** [pəˈpajə] n. 木瓜

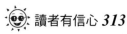

13. **strawberry**
[ˈstrɔˌbɛrɪ] n. 草莓

14. **plum** [plʌm] n. 梅子

15. **tomato** [təˈmeto] n. 蕃茄

16. **lemon** [ˈlɛmən] n. 檸檬

17. **pear** [pɛr] n. 梨

18. **guava** [ˈgwavə] n. 芭樂

19. **carrot** [ˈkærət] n. 胡蘿蔔

20. **pumpkin** [ˈpʌŋkɪn] n. 南瓜

21. **onion** [ˈʌnjən] n. 洋蔥

22. **celery** [ˈsɛlərɪ] n. 芹菜

23. **cauliflower**
[ˈkɔləˌflauɚ] n. 白花椰菜

24. **broccoli** [ˈbrakəlɪ] n. 綠花椰菜

25. **cabbage** [ˈkæbɪdʒ] n. 包心菜

26. **garlic** [ˈgarlɪk] n. 大蒜

27. **potato** [pəˈteto] n. 馬鈴薯

28. **radish** [ˈrædɪʃ] n. 蘿蔔

29. **cucumber**
[ˈkjukʌmbɚ] n. 黃瓜

30. **lettuce** [ˈlɛtəs] n. 萵苣, 西生菜

31. **pea** [pi] n. 豌豆
pepper [ˈpɛpɚ] n. 辣椒

32. **green pepper**
[ˈgrin ˌpɛpɚ] n. 青椒

33. **spinach** [ˈspɪnɪdʒ] n. 菠菜

== 菜 單 篇 ==

1. **entree** [ˈantre] n. 主菜
side-dish [ˈsaɪˌdɪʃ] n. 副菜

2. **appetizer**
[ˈæpəˌtaɪzɚ] n. 開胃菜

3. **specialty** [ˈspɛʃəltɪ] n. 招牌菜

4. **beef steak** [ˈbif ˌstek] n. 牛排

5. **rare** [rɛr] a. 三分熟的

6. **medium** [ˈmidɪəm] a. 半熟的

7. **well-done**
[ˈwɛldʌn] a. 全熟的

8. **spaghetti**
[spəˈgɛtɪ] n. 義大利麵

9. **curry beef**
[ˈkɝɪˈbif] n. 咖哩牛肉

10. **bacon** [ˈbekən] n. 培根

11. **stewed** [stjud] a. 燉的

12. **grilled** [grɪld] a. 燒烤的

13. **boiled** [bɔɪld] a. 煮的

14. **fried** [fraɪd] a. 炸的

15. **roast** [rost] a. 烤的

16. **scrambled**
[ˈskræmbḷd] a. 炒的

17. **steamed** [stimd] a. 蒸的

18. **spicy** [ˈspaɪsɪ] a. 辣的

19. **hamburger** ['hæmbɝɡɚ] n. 漢堡

20. **cheeseburger**
['tʃizbɝɡɚ] n. 起司漢堡

21. **sundae** ['sʌndɪ] n. 聖代

22. **milkshake**
['mɪlkʃek] n. 奶昔

23. **soup** [sup] n. 湯

24. **sunny-side-up**
['sʌnɪsaɪdəp] a. 只煎一面的 (蛋)

25. **salad** ['sæləd] n. 沙拉

26. **juice** [dʒus] n. 果汁

27. **doughnut** ['donʌt] n. 甜甜圈

28. **margarine**
['mɑrdʒərin] n. 人造奶油

29. **pizza** ['pitsə] n. 披薩餅

30. **French fries**
[ˌfrɛntʃ 'fraɪ] n. 炸薯條

31. **sausage** ['sɔsɪdʒ] n. 臘腸

32. **jam** [dʒæm] n. 果醬

33. **nugget** ['nʌgɪt] n. 雞塊

34. **corn flake**
['kɔrn ˌflek] n. 玉米片

35. **potato chip**
[pə'teto ˌtʃɪp] n. 洋芋片

36. **cereal** ['sɪrɪəl] n. 麥片

37. **dessert** [dɪ'zɝt] n. 甜點

38. **soda** ['sodə] n. 汽水

39. **toast** [tost] n. 吐司

40. **side order**
['saɪd ˌɔrdə] n. 單點 (非組合餐)

41. **special**
['spɛʃəl] n. 特餐, 套餐

42. **beverage** ['bɛvərɪdʒ] n. 飲料

43. **topping** ['tɑpɪŋ] n. 加料

44. **vegetable**
['vɛdʒətəbl̩] n. 蔬菜

45. **yogurt**
['jogɚt] n. 優格

46. **noodle** ['nudl̩] n. 麵

47. **dumpling**
['dʌmplɪŋ] n. 水餃

48. **shrimp** [ʃrɪmp] n. 蝦

49. **surf and turf**
['sɝf ænd ˌtɝf] n. 海陸大餐

50. **pork** [pɔrk] n. 豬肉

51. **mutton** ['mʌtn̩] n. 羊肉

52. **pudding** ['pʊdɪŋ] n. 布丁

53. **tofu** ['tofu] n. 豆腐

54. **sandwich**
['sændwɪtʃ] n. 三明治

55. **restaurant**
['rɛstərənt] n. 餐廳

56. **cafeteria**
[ˌkæfə'tɪrɪə] n. 自助餐廳

57. **buffet** [bʊ'fe] n. 歐式自助餐

時 間 篇

1. **month** [mʌnθ] n. 月份
2. **January** [ˈdʒænjʊɛrɪ] n. 一月
3. **February** [ˈfɛbrʊɛrɪ] n. 二月
4. **March** [martʃ] n. 三月
5. **April** [ˈeprəl] n. 四月
6. **May** [me] n. 五月
7. **June** [dʒun] n. 六月
8. **July** [dʒuˈlaɪ] n. 七月
9. **August** [ˈɔgəst] n. 八月
10. **September** [sɛpˈtɛmbɚ] n. 九月
11. **October** [akˈtobɚ] n. 十月
12. **November** [noˈvɛmbɚ] n. 十一月
13. **December** [dɪˈsɛmbɚ] n. 十二月
14. **week** [wik] n. 星期
15. **Monday** [ˈmʌndɪ] n. 星期一
16. **Tuesday** [ˈtjuzdɪ] n. 星期二
17. **Wednesday** [ˈwɛnzdɪ] n. 星期三
18. **Thursday** [ˈθɝzdɪ] n. 星期四
19. **Friday** [ˈfraɪdɪ] n. 星期五
20. **Saturday** [ˈsætɚdɪ] n. 星期六
21. **Sunday** [ˈsʌndɪ] n. 星期日
22. **weekend** [ˈwikˈɛnd] n. 週末
23. **a.m.** [ˌeˈɛm] n. 上午
24. **p.m.** [ˌpiˈɛm] n. 下午
25. **morning** [ˈmɔrnɪŋ] n. 早上
26. **noon** [nun] n. 中午
27. **afternoon** [ˌæftɚˈnun] n. 下午
28. **evening** [ˈivnɪŋ] n. 傍晚
29. **night** [naɪt] n. 晚上
30. **midnight** [ˈmɪdˌnaɪt] n. 午夜
31. **season** [ˈsizn̩] n. 季節
32. **spring** [sprɪŋ] n. 春天
33. **summer** [ˈsʌmɚ] n. 夏天
34. **fall** [fɔl] n. 秋天
35. **winter** [ˈwɪntɚ] n. 冬天

═ 顏 色 篇 ═

1. **black** [blæk] n. & a. 黑色 (的)
2. **blue** [blu] n. & a. 藍色 (的)
3. **brown** [braʊn] n. & a. 棕色 (的)
4. **golden** [ˈgoldn̩] n. & a. 金色 (的)
5. **gray** [gre] n. & a. 灰色 (的)
6. **green** [grin] n. & a. 綠色 (的)

7. **orange** [ˈɔrɪndʒ] n. & a. 橘黃色 (的)
8. **pink** [pɪŋk] n. & a. 粉紅色 (的)
9. **purple** [ˈpɝpl̩] n. & a. 紫色 (的)
10. **red** [rɛd] n. & a. 紅色 (的)
11. **white** [hwaɪt] n. & a. 白色 (的)
12. **yellow** [ˈjɛlo] n. & a. 黃色 (的)

═ 數 字 篇 ═

1. **zero** [ˈzɪro] n. & a. 零
2. **one** [wʌn] n. & a. 一
3. **two** [tu] n. & a. 二
4. **three** [θri] n. & a. 三
5. **four** [fɔr] n. & a. 四
6. **five** [faɪv] n. & a. 五
7. **six** [sɪks] n. & a. 六
8. **seven** [ˈsɛvən] n. & a. 七
9. **eight** [et] n. & a. 八
10. **nine** [naɪn] n. & a. 九
11. **ten** [tɛn] n. & a. 十
12. **eleven** [ɪˈlɛvən] n. & a. 十一
13. **twelve** [twɛlv] n. & a. 十二
14. **thirteen** [θɝˈtin] n. & a. 十三
15. **fourteen** [fɔrˈtin] n. & a. 十四

16. **fifteen** [fɪfˈtin] n. & a. 十五
17. **sixteen** [sɪksˈtin] n. & a. 十六
18. **seventeen** [ˌsɛvənˈtin] n. & a. 十七
19. **eighteen** [eˈtin] n. & a. 十八
20. **nineteen** [naɪnˈtin] n. & a. 十九
21. **twenty** [ˈtwɛntɪ] n. & a. 二十
22. **thirty** [ˈθɝtɪ] n. & a. 三十
23. **forty** [ˈfɔrtɪ] n. & a. 四十
24. **fifty** [ˈfɪftɪ] n. & a. 五十
25. **sixty** [ˈsɪkstɪ] n. & a. 六十
26. **seventy** [ˈsɛvəntɪ] n. & a. 七十
27. **eighty** [ˈetɪ] n. & a. 八十
28. **ninety** [ˈnaɪntɪ] n. & a. 九十

29. **hundred**
 [ˈhʌndrəd] n. & a. 一百

30. **thousand**
 [ˈθaʊzn̩d] n. & a. 一千

31. **million** [ˈmɪljən] n. & a. 一百萬

32. **first** [fɝst] n. & a. 第一

33. **second** [ˈsɛkənd] n. & a. 第二

34. **third** [θɝd] n. & a. 第三

35. **fourth** [forθ] n. & a. 第四

36. **fifth** [fɪfθ] n. & a. 第五

37. **sixth** [sɪksθ] n. & a. 第六

38. **seventh**
 [ˈsɛvənθ] n. & a. 第七

39. **eighth** [etθ] n. & a. 第八

40. **ninth** [naɪnθ] n. & a. 第九

41. **tenth** [tɛnθ] n. & a. 第十

42. **twentieth**
 [ˈtwɛntɪɪθ] n. & a. 第二十

43. **thirtieth**
 [ˈθɝtɪɪθ] n. & a. 第三十

44. **ninetieth**
 [ˈnaɪntɪɪθ] n. & a. 第九十

國家圖書館出版品預行編目資料

初級挑戰單字 1500 / 賴世雄著 -- 初版.
臺北市：常春藤有聲, 2003 [民 92]
　面：　公分. -- (常春藤全民英檢系列；G04)

ISBN　957-8610-91-2 (平裝)

1. 英國語言 -- 詞彙

805.12　　　　　　　　92000626

常春藤全民英檢系列 G04N

初級-挑戰單字 1500

編　　著：賴世雄
編　　審：Rachel A. Black ・ Jerrie C. Shepherd
　　　　　郭章煥・吳乃作
校　　對：常春藤中外編輯群
封面設計：JAZZ
電腦排版：朱瑪琍・劉濰崢
顧　　問：賴陳愉嫻
法律顧問：王存淦律師・蕭雄淋律師
發行日期：2008 年 2 月　再版/三刷

出 版 者：常春藤有聲出版有限公司
　　　　　台北市忠孝西路一段 33 號 5 樓
　　　　　行政院新聞局出版事業登記證
　　　　　局版臺業字第肆捌貳陸號

服務電話：(02)2331-7600　　　服務傳真：(02)2381-0918
信　　箱：臺北郵政 8-18 號信箱
郵撥帳號：19714777　　常春藤有聲出版有限公司
定　　價：350 元 (書+3CD)

＊如有缺頁、裝訂錯誤或破損　請寄回本社更換

A Quick Note

常春藤有聲出版有限公司
讀者回函卡

感謝您的填寫，您的建議將是公司重要的參考及修正指標！

我購買本書的書名是	編碼
我購買本書的原因是	☐老師、同學推薦 ☐家人推薦 ☐學校購買 ☐書店閱讀後感到喜歡 ☐其他
我購得本書的管道是	☐書攤 ☐業務人員推薦 ☐大型連鎖書店 ☐書店名稱＿＿＿＿＿＿ ☐其他
我最滿意本書的三點依序是	☐內容 ☐編排方式 ☐雙色印刷 ☐試題演練 ☐解析清楚 ☐封面 ☐售價 ☐促銷活動豐富 ☐信任品牌 ☐廣告 ☐其他
我最不滿意本書的三點依序是	☐內容 ☐編排方式 ☐雙色印刷 ☐試題演練 ☐解析不足 ☐封面 ☐售價 ☐促銷活動貧乏 ☐廣告 ☐其他
我有一些其他想法與建議是	
我發現本書誤植的部份是	☐書籍第＿頁，第＿行，有錯誤的部份是 ☐書籍第＿頁，第＿行，有錯誤的部份是

我的基本資料

讀者姓名		生　日		性別	☐男 ☐女	
就讀學校		科系年級	科 年級	畢業	☐已畢 ☐在學	
聯絡電話		E-mail				
聯絡地址	＿＿ ＿＿ ＿＿(郵地區號)					

請您填寫完後寄至：
台北市忠孝西路一段33號5樓　　**常春藤有聲出版有限公司**　　**出版部收**

填寫日期：西元＿＿＿＿年＿＿＿＿月＿＿＿＿日

A Quick Note